The Miner Warrior of Luzon

Walter McKay Cushing

Book 1

Rise of Resistance

The Miner Warrior of Luzon

Walter McKay Cushing

Book I
Rise of the Resistance

Chris Ruttan

The Miner Warrior of Luzon, Walter McKay Cushing

Book1, The Rise of the Resistance

Copywrite © 2025 by Christopher Ruttan Press

Contact: caninoridge@gmail.com, comments welcome

Print edition ISBN: 979-8-9859755-3-6

*The guerrilla must move amongst the people
as a fish swims in the sea*
Mao Zedong, 1937

Contents

ACKNOWLEDGMENTS

People and events described in this book are historically authentic. My interest in them stems back to my early adolescence. My family lived in Luzon, PHL from 1963-1965. Memories of the Japanese occupation in World War II were still fresh in the minds of the Filipinos, from whom I chose historical fiction as my genre for the expression of human drama where historical datapoints leave off.

On this endeavor, I give special thanks and recognition to my wife, Carolyn Elizabeth Ruttan, who provided detailed and well-considered editorial support. I thank my cousin, Tim Gustke, Master of Linguistics, who beta read and commented on select sections. My editor, JJ Toner Editing Services of Dublin, Ireland not only edited style and grammar but made valuable suggestions to the plot and story structure. As for graphic design, I am grateful to the services of Leo Baquero, in Santa Rosa, CA., who steered my book through graphics and layout to production. For the final art design for the book cover, my thanks go out to Jonas Peres, graphic designer, Madrid, Spain. I extend my appreciation to the members of my writers' group in Lower Lake, CA for their beneficial critique of my work as it developed from inspiration to copy.

LUZON 1941

Kubagao
Aparri
APAYAO
ILOCOS NORTE
CAGAYAN
Acsimao
Lagangilang
Banqued
Vigan
ABRA
Tuao
Tuguegarao
Enrile
Balbalasang
Bonglo
Tubo
KALINGA
Del Pilar
Candon
Cervantes
ILOCOS SUR
MOUNTAIN PROVINCE
Bontoc City
Labuagan
ISABELA
Santiago
Echaque
Jones
LA UNION
La Trinidad
Baguio
BENGUET
NUEVA VIZCAYA
LINGAYEN GULF
PANGASINAN
NUEVA ECIJA
San Quinton
TAYABAS
TARLAC
Philippine Commonwealth
by PROVINCE and Community
e.g. ISABELA, Echaque
ZAMBALES
PAMPANGA
San Fernando
BULACAN
LAMON BAY
Guaga
Manila
BATAAN
RIZAL
CAVITE
LAGUNA
Corregidore
CAMARINES NORTE
BATANGAS
CAMARINES SUR
ALBAY
Legazpi
SORSOGON

MINDORO

WALTER MCKAY CUSHING

PROFILE

GOLDMNER LUZON 1940

HS FOOTBALL-FULL OF LA FIGHT

CHAPTER 1

Invasion Plan, The Philippines

OCTOBER 1941, IN OCCUPIED FORMOSA, Lieutenant General Masanobu Homma, commander of the Japanese 14th Army, stood before his general staff in a crowded room. The Japanese-occupied port city of Taiboku sweltered in an unusually hot fall heat wave. Outside, the underbellies of the clouds loomed dark and foreboding. Despite having his olive-green uniform pressed this morning, his sweat-saturated shirt stuck to his back. Humidity circulated in the ceiling fan like a misty veil. Cigarette smoke hung thick in the air. Those seated shifted uncomfortably. But all waited with bated breath. Today was supposed to be a pivotal meeting. Yet, Homma's thoughts were of his wife and teenage son. He eyed the clock on the wall at the back of the stark room. She would be home preparing the evening meal. *Please keep our children safe in the trials ahead.* He swallowed hard, looking at the men before him, realizing his thoughts were multiplied many times by the men he would lead into war, leaving their families.

"You are among the first privileged to hear the final Imperial battle plans for the invasion and conquest of the Philippines. Campaign strategies are already underway for war in the Pacific."

Men at the tables hunched forward with intensity directed at him. Homma knew there would be considerable casualties, yet he held his ramrod composure. At 5'10", Homma was above average height for Japanese men. Most of his fellow officers saw a commander with experience in combat. His three rows of campaign ribbons above his breast pocket designated a life dedicated to the homeland, leading him to this moment. He kept his collar high to conceal the burn scar from an enemy thermite bomb. For him, the memories of the atrocities in the Sino-Japanese War were raw. Homma vowed not to let the atrocities happen again. Having served as an observer in France during the Great War, he understood the Western view of military honor, at odds with the scorched earth vision of the fanatical ideologues among his staff. Today's plan had calculated risks of immense proportions.

With a pointer, he turned and faced the large map stapled to the wall. "Under Emperor Hirohito's divine rule, Japan will reap great benefits. In Malaya, this includes the region's rubber and tin production. The greatest prize is the vast oil reserve in the Dutch East Indies." He clenched his fists; his eyes focused with fervent intensity. "This will break the American embargo on oil and gasoline exports. Long live the Empire," which the men in attendance repeated vociferously like a chant.

His chief of staff, Lieutenant General Masami Maeda, was reputed amongst his peers as bookish, heavy with facts. In a rare moment of levity, he raised his hand to interject. "Then we tell the Americans, you keep your oil, and we'll keep your territories."

Applauding erupted from the men in unanimous agreement. Again, Homma raised his hand for silence.

"In the Philippines, the resources include gold, copper, chromium, and agricultural production. The island archipelago occupies a strategic central location in the Asia-Pacific. We will begin the attack on Luzon in the north from Lingayen Gulf. American Supreme Commander General Douglas MacArthur will assuredly succumb to our overwhelming might. Force him to eat his words: "The Philippines are the key that unlocks the door to the Pacific."

More cheering erupted. Homma traced his pointer around a wide horseshoe-shaped bay with Manila, the capital of the Philippines, at the east end. The Bataan Peninsula, a natural levee between Manila Bay and the China Sea, formed the bay's north shore.

"Manila Harbor is an ideal hub for shipping throughout the Japanese Imperial Empire, essential for a sea route between Japan and the rest of the Imperial Japanese Empire. As long as the Philippines remain in American control, Japan cannot safely secure its vital interests in Southeast Asia and the Pacific." He paused for effect. "In the first wave, heavy bombers from Formosa will attack American Air Force installations in the Philippines, destroying all offensive air power capability. Only after eliminating the American military strike capability can our forces take British Singapore without enemy interference and sever all allied communications in the Pacific. After that, all outlying American bases in the Pacific will fall swiftly, giving Japan an outer protection barrier against future American encroachment."

Homma tapped his pointer sequentially at four points on the map: three times on the island of Luzon, the largest of the Philippine islands, at the north end of the chain, and once on the next largest island, Mindanao, at the far southern end of the chain.

"Regiment strength landings by Army and Navy units from Taiwan preceding the main invasion of the Philippines will secure three cities on Luzon—Aparri, Vigan, and Legazpi—and Davao, in the south on Mindanao. They are all port cities with facilities for landing troops and supplies, and with airfields nearby suitable for fighter planes, providing us immediate strike capability anywhere in the Philippines."

Next, he moved the pointer to a large bay with a wide entry north of Manila on the west coast of Luzon.

"This is Lingayen Gulf, where our main invasion force will make amphibious landings. Based on our intelligence, there is minimal defense. Upon securing the beachhead, the 14th Army will move south through the central plains of Luzon to Manila. Our forces can then capture the capital city without sailing past the fortified island of Corregidor guarding the entrance to Manila Bay."

Colonel Masanobu Tsuji, Imperial General Head-quarters emissary, slapped the table. "The weak are the meat. The strong eat!" he said, reciting a bushido proverb.

With rising excitement, the junior officers began nodding fervently in agreement. Tsuji stood, readjusted his glasses, widened his stance, and peered at the throng with venom. The round lenses masked his malevolence. Among his peers, Tsuji was considered vicious. There were stories of opponents who opposed his views— indifferent to his denunciation of western countries as the "White Peril—of being exiled or disappearing altogether.

Tsuji wielded immense political power for his rank. An influential ultranationalist, he enjoyed the authority granted by the Imperial General Headquarters and the confidence of the emperor's younger brother, Prince Chichibu, a former classmate at the Tokyo Military Academy. Tsuji emboldened ruthlessness in his followers—even to the extreme, assassination of officers he deemed insufficiently aggressive.

His known deeds justified much speculation. In the aftermath of the Battle of Nomonhan, he ordered that soldiers captured by the Russians should commit suicide upon repatriation. Rumors circulated that Tsuji planned to assassinate Prime Minister Fumimaro Konoye if his negotiations resulted in peace with the Americans. To the chagrin of senior officers, Tsuji also enjoyed the veneration of a cadre of aggressive, ambitious subordinate officers, evident in the heightened interest of those present as he spoke. A Colonel Hidemi Watanabe shot upright, enthralled. He rose from his chair quivering with excitement, knocking over a glass of water. The gleam in Watanabe's eyes disappeared quickly upon realizing his shameful show of emotion.

Ignoring him, Tsuji addressed Homma. "This is an impressive battle plan, but please enlighten us if you would, General. Tell us how our Imperial forces will prevail over the mighty Americans."

Homma secretly despised him with barely contained animosity. He responded with a wave, dismissing his derisive insinuation directed at his mettle. "Most forces opposing us are poorly trained and equipped Filipinos." His upper lip half curled in contempt. "The American troops are regarded as good soldiers but inclined to deteriorate physically and mentally in a tropical climate. Though accustomed to the tropics, the Filipino troops have little sense of responsibility and are markedly inferior to soldiers. I anticipate a complete rout in our advance south toward Manila."

Around the table, hands rose, but General Homma continued with the briefing. "The initial bombing raid will begin at first light on December 8, followed by a naval bombardment and the amphibious landings."

Colonel Tsuji again interrupted the General with a grunt. "Why wait until December, General? Our forces are primed and ready. The Imperial fleet can reach the area within days if not hours."

Homma fixed him with his gaze. "These are our orders, as conveyed from Imperial Headquarters. I trust you are not questioning the Imperial plan, Colonel."

Tsuji cast his eyes down; he had no answer to that, but the General had impugned his honor, his loyalty to the emperor. He would not forget!

Ignoring Tsuji, finding his influence unsettling, Homma continued the briefing. He pointed to an elongated, concave bay on the east coast of southern Luzon southeast of Manila. "This is Lamon Bay. A smaller force of 7,000 troops will land there and advance northeast toward Manila with close air support. This positions our forces to attack Manila from the north and south in a pincer maneuver, with the enemy trapped in between in their last defense. When pressed, they will scatter, and the stragglers easily mopped up. Once we take Manila, the last remaining obstacle, the island fortress of Corregidor, will be cut off and captured, and the conquest of Luzon complete. The last isolated pockets of resistance left in the archipelago shall soon follow."

Colonel Watanabe led the officers in a round of exuberant Banzai cheers. Homma half-raised his hand, his expression grave. "Our deadline is tight. Imperial General Headquarters expects us to complete the conquest of the Philippines within seven weeks from the first bombing attacks. At the end of that time, half of the 14th Army and the Army and Navy air units are to leave the Philippines for the Dutch Indies to secure the oil fields, leaving an occupation force to garrison the Philippines. We expect that the fall of Manila will have a strong psychological effect, demoralizing further Filipino resistance.

"To facilitate the pacification of the Philippines, Japan intends to win Filipino cooperation through political concessions and inclusion in our Greater East Asia Co-Prosperity Sphere. As envisioned by our esteemed foreign minister, Hachiro Arita, this refers to a self-sufficient block of Asian nations under the benevolent guidance of Japan, sharing prosperity and peace, free from Western colonialism and domination. Stated, Asia for Asians. We also anticipate most Filipinos will applaud the overthrow of the American colonial government." Intuitively, he sensed a dismissive sneer from Tsuji, although his face betrayed no hint of it.

Homma spoke for two hours, elaborating on logistics, the deployment of troops, supply management, and military administration. After completing his briefing, Homma invited questions from his officers, starting with a question from a lower-ranking officer to show beneficence. He nodded to an operations officer. "Yes, Lieutenant Colonel Nakayama."

With his head tilted, Nakayama swallowed visibly and asked, "Negotiations are in progress in Washington. If they show progress, will military plans be abandoned?"

Colonel Tsuji jolted forward at the question as if electrified, with his formidable, wide jaw clenched and his narrow shoulders hunched. He fixed Nakayama with a basilisk-like stare as if he could kill with a glance, like the serpent monster of medieval mythology, or mark him for elimination should he deem him unfit for command. "Fool! The negotiations will continue until the moment we strike. To do otherwise would arouse their suspicions."

Homma gave a slow, somber shake of his head. "Imperial General Headquarters has concluded that negotiations have reached an impasse. America insists Japan withdraw all forces from China, which we will never do. We have offered to withdraw from Indochina, but they have rejected this concession. They refuse to lift their oil embargo, which they believe gives them leverage over Japan. We have less than two

14

years of strategic oil reserves. So action is urgent. There is no turning back from the course of war."

Homma next picked his chief of staff, General Masami Maeda. "What you have explained is the most likely battle scenario. However, what if the American forces withdraw onto the Bataan Peninsula, northeast of Manila, to make a last stand? With Corregidor Island at the mouth of Manila Bay, it would not be easy to flank the defending troops there from the sea. We would then have to defeat them in a potentially costly frontal attack in difficult terrain, which could upset our schedule."

Homma snorted contemptuously. "General Maeda, Bataan is simply an outlying position. There is no evidence there of any prepared defenses. It would be unwise for American troops to trap themselves in such an indefensible position, like cats in a bag. All we would have to do is pull the drawstrings shut."

The officers in attendance chuckled obsequiously.

Colonel Tsuji cleared his throat with a guttural snort. "Humph! General Homma!"

"Yes, Colonel Tsuji," Homma responded blandly as if out of stoic forbearance. Tsuji locked eyes with a challenging stare.

"General Homma, I don't dispute your grasp of operations and the invasion plan. You mentioned issues of military administration, which raises another issue: the custody of American and Filipino prisoners of war. There are over 200,000 troops in the combined American and Filipino armies. Because they lack the sense of sacrifice of the Japanese soldiers, I expect they will surrender in masse. His voice rose stridently. "Since there will be no prisoner repatriation, their continued custody will serve no useful purpose. After we have extracted what useful information we can from the prisoners, I recommend we execute them—all!"

He paused to channel the rising anticipation in the room. In China, we adopted a practical, effective strategy, Sankō Sakusen, the Three Alls: Kill All, Burn All, Loot All. Make sure they never rise again. Japan will be fighting a racial war in the Pacific. Also, exterminate all

15

civilian colonialists as enemy aliens. As for the Filipino soldiers who fight alongside the Americans, their allegiance betrays the Asian cause. Make an object lesson of them, I say, to deter other misguided Filipinos." Bringing his hand down forcefully on the table, his voice rising to a crescendo, Tsuji exclaimed, "I am conveying the wishes of the Imperial General Headquarters in this matter."

Unimpressed, General Homma noted that Tsuji had dropped no powerful names in his bluster. Homma regarded the very suggestion— the Three Alls—as an attack on the moral foundations of the bushido code, especially the strongest of the eight virtues, rectitude, one's power to decide upon a course of conduct under reason. For an instant, Homma stared back, appalled, meeting the monster's gaze directly. He recognized the rising frenzy of the subordinate officers. Sitting beside Tsuji, Colonel Watanabe shouted, "Sankō Sakusen," the call for 'Scorched Earth,' which many junior officers parroted in unison.

Wanting to avoid the scene in which Tsuji thrived, arousing the passions of lower-ranking officers through insolent challenges, Homma replied ambiguously, "Thank you, Colonel Tsuji. The need to properly administer the custody of prisoners cannot be understated." Tsuji glared incredulously, his eyes hard. Homma deeply resented Tsuji's arrogance and his well-earned reputation for challenging superiors—the practice of gekokujo, the domination of a superior by a subordinate, which had prevented his rise in rank above colonel. However, he still had direct access to Imperial Army Minister General Hideki Tojo.

Tsuji said, "General Homma, I should not have to lecture you on this obvious imperative." Homma had no intention of allowing Tsuji to sway any policy deciding the fate of the prisoners. He stiffened but resisted the urge to put the insufferable colonel in his place. He understood that a reckoning loomed; now was not the right time. Let Tsuji dig his grave deeper before burying him.

Lifting his chin, Colonel Watanabe looked proudly at Tsuji with the ardor of the devout. "Colonel Tsuji is right! Fear makes Japan strong. I remember the famine in my youth, during the financial depression of 1930 to 1932. Our beloved Japan had nearly succumbed to economic collapse brought on by corrupt civilian leadership, bowing before the degenerate colonial empires of the West. Destitute parents sold their daughters into prostitution. Never again will Japan beg from inferior races. The Japanese Empire will prove its preeminence and appropriate by divine right what should belong to Japan, the raw material, and markets of Asia, and punish those guilty of betraying the Imperial cause with the unforgiving ferocity of the righteous."

The staff officers applauded his speech with resounding cheers. General Homma stood by expressionless. Colonel Tsuji glanced approvingly at his self-declared acolyte, acknowledging his zeal with an encouraging nod.

CHAPTER 2

Out of the Blue

IN COORDINATED STRIKES, Japanese bombers struck the
Pacific Naval Fleet at Pearl Harbor on December 7, 1941, and the
American air bases 5,300 miles west in the Philippine Islands on
December 8, precipitating war in the Pacific. Three days later, on
December 11, the first expeditionary forces of the Japanese 14th Army,
48th Sea Division, landed at the historic Spanish city of Vigan in
Northern Luzon, one of four Philippine cities simultaneously attacked.
Vigan sat at the delta mouth of the expansive Abra River, a commercial
artery for transport of natural resources from the interior of Luzon to
the end of its journey beyond the China Sea.

Exhibiting an eclectic blend of Spanish and oriental design—
preserved mansions, cobblestone streets, and terracotta Chinese tiled
roofs, Vigan had become a favored tourist destination in American
colonial Luzon along a coastline dotted with secluded beaches. Arched
doorways accessed the 19th century Spanish colonial buildings beneath
overhanging balconies with ornate balustrades shading the shops,
offices, and storerooms on the ground floors and tranquil courtyards
behind. On any normal day, an industrious mix of Filipino, Chinese and
mestizo people mingled busily in the streets, the business district and
hectic waterfront. On any normal day, a steady stream of fishing boats
and interisland cargo and passenger ships passed between the Vigan
waterfront and ports of the Philippine archipelago. But on this day, the

City of Beauty—the colloquial name bestowed by the original Chinese merchants—capitulated without resistance to the Japanese 14th Army occupation forces.

Gangs of drunken Japanese troops rampaged through the streets, perpetrating the gratuitous carnage and atrocities of conquering armies throughout history on helpless civilians. Soldiers riddled the stucco walls with bullets, ordering the inhabitants out of their homes, yelling, "Ou'side, speedo, speedo," and in the presence of family and community, abducting women, and beating anyone attempting to intervene.

Japanese brutality was direct: simply strike their unlucky victims with whatever they happened to be holding, which usually meant the butt end of a rifle. They entered the vacated premises, grabbing anything they considered valuable, destroying what they could not carry away and, when out of sight of the street, committing unimpeded assault on whomever remained inside.

During the last ten years, the evidence of growing Japanese militarism had become increasingly clear to anyone paying attention. In 1937, the world got a wakeup call when global mass media publicized the first shocking reports of Japanese atrocities in China. The "Horror in Nanjing," the headlines said, after out-of-control Japanese troops massacred 300,000 Chinese military prisoners and civilians in the Nationalist capital of General Chiang Kai-Shek's China. For much of the world, the sheer savagery of the reports seemed too implausible to register.

Three years later, by 1940, the last of Japan's civilian government had been swept away in a spasm of ultranationalism with the military cementing its grip on power, whether with the full support or compulsory capitulation of Japanese society. The Japanese military wanted soldiers devoted to the bushido warrior code of extreme sacrifice for the Japanese empire. After three years in China, Imperial Japan had that army, indoctrinated to conduct violence, methodically and on a colossal scale, against societies their leaders viewed contemptuously as inferior, without honor and dignity.

Approaching Vigan on his return to Abra province, the 34-year-old American gold miner Walter McKay Cushing carried too heavy a weight in his heart to care about the collective indoctrination of Japanese society. With ambivalence, he knew he would regret not taking the last ship available home but, reluctantly, had been unable to tear himself away from the ambition that brought him to the Philippines, metaphorically called gold fever, the obsession with getting rich through risky venture. And why not? Fortunes had been made since the first significant strikes in northern Luzon in the 1920s.

Driving north from the mountain city of Baguio in the Cordillera Mountains along the coastal highway 2 to his mine in landlocked Abra, the despondent Cushing approached the Highway 6 turnoff to Abra just before Vigan, his purpose, to destroy his life's greatest endeavor, the Rainbow Mine. Along with all mine operators in the country, following the Japanese bombings of American airbases in the Philippines on December 8, he had received the official orders from the U.S. Military: Dismantle and destroy all mine equipment and infrastructure to prevent the Japanese from seizing the mines intact and operational. A sick, aching feeling of loss welled up inside him.

Unlike the mines in Benquet province owned by corporations, the Rainbow Mine in Abra, a private venture, had absorbed all his life savings. Cushing winced inwardly, remembering the many hard months prospecting with his partner Maurice 'Peewee' Ordun, searching and sifting through the alluvial soils among the rivers and hills of Abra for placer gold leading to the source, the mother lode, for their mine. After all their sacrifices, and just when the mine was beginning to turn a profit, he now realized with a jolt, the Rainbow mine would not be the proverbial pot of gold its name suggested, just another dead end in his life marked only by holes in the ground as dark as his mood. The Japanese bombing attacks had shattered his dreams of opportunity in his adopted land. Nothing could soften his bitterness.

Driving up a high bluff, Cushing looked west toward the sea. Stunned, as if out of the blue, he struggled to grasp the sight of a destroyer-size warship cruising south off the coast moving north, flying the Rising Sun flag of Japan. Suddenly, the roar of orange mussel flash and puffs of smoke welled off its starboard. Sporadically, the main guns fired whistling shells overhead toward the hills, which would erupt in a brief roar and heave of earth on impact, probing as if trying to provoke a response from an unseen enemy. At the instant of comprehension, a sour taste of bile rose in his throat. *Dangerous bastards*, he thought as a round exploded too close for comfort uphill from the highway.

Cushing drove past his highway 6 turnoff to Abra, instead on toward Vigan. Trying to still his premonitions, he stopped on a hilltop overlooking the city. Gunfire and faint screams emanated from the town. Scanning the town through binoculars, his eyes shielded by a tan bucket hat with a turned-down brim, he could see smoke rising, troops in the street, and bodies hanging by nooses from a balcony. As if from Hell, a terrifying déjà vu flooded his brain—The fucking rape of Nanjing, history repeating in the Philippines right before his eyes.

The horrifying reports from China had been of wanton killing of Chinese people and violent mass rape of women by unrestrained Japanese soldiers in the Chinese city. As Cushing understood, the animosity between the Japanese and Chinese in the Far East was deep and permanent. Vigan, with its Chinese enclave, now appeared another flashpoint of this ancient animosity.

An American in the Philippines since 1933, Cushing had found contentment in his new land of opportunity and a fondness for the Filipino people, touched by their hospitality. Even after his marriage ended in divorce and his former wife returned to the States, he had stayed on, never imagining the unthinkable unfolding in the desperate town below. After all, the Philippines was not like China; a powerful, modern American military protected the archipelago. His stomach knotted; his face and neck flushed hot; outrage and anger coursed through him, leaving him feeling utterly impotent as he watched from his hillside observation point. Though not a particularly religious man, he invoked God, imploring the Almighty that the crimes of the enemy, wherever transgressed, from this day on not go unpunished. *There has to be a reckoning.*

He turned the car around and followed the coastal road back south to the Highway 6 turnoff to Abra. The road had been clear of Japanese on his way to Vigan. He hoped his luck would hold on the remainder of the coastal road, but the hair trigger in his brain was set to fire the rage roiling within him.

As he rounded a corner, a Japanese scout car blocked his path. Cushing stopped the car, got out. The shelling had grown fainter to low rumbles as the Japanese ship moved up the coast. Two Japanese soldiers in flat topped peaked hats with stubby visors approached, rifles tipped with imposing bayonets leveled at him. Seeing the imperial Emperor's "sons of heaven" up close for the first time, he quickly took stock of their attire and equipment—gray green twill uniforms, breeches, puttee cloth around their calves, leather belts with bayonet scabbards and ammunition pouches.

Suck it in Walt, he told himself. He smiled and bowed repeatedly. "Konnichiwa [hello]! Tomodachi [friend]" he greeted them, drawing from his lexicon of oriental greetings acquired from his time in the Orient. He tapped his thumb on his chest and pointed at the car trunk. "I have whiskey! whiskey! Umm Yoi, good!"

The soldiers exchanged wary glances and nodded, grasping the universally understood English word "whiskey." One pointed to the trunk and shouted an order in Japanese. Cushing opened the trunk; two cases of whiskey sat plumb in the middle. He retrieved two bottles from a case and handed one to each soldier. The soldiers smiled and seemed to relax. "N cen! N cen! [I sell]" exclaimed Cushing. With liquor being a prime black-market commodity, he assumed the ruse of a black marketer might give him freer movement among the occupying forces. An American of Irish-Mexican descent, Cushing counted on his predominant Mexican complexion to pass as a Filipino. With his jet-black hair and tropical sun-darkened skin, he looked the part. But his damn blue-grey eyes created one flaw in the deception. *More convincing, maybe a Spanish mestizo,* he concluded. *The Spanish certainly left behind enough bastards in the Philippines.*

One soldier slung his rifle, opened the whiskey bottle, and sniffed it. He took a swig, his mouth puckered; he coughed reflexively, but in general looked pleased. The other soldier now held his rifle by the muzzle with the butt on the ground, both grinning in an intense feral manner, malice in their eyes. As the two soldiers conversed among themselves, Cushing, fit to burst, tried to interpret the meaning of their jabber by their nasal tones and gestures, whiskey being the only word he recognized.

One looked puzzled, turned to the other, muttering something about whiskey.

The other spoke with a snap of authority.

While answering, the first to speak furrowed his brows in a disdainful downward arc.

Responding in a raised voice, the other soldier waved his hand dismissively.

Both Japanese soldiers laughed in harsh cackles that grated on Cushing's nerves like a knife blade against the side of a bottle. He suspected there would be no sale.

After a little more chatter, they seemed to come to an agreement. One soldier handed his precious bottle of whiskey to the other. He moved his rifle in an arc, motioning to the trunk of Cushing's car to the scout car. "All," he commanded. Cushing holding up two fingers, pointed at the two bottles they were holding, *fair to anyone but a thief.*

"No! Only two," he objected, realizing too late the rising stridency conveyed in his voice. The soldier's mouth instantly turned into a snarl. He ordered Cushing, through menacing gestures with his rifle and the unrelenting command "All," to unload the cases of whiskey. In a display of aggression, the soldier leveled his rifle and made jabbing feints at his abdomen with the bayonet. "Speedo," he barked.

"Okay," Cushing relented. "All." The sharp point receded. He bowed submissively, "Gomen! Gomen! [Sorry]!"

With a malevolent gaze, the soldier pointed to the gas cap of Cushing's car and muttered to the other, who retrieved a short hose and gas can from the scout car. He didn't need a translation to realize their intention, siphon the gas and leave him stranded in the hot sun, in what physical condition? He suspected his life was on the line.

He turned to the trunk. As Cushing reached inside, he slipped his hands beneath the cloth covering the recessed spare tire compartment. The thunder of an explosion, a shell fired from the destroyer, reverberated from the nearby hills. The Japanese soldier who had just been prodding his backside with a bayonet raised his rifle vertically, diverted his eyes from the trunk, looking over his shoulder.

In an instant Cushing whirled around armed with two matching Colt semiautomatic .45 caliber pistols, in each hand. "Sayonara greedy bastards!" he yelled, firing at pointblank range into the two Japanese soldiers, a volley as unexpected as a clap of thunder on a clear day. The bayonet wielding soldier's chest imploded. Cushing planted a.45 round point-blank in the other soldier's forehead. Knocked violently to the ground, neither had a chance to use their weapons. As the whiskey bottles fell on the road, one bottle shattered on impact, but the other landed intact.

Cushing looked down at the bodies lying in blood on the road. Feeling victorious, his temples pulsed, his heart raced, surging in his chest. One body lay motionless and the other still quivering in involuntary death spasms. He had just killed two of the invading enemy; but at that moment wanted to kill more. But the surge of exhilaration quickly passed, leaving him shaken and feeling profoundly disgruntled. As for righting a wrong, Cushing realized the two soldiers were inconsequential, easily replaced tools of the Japanese Empire. Killing the enemy this way was merely reacting, like swatting mosquitoes one-by-one in response to a malaria infestation.

But in this pestilence with humans as vectors of death, a more effective antidote would be needed. Though firearms were in short supply in northern Luzon, thanks to the mines, dynamite and disgruntled, soon-to-be out of work miners who knew how to use it were not. Whatever resources and supplies the invaders needed to conduct operations or subsist, blow it up. *And some Japs in the process, all the better*, he reasoned. From a forgotten source in his education, a quote came to mind by the Kansas abolitionist John Brown in years before the outbreak of the Civil War, railing, "The crimes of this guilty land will never be purged away but with blood." At that moment, he imagined channeling the ghost of John Brown in all its fury. But instead of the terrible swift sword, he picked up the unbroken bottle, put it back in the case, and slammed the trunk shut, consoling himself, *Fair trade, one fifth of whiskey for two Japs.*

Grunting, Cushing lifted the bodies of the two Japanese soldiers into the scout car, shoving them onto the seats, and tossing their rifles into the car after them, trying to avoid blood stains on his clothes. With Japanese on the highways, it wouldn't do to be caught with their rifles and equipment. *Thank God the little bastards are on the light side*, he thought exhaling a grunt. He shifted the transmission into neutral and pushed and steered the car across the road to the edge of the hill. A strident Japanese voice crackled from the radio in the dashboard, repeating words like commands. With a final shove, he sent the vehicle over the edge where it rolled over in a loud series of crashes on rocks on its way to the bottom. He hoped to be long gone before the Japanese army began a search for the missing patrol. As he looked around, he spotted a farmer in a fallow field watching him. The tao [farmer] flashed him a two-fingered V for victory sign. Cushing smiled and waved his Colt 45s. What comprehension did the man have *of the events unfolding before his eyes?*

On the eve of the Japanese attack, the past months, Cushing had an increasingly uneasy feeling about the general complacency among the Filipino population about the growing threat from Japan. After witnessing a pathetic example of PA (Philippine Army) training, performing military drills with wooden, dummy rifles, he had hoped the Japanese menace had been exaggerated. Now he worried that men so trained would end up on the battlefield without ever having fired a live round from a real rifle. Aghast, he realized the complacency had extended from the top echelons of Filipino society on down. *Don't worry! America the invincible will protect you.* He got back in his car, shaking his head as if to unburden his mind through force of will, and raced away south on coastal highway 2 to the Abra province turnoff.

CHAPTER 3

The End of the Road

ON DECEMBER 27, 1941, AS THE SUN APPROACHED its zenith, a 1½ ton Chevrolet stake and platform truck, with a green tarp covering the stake frame, moved down the rough road from the pine-forested mountains of northern Luzon. Three travelers were approaching the end of their journey, escape from the Japanese-beleaguered mountain city of Baguio. The road over which they had traveled traversed the sharp-crested, interlinking peaks of the Cordilleras Mountains, above yawning gorges, with hairpin turns bringing into view rivers, waterfalls, and rice terraces.

The three former employees of the recently decommissioned Itogon Gold Mine gazed out the truck windows, absorbed by the alluring view of the Cordilleras in a time of great uncertainty. The young woman, a striking, dark-eyed Filipina, did so with brooding apprehension. Isolated flatlands, plateaus and valleys characterized the land to the west. "I am feeling better," she said. "I know the danger has passed."

"I'm glad you are Maria," the craggy featured yet handsome driver, the senior mining engineer, George Barnett replied. "We were fortunate."

"This time," said Maria Lopez, until just days ago an office clerk in the mine head office, wiping tears from her cheek. "And what of the dangers when we join with Walter Cushing and his guerrillas?"

The other passenger, her fiancé James Novak, an equipment engineer, tried to reassure her. "As I explained Maria, Abra puts us further away from the Japs than Baguio."

"For now," she replied dolefully, refusing to be mollified.

An awkward silence pervaded the truck cab; Barnett shifted uneasily behind the wheel. With the truck moving down toward the low elevation of the Abra valley, their view changed from pine forests of the high mountains to increasingly thick stands of tall, hardwood Almaciga trees, endemic conifers with girths up to three meters. "Hey, take a good look. That's Abra province, the promised land," Barnett said, affecting enthusiasm, "A lumberjack's paradise! A fortune in timber begging to be harvested, and the mighty Abra River to float it all down to the coast."

Maria looked at Barnett astonished. "We are fleeing the Japanese, and you are thinking about business opportunity? Besides, we have no lumberjacks. just Juans and Joses," Maria said, with a pouty edge to her voice. "Filipinos don't pronounce J's like Americans."

A bit surly, James thought, but figured she was all right. They had survived their first encounter with the enemy and come through it shaken but unharmed.

James consoled, "Dear, things will get better. We got to believe that?" And to his former supervisor with a smirk, "Always the optimist. Plans for after the war George?"

Barnett chuckled. "Maybe. Before the Japs invaded I was satisfied just working as a salaried mining engineer. Gold mining paid well and provided steady work during the Depression."

"Great while it lasted, for all of us," James gave Maria a solicitous look. "Working for ol' Jan Marsman and company," he said, referring to the phenomenally wealthy founder of the Itogon Mining Company in Benquet province.

"The Itogon Mine provided the seed money for Jan's financial empire and business conglomerate," Barnett said. "Lucky him. He left on a business trip to Hong Kong just before the outbreak of the war. But with gold prices and production rising, us poor mugs just didn't know when to quit."

"No getting out now," James said, his shoulders slumping. He recalled Barnett's words just days ago before he had twisted the handle of the detonator, yelling, "Everybody ready to see your jobs blown to hell? Military orders, leave nothing for the god damn Japs." The explosions ripped through the mine works in rapid succession, throwing dirt, wooden planks, and shredded metal roofing and siding into the air that rained down through the smoke. He replaced the two wires with two more and engaged the detonator again. As the headframe towers folded and crashed to the ground, explosions reverberated from the tram shaft below ground, as if amplified in an echo chamber.

When the smoke cleared, men lifted their heads to the sight of twisted metal and flattened buildings. With his ears ringing, James peered through the dissipating dust, spying a shattered, partial drum hoist and shaft trailing cable—leading edge mining equipment—from the array of Koepe hoists that he had so painstakingly installed. It laid there, a smoldering omen that his life as he knew it was over and the future ahead, alarming, incomprehensible but clearly dangerous, and just beginning.

Barnett now gazed down the road ahead. "Ah can you blame us? Quit? Gold production in 1941 was up, heading for a record, and for the employees, so were our bonuses. Even Maria here had a bonus coming," he said turning his head and winking. She responded with a suppressed giggle escaping through her nostrils. "Maybe after the war, we'll be paid in arrears with accrued interest," he speculated. Maria nodded hopefully; James shook his head cynically.

But they all realized in retrospect, even with the mining industry in the grip of gold fever, the US military had been sending dependents home. The miners were the last expatriates in the country to take the Japanese threat seriously. Gold fever stories were standard fare in the mining industry. Invariably no amount of gold would satisfy the protagonist, who had brought about his misfortune—like King Midas—

by greed. *Are we proof of that?* James wondered, twisting his head with his hand clutching the back of his neck.

"In 1939 when I came over here, I felt lucky to land a job with good pay up in the cool mountains with the best climate in the Philippines. I'd had it with my former job in the depression Minnesota iron range, with all the layoffs and labor strikes." At the memory, James's thoughts plunged deeper into melancholy. The Itogon mine had hired him as an equipment engineer, installing and maintaining the constantly running system of hoists, lifts, and trams. Initially it had seemed clear as day that he had a steady job he could count on, as long as the hoists ran nonstop delivering men and equipment between the depths, and the trams tons of ore to the processing mills on the surface, and the investors kept getting richer. "For me, it was all about a secure job and a comfortable life," James said.

"And no more God-awful Minnesota winters," Barnett said, a bit too cheerfully.

"Yeah, they told me that the climate in the mountain city Baguio would be more like San Francisco than a tropical island." James remembered reading a Baguio tourist pamphlet quoting the first colonial Governor William Howard Taft, the 27th U.S. president, calling Baguio "The Summer Capital of the Philippine Islands." At least eight degrees cooler than in the lowlands, Baguio offered the colonials thankful relief from the sweltering heat and mosquitoes at sea level.

Barnett looked wistfully out the windshield. "For me, it was the end of the gold standard in 1933 that made mining here such a good opportunity. The price of gold against the devalued dollar rose from $20.67 to $35 an ounce at the same time the Depression struck. Gold seemed to be one of the few viable investments in a global market crash."

As the story went, the gold strikes had built Baguio; until two weeks ago, it had seemed like Simila, the mountain retreat of British India. In short order, Baguio became the operations center for the burgeoning mining industry, epitomizing the best of colonial lifestyle in the Philippines. Over forty years ago, when America had divested

Spain of the Philippines, in a lopsided naval victory against an obsolete Spanish fleet, there was nothing much there but native cow pastures. A sleepy Spanish garrison languished in obscurity where the plush Pines Hotel, called the Grand Old Dame of Baguio, now stood. The allure of Baguio at once captured the interest of the new American colonials. At 5,000 feet in the Cordillera Mountains, the central mountain spine of Luzon, Baguio perched well above the 3,000-foot upper limit of the Malaria belt.

With eyes like dark pools, Maria stared through the windshield with a faraway look. "In my hometown of Legazpi, at the southern end of Luzon, some days were perfect—the sun, temperature, and ocean breeze. When it gets cold in the mountains, I think about those days. But if I had not come to Baguio, we would have never met." Her expression of distant sadness gave way to a fleeting smile directed at James.

"If the mine hadn't hired you. After all, who can resist your fawn eyes," James replied, eliciting a giggle from her.

"If I am so appealing, maybe I could have gotten a better paying job. Baguio was full of job opportunities," said Maria, pushing out her lips Filipina fashion in a mock pout. "I can type 60 words per minute, do double-entry bookkeeping, and run a mimeograph machine."

James and Maria had begun a friendship soon after his employment at the Itogon mine. As the welcoming face at the mine head office in Baguio, Maria had exuded a delightful smile, full and friendly on first meeting. Taken at first sight by her dark liquid eyes and comely figure, James had struggled to refrain from staring, awkwardly glancing away or past her. Maria's fine-boned, heart-shaped face with a well-defined edge to her jawline accentuated her dark almond eyes and sensual lips. She wore her raven-black hair shoulder length ending in an inward flip. Maria had appeared a vision of feminine grace, so out of place in the drab office. Before coming to the Philippines, James had heard the tales

31

of dusky Filipina beauty; upon meeting Maria, he concluded she was the living proof.

Maria had pretended not to notice but found his self-conscious attempts at deference amusing and his dark hair, deep eyes, broad forehead, straight jaw pleasing. Before long she looked forward to his visits to the office, his engaging smile, and cheerful banter. He impressed her as a gentleman in a profession known for rough men. For James, the one complication, he had a fiancé at home in Minnesota, though she had developed cold feet about joining him in the Philippines.

When Maria asked him what his last name, Novak, meant, James replied, "It's Croatian for a stranger in a new place." For a young woman from the tropical port town of Legazpi 300 miles away, Baguio seemed as different from the hot coastal plains of her upbringing as it was to James from his starting point in the northern Minnesota iron range 7,800 miles away. She replied, "Then I am Novak too."

On the day he had received the Dear John letter, he had sat in his office rereading it and thought about Maria. It was just as well, he realized, and that evening they had their first date. The first time out socially with her, he learned her story over coffee and pastries. Breaking the ice with anecdotal stories of coworkers and situations at the mine had engendered a pleasurable level of good-natured mirth and comfortable trust.

Maria recounted an amusing office gag by her manager, who had placed a dark, three-foot statue of a Balul, the traditional rice God of the Ifugao mountain tribes, in the office. She told him how the carved, simplified wooden shape of a human with minimal features had been fitted with a small miner's hard hat made from a tin can and a shortened pickaxe in its hand. Maria chortled, "My manager said the Balul had done such an outstanding job protecting family granaries, they hired him to bless the gold mine. Now he's in charge; anything you need just ask him."

James laughed heartily and responded with a story of his own: Intervening in a dispute between rival miners, lowland Tagalos, a reference to the Tagalog language they spoke, and the Igorots, as the lowlanders called the people of the mountain tribes. "A group of miners objected to riding with the Igorots workers on the mine shaft elevators at the start and end of their shifts," James explained. "A shoving match started before I could step in. So, I demanded an explanation. The lowlanders considered their work more skilled and important, so they insisted that the Igorots should allow them to ride first in the elevators." He continued the story affecting the men's speech. "Then an Igorot shouted, 'We muckers gotta clean rubble 'fore de drillers work. Then why we no go down first? We got-a-wait while de drink coffee.'

"Then a lowlander shouted back," James continued, "Dey spit red betel nut juice all over the elevator floor," referring to the stimulant of choice the mountaineers chewed constantly. "We have to step in it. If they in elevators wit' us, de spit on our shoes and clothes."

James recounted how an indignant Igorot angrily replied, "That's a lie!" And another even angrier, "If Tagalo bastards wanna to go first, we happy throw 'em headfirst down shaft," receiving whoops of encouragement from the other Igorots. "At that point, I thought they were going to start fighting." As James knew, ancient tension between the two cultures lurked like an undercurrent. Contemptuous, the lowlanders regarded the mountain people as primitive, even a national embarrassment, as proof, the Igorot's reputation as former headhunters and tendency to favor G-string and loin cloths to trousers in their daily wear.

On the contrary, the mountaineers considered the lowlanders cowardly and devious. It was clear to James the lowland Filipinos feared the tribes, evident by the way they bunched together for defense. The mountain tribes were infamous as fierce fighters whom the former Spanish colonial rulers had been unable to subdue during three centuries of rule, and more ominously for revenge head hunting. Newcomers to the Islands quickly learned the legends, no doubt piqued by morbid curiosity. The American administration, Philippine Commonwealth, and Christian missions had all sought, but without complete success, to end the ancient warrior tradition.

"Well, the Tagalos howled in protest," James recounted. "They demanded that we fire the offending Igorots, something that damn well wasn't going to happen. So, during the shift I painted the elevator floor red. At the end of the shift, I told the men unless they could find any betel nut stains, they all had to ride together."

Maria looked at him dumbfounded, "You did that?"

James smiled and gave her a sly wink. "No, just wish I could. The management told them all to knock it off or there would be firings."

Maria had leaned forward with a shrill, girlish laugh bursting from the waist. "As you Americans say, you are pulling my leg. You are so bad!" Then her face went from jocular to serious. "But management didn't really solve the problem."

"No, they didn't."

"But you will have to deal with the consequences next time it occurs."

"I need to have the respect of the men, both lowlanders and mountaineers."

Their conversation shifted to Maria's story, how she came to Baguio from the port city of Legazpi in the far South of Luzon at the foot of the perfectly symmetrical postcard picturesque volcano Mount Mayon.

"What made you leave, Maria?" James asked.

"Like everyone else in Baguio, for better job opportunity," she said. "But I could no longer live in Legazpi." This was not the answer James had expected. The story came out with Maria holding back tears, as if struggling for face-saving grace. "My parents died, victims of a cholera outbreak." The memory of their sunken eyes and grayish, blue skin as they lay dying surface painfully from her memory. "I did not know how to care for my parents. By the time I understood hydration therapy, drinking lots of water with the right amounts of sugars and special salts, it was too late. I blame myself for being so stupid," she sniffled, her emotions cracking the thin veneer of her composure, tears forming in her eyes. "I do not understand why I did not also contract the disease. We shared everything, the same water, dishes and kitchenware, and washroom."

"I am so sorry," James said gently. At a loss for more reassuring words, he lowered his eyes slowly. He felt drawn to her, a sensation like the space between them closing, wanting to touch her supportively. He guessed her grief would last a lifetime, but admired her resilience, moving on with her life, graduating a proud recipient of a high school diploma.

The American administration had made education its number one colonial social priority in advancing the Philippine nation. Across the country, the massive introduction of public schools even in the most remote regions had brought public education to Filipinos hungry for it after centuries of neglect by the former Spanish colonial rulers. Though undeniably like every other colonial power, America came to the Philippines to harvest natural resources and for a base from which to project its military power in the orient. But unlike the European powers who had stirred bitter resentment among the colonized through blatant imperialism, America pursued a conscious troubled policy, between naked commercialism and the professed belief in the right to self-determination of all people.

By the end of their meet that day, James knew the story of her revival following the death of her parents. After high school, Maria completed a one-year secretarial program at a business school pumping out qualified clerks and secretaries for the needs of the new Philippine Commonwealth, the U.S. colonial government, and commercial interests. With mining contributing immensely to the economic wealth of the Philippines, Baguio became a magnet for Filipino job seekers from other parts of the country.

With only a referral from the vocational school, Maria arrived in Baguio alone at loose ends in a strange city where she knew no one. But at age 19, having good English, office fundamentals, typing proficiency, and classic Filipina beauty, on her first interview, she landed a clerical position at the Baguio head office of the Itogon Goldmine. For James, the rest seemed like fate. With both living alone in this remarkable new place, each hungered for companionship.

The reflection floated wistfully from James's memory. Maria's sullen look returned as she looked out the truck window at the parched dry season countryside of the valley. "I still can't get the sound of the machine guns out of my head. That Jap plane tried to kill us. It would have if the cloud bank hadn't rolled over us."

"But we're OK now," James said; he gently massaged her shoulder, hopefully conveying concern and support. *If truth be told*, James thought, they all felt dread of a world suddenly turned dangerous. For a minute, Maria lowered her face on his shoulder.

Fleeing Baguio, they had watched the picturesque Philippine gold boom city slip out of sight behind amorphous cloud banks sweeping the highland plain. "I will miss Baguio," Maria had said.

Now, a view of the broad plain of Abra punctuated by round crested hills, stretched east to the low coastal mountains of Ilocos Sur province. "Walter Cushing's mine is close, the only paved road on the left," Barnett said.

CHAPTER 4

Outbreak of War

PREVIOUSLY, ON DECEMBER 22, THREE WEEKS AFTER the first Japanese attack on the Philippines, the impending fall of the mountain city Baguio to the Japanese became fatalistically obvious. Early in the morning, the two volunteer observers, American civilians, on Mount Santo Tomas southwest of town, reported the arrival of the massive Japanese attack fleet eighteen miles away in Lingayen Gulf. Originally, the city civil defense had intended the observation post to provide reliable air raid warnings; from its heights, watchers would hear the planes while still twenty minutes away. Now with the first sounds of artillery fire reverberating like muffled drumbeats on the coast, two startled observers roused to a far more ominous threat. One howled frantically into the field telephone, raising army headquarters at the Baguio army base Camp John Hay. "Urgent! The Japanese invasion has begun."

The other observer peered through high-powered binoculars and shook his head in frustration. "A huge Jap convoy has just moved into Lingayen gulf. How many? It's too dark to make an accurate count. Damn, I didn't know Japan had so many fucking ships," he shouted, straining his eyes for silhouettes against a dark sea. "Judging by the shapes, most are likely troop ships. The escort ships are firing on the shore so they're easier to spot. Pounding the hell out of the beach!"

"They're softening up the shore before landing, poor PA bastards waiting for them on the beach. Stay put and report on the hour," came the voice on the other end.

When the observer slammed down the receiver on the field telephone, the other observer muttered cynically, "If the PA have any sense, they'll be running south to our forces around Manila, like chicks to a mother hen."

"Damn!" the first observer exclaimed. "A handful of Filipino troops on the beach are the only force between us and the Japanese. The Japs can just sweep them aside and fucking march up the Naguilian Road here unopposed."

"A complete FUBAR!" The second observer agreed.

"Yeah, Fucked Up Beyond All Repair," his partner muttered the common catch phrase. "By assholes in the rear. Lingayen gulf is the back door to Manila and the beaches, poorly defended. The military didn't think of this?" he shouted pumping his fists furiously into the air. After futile attempts to estimate the fleet size based on a lot of squint-eyed searching through high-powered binoculars for silhouettes or muzzle fire in the night, all they really knew was the Japanese armada was alarmingly big, unable to estimate the actual size of the fleet with any confidence. Over one hundred ships—85 Japanese transport ships, nine naval escort ships, two cruisers and seven destroyers—had moved in the early morning darkness into the calmer waters of the inner bay, unloading an invasion force of 47,000 troops.

On the beach only one PA battalion, the 12th Infantry, faced the oncoming landing craft. The Japanese onslaught easily brushed aside the desolate resistance by poorly trained, ill-equipped reservist troops. With the beach defense in ruins, the PA troops withdrew discarding their few machine guns in the sand, leaving the shore of Lingayen Gulf to the Japanese. Armed with two 155mm howitzers, they had succeeded only in splashing shells ineffectively in the water. As the Philippine soldiers fell back in disarray, the majority retreated in a disorganized stream south along the coastal road toward Manila to join the forces positioned around the city, seeking strength in numbers. A lesser number moved east up the Naguilian Road toward Baguio, on the way conscripted by Colonel Horan's 43rd battalion for help with road demolition and blockade.

The Miner Warrior of Luzon, Walter McKay Cushing

That morning in Baguio, the early dynamite explosions from the demolition jolted the citizens to a rude awakening and a new jarring reality. Assigned to defend the road to Baguio city, the PA 43rd infantry battalion, led by the American Captain Leo Giitter, returned to Camp John Hay after occupying the heights above the Naguilian road, an ideal position to inflict maximum damage on the approaching enemy. Appalled, Giitter's senior officer, the camp commander Colonel Horan had rejected his excuses that he thought his mission was road demolition and that enemy air and flanking attack had compromised his position.

Horan concluded that Giitter's inexcusable inaction warranted court martial, but current conditions precluded convening one. For a plausible explanation, he considered how Giitter had survived the December 8 bombing of Camp John Hay, the first of a series of Japanese attacks in the Philippines, by a freak stroke of dumb luck. A desk had blown back from the concussive force of a bomb, sheltering Giitter from the blast that killed five other men in the office. Horan now wondered if it had left him shell shocked, rendering him useless.

At the sight of the disorganized PA troops returning to Baguio, bitter grumbling spread among the civilian residents. With their nerves on edge, mounting rumors circulated of unopposed Japanese advances, talk included words like 'cowardice' and 'incompetence.' As the withdrawing soldiers moved on by south through the city, an angry man on the street pointed a shaking finger at the troops and yelled indignantly to no one in particular, "Useless PA bastards held a position over one thousand feet above the highway on top of a mountain ridge, with a 60-degree grade into a canyon below—an approach the Japs sure as hell couldn't detour! Look at them scram, leaving us in the goddamn lurch!" he railed, as others of similar view shouted and shook their fists at the PA troops in retreat.

The gossip mill responded with outrage at the sight of the newly promoted Camp John Hay second-in-command, Lieutenant Colonel Everett Warner, a known drunkard finishing off his military career as camp provost marshal of the military police, on a drunken binge racing around town on an MP motorcycle from tavern to tavern. Not lost on the PA troops under his command, in place of his gold major clusters, he now wore the silver clusters of a lieutenant colonel. The troops wondered uneasily about the vagaries of military command and updated his old nickname to his new rank Colonel Bottle.

"We are on our own!" both the PA troops and Baguio citizens collectively concluded as reality set in. The only other functional military unit in the area were sixty Philippine Scouts, an elite unit led by a Captain Ralph Praeger, Company C, 26th Cavalry. Their mission orders had been to secure the two roads into Baguio. But with the collapse of Cpt. Giitter's 43rd road blockade, HQ on the fortified island of Corregidor must have realized that a coordinated defense had become hopeless.

Besides, Philippine Scouts were too valuable to waste on suicide missions with no chance of success. All volunteers, high school graduates, the Scouts were the best-trained, best-disciplined Filipino troops in the Islands, with high morale and expert weapons proficiency. But with only 12,000 Scouts on active duty in the entire Philippine islands, they were too few to make a significant difference. HQ on Bataan ordered Cpt. Praeger to withdraw his scouts north to the Bontoc sub-province to recon the inland roads for enemy presence, leaving 84,000 Baguio residents trapped in the city entirely undefended from the advancing Japanese, and hoping for humane treatment as civilians from an enemy that had not signed the Geneva Convention.

As the PA command structure broke down, the herd instinct replaced discipline. Amidst the confusion, the 43rd conscripts fled the city in commandeered vehicles leaving Baguio city to its fate with Colonel Horan, now in command of nothing as it appeared to Baguio residents, chasing ignominiously after his men. In one act of defiance of the oncoming Japanese, the fleeing PA troops blew the local oil tanks. With black, oily smoke billowing skyward and orange flames leaping high above nearby buildings, they retreated south intent on reaching the main body of troops assembled around Manila.

With any formal semblance of law and order in collapse, the looting began. Howling rioters in groups ran in and out of buildings, through battered doors and shattered windows snatching and lugging away merchandise of opportunity. They overwhelmed a hastily assembled posse of local businessmen, flailing haphazardly with axe handles and a jerry-rigged water cannon on a tanker truck to restore order.

Colonel Horan had sent a final message to General McArthur's Headquarters on Corregidor: "My right hand is in a vice, my nose in an inverted funnel, constipated my bowels, open my south paw." Not knowing what else to do, he waited by the radio for the inevitable evacuation order. In their circumstance, the populace could not have given a hoot that General MacArthur had responded, "Save your command!" The derisive new nickname of those facing internment by the Japanese chose for Horan would stick like glue, 'The Colonel Who Ran.' For the abandoned Americans and occidentals, the fall of Baguio meant a loss too overwhelming to process as they waited for the Japanese to arrive, take them prisoners, and strip them of everything: their freedom, property, security, and safety. Not even their lives seemed exempt.

Back in Abra as Barrnett's truck trundled along the Abra throughway, on the last stretch before Cushing's Rainbow mine, James reflected on the first time he had met the independent gold mine operator at the Pines Hotel bar. It had been the evening of December 7, 1941, one calendar day ahead of the U.S, west of the International Dateline. Cushing had bought surplus ore crushing machines called jaw crushers from the larger Itogon Mine, which had replaced the smaller outmoded ore processing equipment with higher volume impact crushers. The business social occurred spontaneously after the equipment sale to the socially gregarious Walter Cushing. Though the deal had been small, representatives of the Itogon mine management attended, curiously interested in Cushing's gold mining venture in neighboring Abra.

The Pines Hotel represented one of the finest examples of boomtown gold wealth in Baguio. For a Sunday night, the atmosphere at the hotel had been unusually festive on the eve of the Catholic holiday, the Feast of the Immaculate Conception, with a day off work for most. Outside in the evening air the aroma of piney balsam wafting through the city had reminded James more of the pine forests of his home of origin in northern Minnesota than a scene from a tropical Pacific Island. Baguio boasted the nickname City of Pines for the stands of indigenous pines flourishing in the highlands of Benquet province. On that night, the problems of the rest of the world had seemed further away than James cared to imagine.

He had been nursing a scotch on the rocks when a familiar clear, resonant voice carrying above the din of the barroom broke his reverie. "Yoh James, over here." He spotted the wiry, broad-shouldered form and craggy, etched face of his boss, senior mining engineer George Barnett. "Come join us," he shouted, waving his arm at a table where four other men gathered, the solid form of the crusty Itogon Mine Supervisor Dave McConnell, and two midlevel managers, Pete Mason, and Bill Jenks.

A fourth man of tan-brown complexion and dark hair, unknown to him, gave him a broad smile. "Look who I found hanging out at the bar. Most of you know our hotshot equip engineer James Novak," Barnett said. The men at the table looked up from their drinks. "James, let me introduce you to Walter Cushing." The short, swarthy man, about 5'6", a wiry physique, rose to his feet extending his hand. James guessed Cushing might easily pass for a Filipino, but for his blue-grey eyes. Cushing greeted him with a hint of a Texas drawl, "James ma-ah pleasure!" pronouncing 'my' in two syllables, cluing James on his origin. His firm handshake and broad grin projected infectious enthusiasm, his eyes radiated energy.

"Walter's manager of the Rainbow mine, wildcatting for gold in Abra province. Walt bought our surplus jaw crushers collecting cobwebs in a warehouse," McConnell said.

Barnett whistled softly, "Abra, a bit speculative up there. Best of luck."

Cushing smiled enigmatically, "The corporations got Benquet sewed up like a piece of cloth. It's new opportunity."

"Oh, virgin territory?" said Barnett.

"Naw, not quite that pure," Cushing drawled. "If it were, it wouldn't be worth the bother. It's known there are pockets of gold-bearing quartz, though the diggings probably not as rich as in Benquet."

Mason said, "The jaw crushers are in good condition. Perfect for mining gold quartz that you got but not adequate for Itogon hard rock mining. As long as you're shopping, have you heard the new order from the colonial government? All mines must have a mandatory six months' stockpile of supplies—you name it dynamite, machine parts, carbide, cyanide. Until the Jap scare blows over, they see fit to tell us how to run our business—buy more supplies in case we're blockaded."

"Makes you wonder if there's collusion between the government and the suppliers," Barnett said. "Dough being spread around."

McConnel grumbled, "There's always that George. To them the industry is like a plump chicken prime for plucking, a damn nuisance, but the cost of doing business. Our operations are in full production, and I want to keep them that way. Besides, no need to bargain with the bloody Nips. It would take three months for our navy to find the pissant Japanese fleet and three weeks to sink it," he said, repeating the cliché wisecrack making the rounds.

"It's ironic," Pete Mason quipped. "If the Japanese invade, the colonial government might just tell us to destroy all the supplies we just bought."

"That's the least of our worries," McConnell said with a smirk.

James noted uneasily that the dismissive attitude to the Japanese threat seemed pervasive, alternatively referred to as a scare, combined with cynicism about military wisdom. At the bar, James had been talking to a middle-aged couple. The wife, Edith, expressed her concerns. "Yes, I read in the newspaper the military actually commandeered two cruise liners to evacuate military families. Stirred up a row with eager-to-leave civilians who thought they were getting bumped unfairly."

Her husband Tom, a stocky, broadfaced man with a hairline close to his eyebrows, introduced himself as a mining supplies salesman, James guessed trying to generate sales from the new military directives to the mines. Tom complained truculently, "Ah the Philippines is full of businessmen worried about being trapped here by the Japanese." He took a copious swig from his highball glass. "I say they're giving the Jap too much credit. Running roughshod over China is one thing but tangling with America is a whole different ballgame." When the restaurant announced their table ready, James wished the couple a pleasant evening. In parting Edith gave him a look of trepidation as if wishing she were somewhere else.

Although he had hoped Tom was right, he had his doubts. The signs of preparation for war were everywhere if one cared to look, with the Baguio civil defense ordering practice blackouts, in which residents hung black cloths over their windows. Brent, the Episcopal international boarding school for middle and high school students, had closed and its staff departed. Baguio residents had begun to regard Japanese merchants with suspicion, suspecting them of fifth column activities. Following the decision by the Roosevelt Administration to freeze Japanese assets, Pacific Commercial, the largest and one of the oldest U.S. companies in the Philippines, made the decision to liquidate its holdings, sending tremors of uncertainty throughout the Philippine economy.

"It's been six months since the American military began sending dependents back home. Washington thinks civilians leaving would look bad to the Filipinos. Some nerve!" Jenks said.

"The military doesn't tell us civilians everything they know," Cushing said, as a loud, jarring crash of glass interrupted their conversation. A stocky major, the gold cluster insignias of his rank on his lapels and the face of an alcoholic, red puffy cheeks crisscrossed by spidery red veins, stumbled into a waiter sending a tray of drinks crashing onto the floor. "Watch…the fuck ya goin,' goddamn googoo," he drunkenly roared, slinging the racial slur for Filipinos coined by the American occupation forces in 1898.

"Who the fuck is that?" Cushing asked.

"Camp John Hay second in command, the distinguished Major Everett Warner," Barnett said with deadpan sarcasm. "The Filipino troops call him Major Bottle."

"Hah! George here knows all the scuttlebutt," McConnell chuckled.

"Isn't Colonel John Horan in charge of Camp John Hay?" asked Mason.

"Yes, he is the commandant," Barnett answered, blandly.

"How does he put up with that stumble bum?" Jenks asked. "What's Horan's reputation?"

"I gather he's an able administrator, but then again the U.S. military doesn't assign their best officers to command a rest and recreation camp," Barnett replied.

"No kidding! A damn country club for the U.S. military. They come up here to escape the heat and mosquitoes in the lowlands," said McConnell. "They play soldier a few hours a week to keep up appearances. There's a battalion of PA there, more familiar with hedge clippers and dust mops than rifles."

"So, if war comes, we got a paper pusher, a drunk, and an army of domestic servants to man the defense of Baguio," Cushing remarked, ruefully.

McConnell squinted disagreeably, "America has more than enough men and modern equipment in the Philippines, and Pearl Harbor is just a quick trip across the Pacific. The Japs know it."

Jenks spoke with authority, "Plus the geography and terrain is a tremendous deterrent to an invading army, even a large one. With hidden bays and coves and a maze of sea routes through the islands, the Philippine archipelago is as porous as a sieve to the undetected movement of vessels. The mountainous interior and valley farmlands make the concentration of troops impossible without robbing them from one area to secure another," he pontificated. "From Peter to Paul. I can't imagine the Japs even able to garrison the coasts."

Cushing replied, "Seems like the miners are the only expatriate community in the Philippines that don't take the Japanese seriously."

McConnell waved his hand. "Don't get me started! Blame it on gold fever. We're not the grizzled prospectors in the pulp westerns. The truth is the top mines here are as modern and systemized as any in the world. We're sitting on the second most productive gold field in American history, thanks to our colonial interests in the Philippines. We built the mines, and mines built this town. We're not going to give it up to some nearsighted Nips who can't shoot straight."

"Hitler's successes in Europe may encourage them," Cushing said. "What else can you expect with their Axis alliance with Germany? The Japs took Manchuria, a large chunk of China, and are now running rampant over Indochina."

McConnell looked unimpressed. "They just have a bee up their butt because America won't sell them no more oil."

Cushing nodded, "Or let them sail through the Panama Canal. Pretty light penalties for their unspeakable savagery in China!"

McConnell nodded his head in agreement. "The Japanese invaded China defended by a poorly equipped, poorly trained Chinese army and still haven't defeated them. Pathetic! I wouldn't worry about them conquering the Philippines."

"Which we're all hoping that won't happen," Cushing said, glancing down at his empty glass, recalling his own observations. "From what I've seen, poorly equipped and trained seems to sum up the readiness of the PA troops."

Barnett looked for the waiter. "Another one, Walt?"

Cushing waved his hand dismissively. "After Major Bottle, one punch drunk rummy tonight is enough." A round of hearty laughter rocked the table.

Cushing looked reflective for a moment. "Before I go, I have to tell you how impressed I was with the tour of the Itogon mine. All those synchronized Koepe drum hoists running the operation! Double-drum mounts reeling and unwinding cable simultaneously, diesel driven, hydraulic braking, 6,500 feet of steel cable per drum. Wow! You got a whole array of them. When they're surplus, I'll buy a couple off you."

"I'm sorry, you'll have a long wait Walter," McConnell chuckled, motioning with his hand. "The way James here maintains the hoist in tip-top running shape, they'll be the main stay of our operation for a long time. He also oversaw the installation, knows them like the back of his hand."

"Impressive job James! Must keep yah hopping busy."

"Yes sir Mr. Cushing, the way I like it," James said, wondering if that sounded too hackneyed.

"We'll keep in touch. If you ever get an urge to move on, talk to me. I could use a good mining engineer. Profit sharing included."

McConnell eyed Cushing incredulously, "You can't have him! He ain't surplus equipment," he roared, eliciting laughter. "Ha! what profits?"

"On the level, if I were sitting on a rich vein in Abra, I'd be a fool to mention it in this bar. The way the Benquet mining companies gobble up the little guys, they're worse than a den of thieves," Cushing guffawed, winking to mute the reproach. The mining laws enacted by the colonial government favored corporate mining companies and before long the native mine operators—with their crude alluvial placer mining techniques, panning, sluice boxes, and shallow dog hole pits—were considered simply squatters. The gold boom fueled rampant speculation as investors eagerly snapped up gold claims. Fabulous bonanzas created inflated demand for gold mining stocks. Not all legitimate, fraudulent claim staking fleeced more than a few unwary investors.

James considered Cushing's remarks. "You seem to know your equipment."

"James, I was born into mining. My father was a mining engineer for a company headquartered in El Paso, Texas. He worked their mines in Mexico where he met my mother. My father is Irish and she's Mexican." James looked at him with heightened interest. "For a while,

47

conditions were tense south of the border." Cushing garrulously continued, "One time, Pancho Villa's men commandeered our train on the way back to Texas. My pa made me hide under the seat, though it proved unnecessary that time. A massacre of Americanos happened on another train when some smart-mouthed Texan called the rebel captain a greaser. After that, everyone riding the trains knew to mind their tongues in the company of rebels."

Feeling the effects of the drinks, Cushing's smile went wan as he reminisced. "After the Tejano border violence of 1910 to 20, Texas passed anti-Mexican laws. Texas Anglos had become deeply suspicious of Mexican Americans after Pancho Villa's cross border probes and Germany's courting of Mexico. My father decided Texas was no longer a good place to raise a mestizo family and moved us to Los Angeles. My brothers and I had been getting into too many fights. At least mixed marriages were legal in California so long as the couple didn't marry there."

"My parents came to Hibbing, Minnesota on the iron range from Croatia. East Europeans were not too popular with all our neighbors, though not much fisticuffs, expect at the hockey rink where we played. Some knuckleheads thought hockey sticks were good for hitting things other than hockey pucks." James said, raising his eyebrows conveying disapproval. "Sometime the American melting pot doesn't meld so well."

"Sounds like we see things a lot in common."

With a flash of annoyance in his eyes, McConnell bunched his fist, but his grimace quickly returned to a smile. "Say, what's a young buck like you doing hanging around with a bunch of old duffs like us. Tomorrow's a holiday. The dance floor in the Crystal Room is twitchin' with the crème de la crème of Baguio." The music drifted into the bar, a mix of swing and tango. He leaned forward, giving James a conspiratorial wink. "If I was your age, I'd be out there trying to hitch up with the daughter of a wealthy mine investor." The men at the table roared with laughter.

"Old Duffs!" Cushing responded in mock affront. "Speak for yourself. I'm single. Hell! Maybe I should be out prowling the dance floor."

"Now Walt, no need to scare the young ladies." The other men at the table hooted derisively.

The evening ended with the five men joking and ribbing each other like good fellows. That night, the residents of Baguio went to bed with no premonition that the next day would be any different from the last, blissfully unaware of the Japanese naval fleet massing three hundred miles north of Pearl Harbor and the Japanese bombers, based on occupied Formosa, fueling and arming for a strike on the Philippines 10 hours later.

On the morrow the Japanese airplanes unleashed multi-airstrikes in the Philippines. Baguio's Camp John Hay, though a small side mission, earned the distinction as the first target in the bombings. The rumor circulating after the attack claimed that the Japanese figured General MacArthur had been vacationing there. Maybe the Japanese reasoned they might get lucky and bag the big prize, worth a try. Their primary objective for bombing the American military airbases in the Philippines was to destroy American air power in the Far East.

CHAPTER 5

Bombing of Baguio

AFTER A NIGHT OUT DRINKING WITH MINING COL-LEAGUES, James awoke late in bed with Maria snuggling against him with her back to his chest. Golden fingers of light filtered through the pines shading the east-facing window of his bungalow. Content, he draped his arm over Maria's slender waist enjoying the warmth of her bottom spooning against his groin, stimulating him to arousal. As she wriggled happily in his arms, he cupped her supple breast. "Maria, I can feel your heartbeat."

"Our hearts beat as one," she sighed, snuggling in his arms, enjoying the masculine strength of his embrace enfolding her. Suddenly she became aware of time passing.

Turning to him, she frowned, "Oh my," she said. "I will be late for church."

"Monday?" James responded.

"Have you forgotten? December 8th is the Feast of the Immaculate Conception. Why do you think we are not at work?"

"I haven't forgotten," James said, gently stroking her inner thighs. "It's not often that I get a three-day weekend because of a religious holiday. And making love to you is a sacrament."

"Such a smooth talker." Maria sighed pleasurably. "There will be a parade, fiestas, and lots of food. You said you would come."

"Well, if there is free food, I'll join you."

"Your stomach! Is that all you think about?"

"That's not all I think about," James said in a roguish voice, tracing his fingers over her hips, his hand lingering between her thighs as she quivered to his touch. "First one pleasure and then another."

Maria rolled over, reciprocating with her own intimate caresses. With her breast pressed to his chest, James held her firmly, enjoying her every breath, pressing against her with throbbing urgency. "I will have much to confess," she said with a moan, arching her back in response. Though she said this lightheartedly, James knew Maria wrestled with internal conflict, ambivalently between her deep Catholic faith, the conservative sexual mores of her society, and in the ardent passion of youthful desire, her love of James. So, she had set aside her qualms and became his lover. "Just don't call me your mistress," she had admonished him.

"No, I'll leave that to the gossipmongers," James had replied. He smiled impishly, "You should keep some secrets to yourself in confession. We don't want the priest to know what a sweet little lovemaker you are, ripe as the most delicious fruit in the Garden of Eden."

"That fruit was forbidden. You are so bad!" Maria feigned reproach, raising herself and slapping him playfully across his shoulder.

"And besides this kind of thing is a bit out of his league."

"League?" Maria asked.

"It's baseball talk, and the priest doesn't play. It might be unkind to remind him what he's missing."

Maria wrapped her arms around his neck, "No baseball? Poor man." She giggled.

With Maria pressed against him, her soft shudders and caresses stirring him, James reached for a condom on the nightstand. He hesitated. A low rumble of approaching airplanes in the distance came from the sky, their engines clattering louder. Suddenly, the sound of explosions reverberated across the city. "What the Hell!" James exclaimed; together, they leaped from the bed grasping for bathrobes. Stepping through the door, they looked east toward Camp John Hay, where dark clouds of smoke and dust rose above the treetops. The

51

explosions lasted briefly before the whir of the Japanese bombers' radial engines faded and the planes were no more than retreating black specks in the sky moving south.

Throughout the city, shrill air raids sirens wined uselessly after the raid had ended. Up and down the street, faces appeared at windows. People rushed from open doors, conferring anxiously with their neighbors. One bomb had detonated in a jolting blast with swiftly rising plumes of smoke just beyond the trees near James's bungalow, jarring the residents in the neighborhood from their complacency.

"I'm turning on the radio." James said. They rushed back inside. Over a crackling frequency, Manila Radio broadcasted an abrupt report that the Japanese had bombed Pearl Harbor. James and Maria sat transfixed to the radio. From the broadcasts, it soon became clear that the Japanese air raids in the Philippines had been part of a two-pronged attack. Over the next few days, the enormity of the Japanese attack on Hawaii would filter sporadically over the radio. Japanese naval attack planes had sunk or damaged twenty American warships, destroying most U.S. aircraft on the ground, killing 2,403 American servicemen and leaving 1,178 wounded. President Franklin Delano Roosevelt would later declare December 7, 1941, "A date which will live in infamy."

While airplanes of the Imperial Japanese Army Air Force were returning from Pearl Harbor to their aircraft carriers, on the Japanese occupied island of Formosa, ground crews were fueling bombers and loading bomb bays for attacks on Luzon 450 miles due south. By destroying the American airplanes on the ground, the enemy had left the American forces vulnerable to nearly uncontested air attacks.

By December 23, it had become all too clear how underequipped and inadequately trained PA forces were to repel or even hold a line against the Japanese troops. With conditions worsening daily, James and George Barnett met over drinks at a local tavern where George proposed his plan to flee Baguio. With no other viable options for him and Maria, everything else seemed irrelevant amidst rapidly deteriorating circumstances in the increasingly besieged city. They would find relative safety of Walter Cushing's Rainbow Mine in Abra province Barnett reassured, though questionable in James' mind. "Walter Cushing is putting together an irregular, guerrilla militia. Abra's remote and currently overlooked by the invading Jap forces, the perfect place to avoid detection." James wondered how long that would last once Cushing put his plans for a guerrilla militia into action.

The tavern owner had insisted they pay for their drinks in silver pesos, a practice that had become increasingly common in the last two weeks among the merchants of Baguio, who believed silver to be the only currency hedge against expected wartime inflation. The cost of everything, including their drinks, had nearly tripled as merchants saw their last desperate chance of earning a living slipping away. Both men stared into their drinks. "So, George, how'd we end up in this fucked up situation?"

Barnett shrugged. "A lack of common sense. It's beyond me why anyone should be surprised by the Jap landing at Lingayen Gulf. It's the logical place if they intend to take Manila. They don't have to sail past the big guns of Corregidor Island into Manila Bay. They just enter Manila through the back door, like the fucking Germans going around the French Maginot line through Belgium in 1940." He shook his head in consternation. "The only thing slowing their advance on Baguio is a bit of road and bridge demolition. When the Japs take Baguio, they cut Luzon in two, north and south. So, the poor PA troops fleeing Baguio are making a last-ditch attempt to escape south to the security of our forces around Manila."

"The same straggling PA troops entering town on Naguilian Road? They ain't stopping to defend us?"

"No took a powder and so should we. There's no organized defense! Believe me, you don't want to be here when Baguio falls, a few days from now. If you are coming with me to Abra, it's now or never."

"What's Abra? The new Hooverville? And the alternative, a few months wait in a Japanese internment camp until the cavalry comes to the rescue?"

"A lot longer than that! It's damn sure their intern camps will be a lot worse than any depression shanty town."

"Huh?"

"The navy lost its best warships at Pearl Harbor, and now the Philippines is literally behind Japanese naval lines. Before any rescue, the navy has to rebuild the Pacific fleet, and it seems like everyone in the Philippines is forgetting that Germany declared war on America on December 11." Barnett furrowed his brow like a man tired of explaining the obvious to the oblivious. "With American resources spread thin, our European allies, the Brits and the Frenchies, get first dibs. The Philippines is on the backburner. Asia and the Pacific will just have to wait until our navy is strong enough again to punch through the Jap Pacific blockade."

"What about the American troops stranded here? Aren't they a moral priority?"

Barnett's mouth compressed as if stifling a laugh, James guessed cynically. "Yes, but if you have to choose, it probably makes more sense to leave them stuck here in harm's way."

"What do you mean? If the Japs take the Philippines, Manila harbor becomes a hub for shipping between Japan and the rest of conquered Asia. How can we abide that?"

Barnett returned James's gape coolly through lowered eyelids. "Think of it like punting in football. The further the punt, the more yardage the offense has to move the ball to the goal line. If our troops can't beat them now, we can at least put the Japs in a bad field position. As long as Corregidor holds out, their hub through Manila Bay does not become operational, regardless of whether they take Manila from behind."

"Bad field position for what? To keep Australia safe!" James responded, his face twisting petulantly.

54

"Without a safe base of operation in Australia, there is no rescue for the Philippines.

James gave a mock salute. "Well General, what should our sacrifice be for our Aussie friends?"

Barnett smirked. "For now, join Cushing's irregulars, a militia he created of local miners and PA reservists in Abra. He wants to harass and tie up the Japs in Northern Luzon—create a diversion to take pressure off the defense of Manila."

"Hmm definitely sounds like a punt," James said, leaning his head forward. "By irregular, what do you mean?"

Barnett explained, "Any combatant not part of the regular military. In our case, he intends guerrilla warfare—hit and run, sabotage, blend into the land. Guerrilla is the Spanish word for little war, the tactics the Spanish peasants used to drive Napoleon's army of occupation out of Spain. Using guerrilla tactics, a handful of troops can tie up a much more numerous enemy, forcing them to expend men and resources. That's the strategy. But there is a catch. Guerrillas are not self-sufficient. They must have the support of the people to survive."

"Like Robin Hood and his merry men."

"Well, the jungles here make Sherwood Forest look like a well-kept garden. To quote Mao Zedong—you know, the communist rebel commander in China, 'The guerrilla must move amongst the people as a fish swims in the sea.'"

James snickered, "I never took you for a red."

"I'm not. I hate the commie bastard and all he stands for," Barnett responded indignantly. "But he said one thing that makes sense in our current situation. It's time to start swimming the sea."

James looked doubtful. "The way Americans stand out, we're more like fish out of water. That will be our situation if the people don't support us!"

Barnett said with conviction, "If the people are outraged, we gain their support."

"The Japs are certainly doing that." James shook his head. "And how do we get to Abra? The Japs control the Naguilian road and coastal Highway 2."

"The Mountain Trail!"

"Halsema's Highway?" James huffed in response to Barnett's use of the informal name for the for the 140-mile-long trunk highway over the mountains connecting Baguio to Bontoc City. The former Baguio mayor James Julius Halsema, oversaw the construction during his 16-year 1920 to 1936 administration. Before Halsema had constructed the road, a narrow mountain trail formerly provided a wagon route for native traders transporting produce to the highland cities of La Trinidad and Baguio. It traversed some of the most rugged landscape in the country. "They say half the year it's closed because of washouts or landslides," James said.

The Mountain Province within the range of the Cordillera Mountains included a mix of the most primitive people in the Philippines. Igorots, as the Tagalog speaking lowland Filipinos referred collectively to the tribal people of the highlands, translated as mountain people. As Barnett had explained, the mountain tribes considered it a slur. "They've been fighting each other from before recorded time, have their own names for themselves, and it ain't Igorot."

"The further north you go the worse the road gets," Barnett said.

Halsema had built the highway to provide access for heavy vehicle traffic to and from the copper mines but continued it on to Bontoc city ending at the intersection with Route 4, a rough throughfare cutting across the breadth of Northern Luzon. The benefit to the locals, the road replaced the precarious wagon trail, an inducement to obtain their construction labor cheap. All hoped someday trucks would carry their produce to market, ending the wagon caravans.

Beyond the mines, the road narrowed to a landslide-prone rocky track blasted out of the side of vertical cliffs with sheer drop-offs, a hopeful prototype for future expansion. Though never having travelled the road, James was acquainted with its breath-taking descriptions. Rice terraces lined the mountainsides, carved into the mountain by ancient natives using primitive tools. On 8,914-foot Mt. Timbak, the third tallest mountain in Luzon, the highway peaked at an elevation of 7,200 feet. When the clouds and mist cleared, the views from the road above deep gorges extended all the way to the China Sea, the sunsets considered as breathtaking as the nighttime highway was dangerous.

"Oh, and when in Bontoc country, hold on tight to your head," Barnett said, smiling mischievously. "Traditionally headhunters, the Bontocs still practice it occasionally. It's said, young Bontoc men could not marry until they'd taken a head, a rite of passage for adolescent Bontoc boys to manhood."

James shook his head, "Some courtship. If necessary, how do we pacify them?"

"Gifts, tobacco, alcohol. You have any firearms?"

"A 38-caliber revolver."

"Better than nothing until you can get a Colt .45 pistol, a proper weapon for stopping jaramentado [running amok] Moros in their tracks." James knew the legend of the 1911 introduction of the pistol: the original U.S. occupation forces learned the hard necessity of effective .45 firepower when fighting at close quarters with the fanatical Muslim tribes of the southern island Mindanao.

"How are you with firearms, James?"

"Done my fair share of deer hunting."

"I figured as much. I'll bring a couple of Springfield rifles; .30 caliber is the most common large bore ammunition in the Philippines."

"I'll get the supplies together, appropriate a mine truck—didn't blow everything. I'll pick you two up at first light tomorrow. Tell Maria one suitcase only."

Feeling flustered, James asked "How should I reassure her?"

Barnett looked pensive. "Tell her the Japs are focused on securing the coasts. They haven't moved much into the interior, and there are no indications they intend to, soon. Hopefully, Maria will find that persuasive."

"I appreciate your invitation. But life in a guerrilla camp? Is that any place for a woman?"

"Well, if the Japs get the personnel records from the mine, she could be in danger. The Japs might single out Filipino employees of Americans as lackeys and traitors to the Asian cause. You'll be more dependable if you're not burdened by that distraction." Barnett playfully punched James's shoulder. "Besides, nights in the mountains can get cold."

"Yeah! Where's your woman?"

Barnett chuckled, shooting him a crooked grin. "That's a long story."

"I guess we'll have time for long stories. How do I explain to her how long we might be on the lam?"

"Sometimes with women it's best to tell the truth in stages."

"Oh well, that explains why you ain't hitched." James smirked. Barnett half-smiled as though reluctant to dredge up old memories. He needed a partner for the journey, and James, as his direct subordinate at the mine, proved a known quantity, solid character, and not burdened by the responsibilities of family.

"Well, so the three of us cut and run. The rest of Baguio are on their own."

Barnett's shoulders slumped and his mouth twisted. "Baguio is a lost cause. That's why the military evacuated. Saving the people would be like trying to clean up shit creek one turd at a time. The Japs will roundup and intern all the Americans and allied foreigners as enemy nationals. I know it stinks, but I don't want to be one of them. I'm leaving. You and Maria are all I'm prepared to handle. But try not to knock her up in the meantime," Barnett said with a wry smile.

James smirked, "Latex has been around for nearly ten years, boss. No more need any more for those pig skins." He raised his glass. "To the trials of the road."

Barnett smiled, "All for one and one for all, D'artagnan," Barnett reciprocated with a clink of glasses

CHAPTER 6

The Mountain Trail

WHEN JAMES HAD PROPOSED THE PLAN TO MARIA, her voice wavered with palpable apprehension. "You want us to go off with George Barnett to fight the Japanese?"

"Not necessarily. This is the only way I can get us out of Baguio. I want us to be safe."

"Safe? You sound uncertain. Walter and George want to wage war. Do you think they will give you a choice." She stared at him wide-eyed in disbelief before narrowing her eyes critically.

"We are not going to surrender and put ourselves at the mercy of the Japanese. They were very cruel to the people in Vigan, and their atrocities in China are well known. I would not trust them to treat us well. So, we will flee and take our chances with the guerrillas forming in Abra."

"Why do you have to fight the Japanese?"

"Why me? It has to be somebody. I'm an American, it's my duty."

"You will defend the Philippines even when our soldiers flee?" Maria clasped his hands, her wide eyes betraying dismay. "You are not a soldier!"

"I will be when the shooting starts Maria," James said too quickly.

Looking back at him in alarm, her dismay spread from her dark eyes to her whole face, her lower lip turning pale between her teeth.

"I do not want you to get shot!" Her chin trembled.

"Maria, you need to understand the nature of guerrilla warfare. The guerrilla fights by stealth, picks his time and place, hits and runs, and lives to fight another day." As he tried to explain, he felt he was only succeeding in digging himself deeper into a hole, without the tact to ease her anxiety. He couldn't shrug off the bleak truth.

"You mean you provoke the enemy, but you don't defeat them. You think the Japanese will leave because you blow up a few bridges?"

"No, but we can tie up a lot of Japanese troops here in the North that would otherwise be on their way south to fight our troops."

"You flee to draw the Japanese to you? This is not a children's game of hide and seek. Can Cushing's small group make such a difference?"

James waved his hand as if brushing away frivolous objections. "Just like a woman! Deny the problem and it goes away." Maria's jaw tightened and her lips pulled back.

Catching his temper James changed tact, now speaking gently but firmly. "The other reason Maria, this is no longer a choice for us. It is a last resort. The military has deserted us, so the Japanese are going to capture Baguio any day and intern every last American they catch and punish Filipinos they believe too cozy with Americans. Aside from a few potholes dynamited in the Naguilian road, there ain't nothin' slowing them down."

James pulled Maria to him, his eyes locking her gaze in his. "Abra is further away from the Japs than here. Eventually American forces will drive out the Japanese. *Saying anything more specific would be a lie*, he thought.

"And if they do not, what then?"

"America will have to defeat Japan here. The Philippines is strategic to everywhere in the Pacific. Exactly when, there are no certainties. For now, we run and hide."

Maria stiffened in his embrace. "George Barnett is a very determined man with a mission. He will not be content to just hide until the Americans return. No doubt, he will put you at risk."

"I am determined too, Maria."

"I see! Going off with him puts us in his debt. He will take us from one danger to another," she hissed, her eyes suddenly becoming wary.

"But now the greater danger is staying here. We are leaving tomorrow just before dawn." He held Maria close; her breasts rose and fell rapidly against his chest with her breath.

She stayed silent, briefly, slowly shaking her head. "Yes, danger is everywhere. But you are my love. Where you go, I go." She freed herself from his embrace. "I must prepare food for the journey, chicken adobo," she said, referring to the popular Filipino dish of chicken prepared in a vinegar and garlic marinade.

"You know how much I love your adobo," James replied, receiving an appreciative smile.

On their last night in Baguio, James and Maria made love, urgently sharing the warmth of their bodies, locked in each other's arms, retreating briefly into the fleeting refuge of lovemaking, consummating in pleasurable shudders. They spooned together for the last time in James's soft bed. "Every pot has a matching lid," Maria said dreamily. "I am incomplete without you." James wondered uncertainly when they would again enjoy intimacy in the comfort of a warm bed and crisp bedsheets.

On Christmas Eve, 1941 James and Maria awoke just before dawn. He reminded her, "Maria you are not dressing for a day at the office—work shoes, trousers, and shirt. Find something you can live in for days because we are going to get grubby. Barnett will be here any minute."

"I understand." She emerged from the bedroom, with her raven hair gathered in a ponytail. Excitement beamed from her eyes. "Look, I am no longer a city girl." The loose-fitting khaki shirt and slacks did not diminish the feminine sensuality of her figure.

"How are the shoes?"

"A little loose."

"It ain't easy finding work shoes that fit your dainty feet."

Maria giggled, for an instant as if forgetting her apprehension.

Just as the dim light of dawn had begun to replace night, Barnett's truck rumbled to a stop outside the bungalow. A tarp stretched over the stake frame, like a covered wagon. A winch replaced the front bumper. Barnett yelled, "Come on kids. Time's a wasting. Let's go!"

Maria slid onto the bench seat of the truck between Barnett and James. "Glad you are on the small size, Maria. Would be rather cramped with three full grown men!"

"The truck looks jam packed in back. What all we packing?" James asked.

"Everything a well-prepared boy scout would need to flee from the Japs—food, tent, extra gasoline, sleeping mats, field stove and utensils, flashlights, batteries, even fish netting."

"Do you get a merit badge for that?" James asked. Barnett chuckled.

"Are we going to fish for food?" Maria asked.

"Maybe. And you can also toss it over a bush to catch a bird, dual purpose."

"George, what else you got back there?"

"Dynamite," Barnett replied.

"Is it dangerous?" Maria asked.

"Not unless you insert a blasting cap in it." Maria's mouth formed a silent 'oh.'

They drove past the outskirts of Baguio, their senses heightened moving into an uncertain future. Leaving the neighboring town La Trinidad, the truck climbed the gently sloping road into the foothills, past the locked gates of Camp Holmes, the vacated headquarters of the PA 11th infantry in retreat. "The military's abandoning Benquet province without a fight, like rats off a sinking ship," James muttered gloomily, his face clouding over.

"Yeah, rats are always the first to sense impending danger," George Barnett scoffed, steering the truck up the winding road.

James noted the absence of traffic on the road. "George, strange were not seeing other vehicles leaving town."

"I'm guessing that anyone mobile is heading south toward Manila. That's where our troops are. They think they'll find food and protection there, not in the desolate boondocks of northern Luzon. I'd be reluctant to head north if I hadn't made prior arrangements."

"Isn't south where the Japanese are headed?" Maria asked.

Barnett gave a grim nod. "Yup!"

They stared out at the country ahead. In the view from the road, the stonewalled rice and vegetable terraces appeared to rise up the mountainsides like giant green stair steps. "The mountaineers built them rock solid!" Barnett said. "You got to admire their engineering skill." He pointed up the mountain. "Natural irrigation. The cloud forests above the terraces supply the water."

James glanced up the mountain to the misty tops. "You mean rain forests."

No, a cloud forest combs the water out of the clouds; a rain forest gets precipitation directly."

Sitting between the two men on the bench seat, Maria ducked down, tilting her head sideways to look up the mountain through the window, her almond eyes darting from side to side. "Why would the cloud forest not remain?"

"Logging," Barnett answered. "Progress ain't necessarily good for the Igorots who live in balance with nature." For the first time, James considered that gold and copper mining could not be good for them either, with the land disturbance and cyanide chemical waste seeping into potable water sources. The once fish-rich, crystal rivers now ran polluted with muddy runoff.

The truck chugged up the steepening road, the differential growling on sharp rising inclines. "Hey George, follow the yellow brick road."

"It's gotten me this far," Barnett said.

Maria laughed merrily, easing his concerns about her mood. "The Wizard of Oz! It was supposed to come to the Baguio cinema." Then she frowned, "I would have loved to see that movie."

"First thing we'll do when the war is over," James promised.

"Believe me, Mountain Province ain't Oz," Barnett retorted. "The Munchkins here carry head axes. Headhunting used to be a big problem."

"What do we got to keep them friendly?" James asked.

"Gifts, tobacco, and Tuba."

Maria wrinkled her nose. "Tuba eww! You are not going to get drunk with them?" Akin to American moonshine, making Tuba amounted to a backyard operation distilling potent liquor from the sugar-rich sap of the Nipa palm flower bud. Double distilling could raise the alcohol content to 155 proof, with the accompanying risk of alcohol poisoning.

Barnett flashed an amused smile. "The Bontocs have a nasty reputation as headhunters. Be hospitable with them rather than our heads stuck on a post."

"That's right! We definitely don't want to offend our Igorot hosts," James snickered. Barnett had his own take on the ethnic tension, once saying, "The one thing the lowlanders can't stand about the mountaineers, they remind them that they too were barbarians 300 years ago."

Clearing her throat disapprovingly, Maria said, "Hmph, I think that is just an excuse for you men to get drunk. I do not believe they will cut off your heads because you do not drink with them. Otherwise, their stakes would have many missionary heads," she said with considerable earnestness.

"A matter of fact, they do," Barnett said with a wink. "A missionary head makes a fine trophy. And what makes you think missionaries don't drink?"

With the window rolled down, James shouted into the mountain air, "Hello! Heads to spare! Spare heads here! Come and get 'em!"

Barnett snickered; Maria crossed her arms tightly and pouted. "You two are bad men and I am stuck here between you. I just hope you don't go blind drinking that stuff."

"I'm already blinded by love, my dear," James quipped. Maria rolled her eyes as though having heard one too many of his witticisms dismissive of her concerns.

As they ascended into the mountains, the view revealed the crisscrossing wedge-shaped peaks of the Cordillera Central range, one behind the other, stretching as far to the east as the eye could see. Maria looked back at the mountain city of Baguio. Giant clouds spilled into the highland valley from the opposite mountain tops, shrouding the city from view. "Goodbye Baguio," she murmured sorrowfully. "I hope America comes to our rescue soon." Her remark met with silence.

On tight mountain switchbacks, the road seemed to disappear over the oncoming cliffs. "How do they get busses around these curves?" Maria asked.

A clever Igorot mechanic Bado Dangwa, owner of Tranco line, designed a bus chassis with a short wheelbase," Barnett said. "When the bus rounds a tight corner, the back end swings over the cliff. Passengers in the last three rows sit there with their asses hanging in midair."

"They must have quite a view," James said.

"No thank you," Maria said. "I prefer mine over solid ground." Barnett and James burst out in hearty laughter.

From the mountain tops, narrow ridges spread downward in various directions like the tentacles of an octopus reaching into the valleys below, lost beyond sight in the canyons and gorges. In places, rice terraces lined the crests of the ridges; flora of ferns and moss-covered trees crawled up the steep sides encroaching on small hamlets. Clumps of thatched roof huts on stilts perched close together like fields of gigantic mushrooms.

"All this moss over everything, 'Bagiwis' the natives call it, is how Baguio got its name," Barnett explained.

"It makes the tree trunks and branches look thicker," Maria said.

James admired Barnett's skillful control of the truck down the steep inclines in the road, alternating between braking and down shifting. "You'd burn out the brakes if you rode them the whole time," James said with the truck wining in low gear downhill.

Barnett nodded. "That's a definite hazard driving this road." James's sense of ease began to fade noticing Barnett restlessly twisting his head from the windshield and side windows, his firm jaw tight and flinty eyes scanning the countryside as if sensing something amiss. Grey, swollen clouds scudded across the sky on a rendezvous course with the mountain peaks. But he realized it was not just the road conditions or the weather on Barnett's mind. From working with him at the mine, James had learned his intuitions were usually reliable. For Maria's ease, James cheerfully tried to point out coincidental images in the landscape like Rorschach interpretations, hiding his apprehension through false nonchalance. "Look Maria, that ridge looks like the spiny back of a lizard…and that mountaintop, like a sleeping woman.

"Ha! You see boulders and think of a woman's breasts. What am I to do with you?" she said, now eliciting edgy laughter from the men, though seemingly oblivious to their forced tenor.

They had been on the road three hours when the distant drone of an airplane engine growing louder emanated from the west. "I heard it earlier, faintly, but hoped it was off somewhere else," Barnett said, his voice deadpan. "James, get the binoculars! ID it if you can." The sun glinting off the sleek fuselage, making identification of the single engine plane difficult at first, but as it banked into a turn in flight, James spotted the rising sun insignia on its wings.

"It's Jap!" James exclaimed. The war plane turned in flight putting it on a course with the road as it swooped toward them. "It sees us!" Simultaneously, as the plane appeared on course with the road, the fog advancing before the grey rain clouds rolled over the road. The plane veered to avoid the cliff above at the same time as the first grey mist from the advancing rain clouds reached the road. Now more decisively, the plane turned back racing the full mass of wet clouds to the road. With the first misty shroud enveloping the truck, vision dropped to barely beyond the hood. Barnett braked the truck to a skidding halt. "Everyone out. Now!" he roared. Without further prompting, all three lurched out of the doors, James pulling Maria by the hand after him. The clattering roar of the airplane, now invisible, sounded alarmingly above them, as if bearing down on top of them. "Hit the deck!" The three companions flattened themselves on the wet ground. Machinegun rounds ricocheted off the cliff behind them where they had been not 30 seconds earlier. The engine roar of the plane lessened and quickly faded into the distance.

Maria rose to her feet. Her hair hung wet, dripping on her shoulders and down her back. The rain had soaked through her khaki shirt and slacks, now mud splattered, and her dark eyes dilated in fear. When Barnett gave the "all clear," they piled into the truck and sat momentarily out of the elements, waiting for their reluctant nerves to calm. James wiped a smear of mud from her cheek. "There now honey, you're all right."

She began to sniffle. "My heart is pounding. Can't you hear it?"

"He couldn't see us in the clouds," James said.

"Or the cliff, damn lucky break," Barnett said. "He wasn't going to risk slamming into the mountain in this soup, so he fired a few wild shots and flew off."

"Talk about coincidence, the timing's too perfect!" James said.

"It was God's hand," Maria said. "The clouds were heaven sent. God still has a purpose for us." Maria rested her head on James's shoulder, with James waiting apprehensively for her trembling to subside.

"I'm sure you're right. You just might make a good Christian of me yet."

"I try."

"Until then, will you settle for a good man."

"I already have," Maria said somberly, stifling a sob. "Why attack us? We are civilians."

"The green stake cover must make the truck look like a military vehicle. The Japs are trying to seal off Baguio," Barnett said with grim finality. "They are flying the roads looking for any troop movement near the city. They must know our troops are operating in the Bontoc area."

"When we get to Cushing's mine in Abra we'll be safe."

"Safe!" Maria exclaimed, her dark eyes flashing. "They don't care if we look like a military vehicle or not. Just something to shoot at. Walter Cushing wants to start a guerrilla war with you and George part of it. My God!"

"I'm sorry Maria, but there are no good options, just some not as bad as others."

"The war will follow us wherever we go," she said with sullen resignation and a haunted look in her eyes.

After seven hours on the 140-mile road, they descended into the region of the Bontoc tribes, down toward a wide valley extending east. A bridge crossed a tributary river at its confluence with the larger Chico River, which stretched east in a straight line for miles between green-sloped mountains, then disappearing in a turn to the north. Wisps of smoke rose from the nearby valley. "That's from Bontoc City, the capital of Bontoc," Barnett said referring to one of the seven sub-provinces that formed the mountain province, each home to a different tribal group. "First leg of the trip is almost over."

Upon first sight James scoffed, "That's a capital?" A thatch roofed village appeared below the descending road on the west bank of the Chico River. They drove past groups of muddy men and women walking along the road on their way to and from work on the rice terrace walls. "Maintenance season," Barnett said. "The terraces got to hold firm against the weight of the torrential rains beginning in late spring, the start of rainy season."

The women carried baskets on their heads. Although their hips and exposed breasts swayed, the baskets remained steady on their heads, a feat of perfect balance and posture at which James marveled. "Wow! Perfect poise!"

"Like the daughters of Europe's finest learn in Swiss finishing schools," Barnett said. In the waist bands of their G-strings, lithe muscular men carried head axes, the concave curved blades designed for greater surface contact when slicing rounded objects, whether firewood or human necks and limbs. Opposite the cutting blade, a prominent spike protruded. "To hook a shield in battle and yank it away," Barnett explained. "Nowadays the axe is more a symbol of warrior tradition than a serious weapon of war."

"Thank God," Maria muttered. "I hope that's one tradition that isn't revived."

The Bontoc dwellings and structures spread out on a gentle grade at the foot of the Cordillera Mountain range above the Chico River. The typical houses of the Bontocs were thatch pyramidal structures built on rock foundations that, from a distance, looked like pointed haystacks. As the east side of town came into view, several brick and wood framed buildings became visible bordering the road. "The business district," Barnett said.

Against the backdrop of a terraced mountainside, a protestant mission, consisting of a collection of white buildings built around an open plaza, appeared to have been plopped down amongst the haystack homes, granaries, pig pens, and terraces of the Bontocs, which swarmed right up to the edge of the mission grounds. A church buttressed a steeple tower, peaked with a cross reaching prominently above all other structures in the town. The white stucco buildings surrounding the landscaped plaza screened the view of the Bontoc city from within, perhaps offering the resident clergy *a secluded sense of civilized grace*, James guessed.

Barnett spoke like a docent. "Bontoc is one of the few places the protestant missionaries have a chance in an otherwise Catholic country, up here in the mountains with the last of the pagans. In spite of converting to Christianity, the Bontocs still cling to their old animist beliefs and deities. They don't see any conflict in spiritual duality."

Interlocking stone construction characterized the Bontoc City, for walkways among their stone foundation homes, animal stalls, and peculiar, raised paved stone platforms of diverse sizes and shapes, which punctuated the town like markers, puzzling James. "There seems to be one in every neighborhood."

"They're a meeting place for their 'atos,' what they call their neighborhoods. A group of atos make up a village," Barnett said. Despite the ato divisions, James thought the paths and tracks through the town lacked geometric uniformity. "Each ato has its own council, which deliberates on ato matters, politics, and justice. The platform is also a site for ritual ceremonies, including animal sacrifices. That shack perched on each is the ato men's club, no women allowed. But in Bontoc City, the traditional poles for displaying enemy heads are absent."

"Village ordinance?" James suggested.

Maria sneered indignantly. "How could they call this place a capital if they allowed that?"

"Probably we'll see the head poles once we're out of the town proper."

Maria shuddered morbidly. "If there are heads on the poles, I don't want to look at them."

Barnett parked in front of Bontoc City's one inn. Metal percussion sounds drifted from a grass plaza off to the side of the market, a collection of crude stalls. There, loud, frenzied groups of Bontoc people danced in circles, beating on clanging brass gongs. They danced in synchronized steps to the beat. Their chants repeated over and over like incantations.

Maria stared in awe. "Is there a purpose to their dancing?"

"It's part of a religious ritual," Barnett said. "In times of crisis, they dance to appeal to their ancestors and gods to cure ailments, ward off bad luck, ensure harvests, and for success in war."

"I hope they're not that foolish. Spears and axes against guns?" James said, watching the men beat on symbol shaped gongs. The men moved in a circular direction in synchronized steps bodies swaying. Women in wrap skirts danced to the beat, moving in their own circle inside the men's circle to their own gender-matched steps. In each circle, one woman appeared to lead; the other women took their cues from her. They responded in a wave motion, swaying from side to side like a chorus line as the dance steps changed. The women raised their hands from their hips fluttering, weaving their arms in sinuous motion. In contrast, the men in the circle danced in boisterous, jarring leaps.

A sign posted on the inn read Mountain View Hotel and in both English and Tagalog, 'Food and Lodging' and "Pagkain at Tirahan.' In the interior, the scent of coffee, tobacco, and cooking oil, and unknown pungent smells permeated the premises. With the interior unoccupied, inn business clearly had suffered an exacting toll of the war. The fidgety proprietor, a short, stocky man with a bald, wrinkled pate like a brown leather cap, nevertheless greeted them with forced geniality betrayed by a worried grimace, "Magandang hapon! [Good afternoon]. I am Alfonso. At your service."

Bontoc tribal relics decorated the walls of the restaurant, spears, a battle axe, colorful basket like hats the men secured on the back of the head. Close inspection of a brass gong, "gangsa," Alfonso said, revealed a handle made from a human jawbone with the teeth still intact, attached to the gong by a looped cord. The jawbone, James guessed, functioned like a hilt in the hand of the holder when the fist wrapped around the cord. "A delightful relic," he said. Maria raised her upper lip disagreeably viewing the heirloom silently.

The proprietor ushered them to a table. "Today we serve chicken adobo," he said, though the restaurateur's portions had more vinegar-based marinade than chicken. "Definitely not your home cooking Maria!" James said eliciting from her a hint of a smile.

How's business?" Barnett asked.

"Slow, not many travelers since the start of the war." The proprietor probed them with questions about Japanese advances. Which way were they moving? Had they reached Baguio? When might that happen?

"Jap troops are sealing off the roads to Baguio. Their planes are flying over the roads and attacking vehicles. Don't go there," Barnett warned him. "How are the Bontocs taking it?"

Following the proprietor's gaze, they looked out the window. "They know unsettling changes with evil portent are underway. You see how they dance! Nonstop in the plaza for two days, reading superstitious omens in entrails, appealing to their barbaric god and creator Lumawig. Just when we thought we had them Christianized, their first reaction is to retreat into paganism—pray to the spirits of their ancestors and deities for protection and vengeance. If they believe the U.S. military and PA have lost the war, I worry what will happen to law and order. Will they become headhunting savages again and conclude their Lumawig wants something more than pig heads as offerings." Swallowing his fear, his Adam's apple bobbed.

The rooms were frugal, with two narrow beds on rollers that could be pushed together, though too tired and glum after an anxious day, neither James nor Maria felt so inclined. Christmas morning, as they drove away from Bontoc city along the rough, potted road beside the Chico River, gloomy clouds hung low and misty air fanned the valley.

"Is there no peace on earth, joy, good will toward men?" Maria asked sadly.

"Blessings to all, except the bloody Japs," James muttered.

"Deliver us from evil," Maria said, gesturing the Trinity.

"The Kalinga-Abra cutoff should now be passable in dry season," Barnett said. "It means we don't have to drive all the way to Tubac in Kalinga sub-province to catch the road into Abra. That will avoid some hazardous river crossings and road washouts."

"Named after the Kalinga tribe, no doubt," James surmised.

"Affirmative! Another tribe with a long, infamous history of headhunting."

"Then please take the Kalinga Abra cutoff, by all means," Maria said.

In the lower elevations of the Chico River valley, pines gave way to tree ferns thirty feet high, and eight-foot stands of cogon grass, undulating in the breeze. Through breaks in the grass and trees, the ato communities and rice fields at various elevations appeared on the hillsides. The road passed near an ato that on first glance appeared ordinary, just residents performing run of the mill chores, men moving between the ato and the fields, women weaving fabric with primitive hand looms. They sat on the ground stretching the fabric by leaning back against a taught harness around their lower back, hand-passing yarn horizontally through the threads and tamping it down with perpendicularly inserted sticks.

As the ato ceremonial rock platform came into view, James exclaimed, "Holy shit!" A severed human head appeared to stare back from the top of a raised pole, its long dark hair fluttering in the breeze.

Barnett glanced away from the road. "It looks fresh."

Maria moved her hand to her mouth. "Oh my God, an awful expression."

James whistled through his teeth. "Maria, I thought you didn't want to look at them."

"I think I will see worse things before this war is over," she said, prophetically.

Mesmerized by the sight of the impaled head, Barnett slowed down. Several Bontoc men ran toward the road waving spears in aggressive displays and shouting. He accelerated, driving away. "Seems like we've been warned. Mind your own business!"

CHAPTER 7

The Road to Abra

FOLLOWING THE DIRECTIONS GIVEN by the proprietor from the Mountain View Hotel, Barnett drove northeast on the poorly surfaced Route 4 toward the Abra province cutoff. Alfonso had told him the cutoff required crossing the Pasil River and that no bridge existed. "No problem!" he had assured him insisting that a man with a raft where the road met the river could ferry a vehicle across. Beyond the village of Labuagan, the river flowed slowly past the rocky shore, severing the road.

"The villages don't have Spanish names like they do in the south," James observed looking at the map. "The native names are harder to pronounce."

"The further north you go in Luzon, the more names are from tribal dialects, less Spanish influence. Ah, there's the raft," Barnett said. A rectangular flat platform, buoyed by thick bamboo trunks lashed together, provided a floating platform with multiple thin sheets of wood laid cross-grain over each other, forming a rudimentary plywood. The companions stared dubiously at the raft.

James frowned with disdain. "That's a ferry? The water's low. Could we drive across?"

"Doubtful. As soon as the exhaust pipe is submerged, the truck stalls," Barnett said. "And the winch runs off a drive from the transmission. Without a running engine, you're stuck."

"Someday someone will invent a reliable electric winch," James grumbled.

A path through the long, spreading leaves of a banana grove led to an open clearing with a squat hut with a thatched nipa palm roof. A man appeared, giving a two-fingered whistle, then second man hurried down the path after him. "I Filipe and he Calao," the first man introduced himself and his assistant. "You cross river?"

"Yes, if your raft can carry our truck?"

"Yis!" Filipe said emphatically, nodding his head vigorously, which James did not find entirely reassuring. From his work in the mines, he had become too familiar with Filipino reluctance to respond with a contrary 'no' considering it disrespectful, leaving one not always sure in advance if they understood his instructions. Filipe and Calao shoved the raft into the water, with the end just off the edge of the bank. "You drive now on raft!"

Barnett eased the truck onto the raft, which rocked and bowed disturbingly in the middle. With the forward end of the raft submerged beneath the waterline, Calao pushed it away from the bank with a long pole while Filipe hauled, his arms bulging, on a line of manila rope strung across the river. In response, the raft rocked precariously. "I can't imagine doing this in the rainy season on a swift moving river?" James said.

Maria splayed her legs for balance and gripped the truck tailgate. "If we get desperate, there's no telling what we will be willing to do. I think we will find out soon enough," she said prudently, her voice quavering apprehensively. Since the airplane attack, her gloom overshadowed her buoyant nature. Uneasy, James felt helpless to lift her spirits.

The raft reached the opposite bank without mishap. Barnett dropped four silver pesos in Felipe's hand. He grinned broadly, displaying a mouth full of betelnut worn, red-stained teeth and gums from a lifetime of chewing the intoxicating stimulant. "May God protect you on your journey," Filipe wished them, with a reverent nod of his head.

"I hope divine intervention won't be necessary," James muttered, considering their narrow escape from the airplane strafing attack. If

75

Maria believed that it was God's will, he hoped that would help her. He was not about to argue coincidence. Barnett gave Filipe a jar full of clear liquid, which he sniffed before taking a sip; a red betel nut grin quickly replaced his initial grimace. "Ah Tuba!" He handed the jar to Calao, who grinned like a cracked coconut after a full gulp.

"Good luck to both of you. I am sure we will meet again," Barnett said. As he drove the truck off the raft, it tottered disturbingly before the wheels gripped firm ground." He drove away from the riverbank with Filipe and Calao waving goodbye. Having made her feelings clear about Tuba, Maria sat resigned, frowning, her arms crossed tightly, as if realizing the values that had governed her life were coming undone.

The rough mountain road ascended past jagged peaks, in and out of the shade of rising mountains and yawning gorges, with each hairpin turn bringing into view isolated valleys, lofty plateaus, rice terraces, or sparkling waterfalls. Coming around a bend, Barnett stopped quickly before a short section of the road, narrowed by erosion, above a steep canyon. He got out and stretched a tape measure across the road. "We can do it!" He pulled out a length cable from the winch and directed James, "Wrap the line around that tree and secure it with the grab hook."

After securing the cable, James returned to the truck. "Maybe I should sit in the passenger seat for counterbalance," he said, opening the passenger door.

"Stay out!" Barnett barked, looking at him with exasperation. "Just motion to me if the truck gets too close to the edge."

"Please do as he says," Maria implored, thoroughly alarmed. Keeping the winch cable taught, Barnett inched forward as James waved him away from the cliff. Rocks loosened by the front tire slid over the edge of the road into the chasm. He stopped and took a deep breath before resuming his forward creep over the precarious surface. Once the truck had cleared the narrow section, Maria squealed with relief, "Bravo!" Clapping her hands, her spirits buoyed, leaving James confident that she was pulling out of her initial shock following the attack.

Upon reaching the Abra valley, they drove past rustic villages in northern Luzon, called barangays. Most consisted of the usual rectangular houses on stilts, with walls of woven bamboo slats called sawali. The peaked Cogon thatched roofs stretched in broad overhanging eaves well beyond the walls, a practical design for shedding rain and casting shade. For protection against rodents, flooding, storage and a pen for livestock below, the houses rose elevated on sturdy posts. From open, wooden-shuttered window frames, adult faces peered out as they drove past. James thought uneasily, *do they wonder what kind of devil would be driving the roads, in uncertain times?* As if they now found the sight of travelers on roads foreboding. Maria shuddered, a tremor passing through her shoulders, "Maybe they think we signal danger, like seagulls flying inland before a bad storm."

Before the Japanese tempest, James concluded.

Heedless, barefoot children ran to the road, waving and shouting the Filipino endearment, "Americanos, Americanos! Hey Joe!"—Girls wore white cotton wrap skirts with blue edging and sleeveless blouses and the boys, loose-fitting white pants, with dirt stains from work in the fields, ending below the knees. Barnett tossed candy from the window, sending the children scampering in glee.

"George, you think of everything!" Maria gave him a glowing smile; a reprieve James hoped from her earlier morbid concerns about his intentions.

In the arid height of the dry season, they drove past deserted rice fields solid with cracked mud that spread like a dry lakebed from the low, dry, brown mountains to the south. The mountains sprouted smaller, equally brown conical knolls and hillocks like goose bumps, the geological signs of timeless erosion. James swiveled, scanning the countryside. "I wonder what this place is like in the rainy season?"

Barnett gave a malevolent laugh, "Ha! Just wait. Actually, Abra's a bit drier than average for the Philippines, but still gets torrential rain, and muggy, steaming hot days in the summer." Barnett gazed out the windshield, searching. "The Rainbow Mine is off a road running south toward nearby hills. You can't miss it. It is the only turnoff with a gravel-paved road. Beyond's the town of Lagangilang."

"What's Lagangilang like?" Maria asked.

"A farm town with an Ag school and some Protestant missionary presence. It used to be the capital of Abra until they switched it to the town of Bangued closer to the coast. Well, what do you know!"

He pointed off-center at ten o'clock. "That appears to be our road up ahead." The road ran south straight toward a range of hills. He turned left and crossed over the seasonally shallow river on a crude but sturdy log bridge. "The Lingas River." Barnett pointed out. "This must be where Walter Cushing found the richest deposits of placer gold."

"Placer gold?" Maria asked.

"Gold deposits formed by water moving small gold particles into streams and rivers. The gold washes through underground fractures from the hills to the river. After you find the placer deposits, then you look for the mother lode in the hills. That's how the rich gold strikes in Benquet province near Baguio were discovered back in 1927." As they came over a low rise, a collection of galvanized metal-roofed buildings appeared against the backdrop of a hill. "That's Cushing's mine."

Barnett braked to a halt down the road from Cushing's Rainbow Mine, now an improvised military base. "Cushing has a perimeter of men around the mine. They have orders to open fire on any unidentified vehicle that doesn't stop. We wait."

From the vicinity of the buildings, an engine sputtered to life. A man on an Indian motorcycle puttered slowly toward them. The glint of rifles reflected from the scrub brush and rubble piles behind the advancing motorcyclist. The short, wiry rider stopped in front of the truck and dismounted with a smart downward kick of the side stand. Barnett stepped out of the truck to greet him. The rider asked, "What is the code?"

Barnett responded, "Everywhere but nowhere."

He nodded. "Follow me."

When Barnett got back in the truck, James asked, "A prearranged code phrase? I prefer 'Swordfish,' the password for the Speakeasy in the Marx Brothers movie Horse Feathers." He spoofed Chico's lines, "I give you three guesses. It's the name of a fish. Sturgeon? Hey, you're crazy! A sturgeon, he's a doctor a cuts you open when a you sick."

Maria and Barnett chuckled. "I saw the Marx Brothers at the cinema," Maria said. "They are clever, not silly like the three stooges you so enjoy…men bopping and poking each other, in the eyes. Really? Is that funny? Maybe to hooligans who gamble their money away at the cock fights."

"Oh, so now I'm a hooligan." Her teasing left James feeling relieved, signifying a cheerful return to her old self.

Barnett grinned, "Well, this ain't a speakeasy or cock pit. I hope your tastes in humor don't cause you no marital discord. Actually, 'everywhere but nowhere' is the basic strategy of guerrilla warfare Means the same as hit and run, just more poetic."

They followed the motorcyclist past the defensive line, where several riflemen guarded access to the mine premises. Barnet parked the truck next to a long, two-story, tin-sided building, as directed by the motorcyclist. Barnett frowned, looking at the gas gauge hovering just above empty. "The truck sucks fuel on the steep climbs." Maria gave him an unsettled look. "Not as bad as it looks. We still have fuel in a gas can. And I could dump the Tuba into the tank," he said winking at her with a wry smile. "High octane stuff."

After the long, trundling drive and moments of danger, all three felt relieved to be free of the dusty truck. The camp bustled with activity. A tropical sun beat down from a powder-blue sky. Men squatted on a tarp under the shade of a mango tree, disassembling and reassembling rifles, wiping the parts with oily rags. A short, lithe American man, his face handsome but weathered by the elements, moved among the men observing and issuing instructions. Then Walter Cushing stepped out the door of the staff house, greeting them enthusiastically. "Welcome to the Rainbow mine. I've been expecting you." He glanced at Maria with a quizzical squint.

"It's good to see you again, Walter," she said. "I remember you from your visit to the Itogon mine office. You were buying our used jaw crushers. I didn't know if you would remember me."

"How could I forget?"

"Those fawn eyes of yours again," James said in a low cooing voice.

Amused, Cushing gave an 'awe shucks' shrug.

"Walter! Good to see you again," Barnett greeted him.

"What took you so long?" Cushing asked. His mouth split wide open, his grey-blue eyes smiling with mirth in synch with his grin.

Affecting a nonchalant tone, Barnett said, "We stopped to see the sights."

Cushing brayed. "I forgot. It's the tourist season."

Barnett glanced from Maria to James. "I guess we should tell him what happened. We almost didn't make it." He paused, collecting his thoughts, "A Jap plane nearly blew us off the road. The only reason we weren't, a cloud rolling over the road at the last minute, saved our bacon. The pilot couldn't see us or the cliff in the soup. He fired a few wild shots and flew away."

The haunted look reappeared in Maria's eyes at the mention of the attack. "I'm sorry, Maria, you had a frightening close call. I would have been scared spitless," Cushing said, softly, but winked.

Maria fluttered her hand dismissively, with a hint of a smile. "Oh Walter, I don't believe anything would frighten you."

With his voice low and soothing, he said, "Maria, I can assure you there are no enemy planes over Abra. I am glad you are safe."

Her expression seemed to be saying, "Now! For how long?" She would not be so easily appeased. "Before the airplane attacked, I was just enjoying the view," she said. "I had never been on the road they call the mountain trail. We were so high, well over two kilometers, and not even to the top of the mountain. Can you believe it? I was thinking this is such a glorious place with all the peaks stretching one after another as far as the eye can see. I had just told James, you can see the hand of God everywhere, feeling safe under his grace. And then there was the

80

airplane and machine gun bullets striking behind us," Maria murmured. Her eyes returned to a bitter flat stare, her mouth compressed.

"I'm sure God was watching, Maria."

Maria gave Cushing a full smile, for the moment a release from fear, the sparkle returning to her eyes and dimples to her cheeks.

"Well, everyone, come on in out of the sun. Have some refreshments." Cushing looked at the other American supervising men cleaning rifles and whistled, "Hey Peewee, friends of mine from Baguio." The American came over. "Meet my partner, Maurice Ordun. Maurice, meet George Barnett, James Novak, and of course the lovely Miss Maria Lopez." All present shook hands.

"We've got a load of dynamite in the back, 500 pounds," Barnett said, returning to business.

"Peewee, more dynamite! Get some boys to unload the truck, stash it in the forward shaft, not too far back. Fortunately, I didn't follow all military directives 'destroy your mine' to the letter."

"I can see that," Barnett said sarcastically, scanning the relatively untouched premises.

"Believe me, I'll have plenty of time to blow the rest. Besides the Japs are mainly interested in the big mines in Benquet." *Who's enforcing military directives?* James thought with irony. Cushing ushered them inside the staff house into a large room divided into an office and a lounge with foldout tables and chairs. "Something to drink. Beer, Coke?"

James and George asked for beer. "Coke Maria?" James asked.

"No, a beer."

"I didn't know you liked beer, Maria."

Her eyes twinkled. "I find it soothing, like a tonic. Another bad habit I learn from you."

Cushing smirked. "The start of a fine relationship." He feigned a stern look at James. "Well young fellow what are your intentions with this exceptional young lady?"

Maria smiled back mischievously. "We are engaged."

81

"Well, that explains your being here. What a shame! Otherwise, I'd propose to you myself."

"Oh, how shameless," Maria mocked, eliciting a round of laughter. Ordun came in and joined them at the table where they sat sipping their San Miguel beers. "Things are a bit rustic here," he said. "We're just starting to get organized."

"It looks like you've collected a few firearms," Barnett said.

"It's a good start. So far, we have armed over two hundred men," Ordun said. Barnett whistled. Ordun continued, "Getting guns and ammo has been a bit of a scavenger hunt."

"The men are mostly local miners, some reservists who never got the call to duty, and constabulary troops from an abandoned post near Bangued city," Cushing said. "Seems their commanding officer thought the Japs were about to invade Abra and fled, deserting his post and men. We picked up some Enfield 17s, Springfield 03 rifles, a few BARs Browning Automatic Rifles, grenades, and several thousand rounds of .30 caliber ammunition."

"It was close," Ordun said. "As we were pulling out of town with the loot, two truckloads of Jap soldiers pulled into the other side of town. The civilians created a diversion hailing the Japs, welcoming them as liberators to the capital of Abra," he snickered.

"We think we can put the guns and men to better use without their AWOL commander. He's the same bastard who wouldn't let me dynamite the delta river bridges south of Vigan." Cushing slapped his forehead as if struck by the absurdity. "It would have bottled up the Japs in the north, at least for a while. The CO had the nerve to call me a fifth columnist."

"What is a fifth columnist?" Maria asked. "I have heard that name a lot recently, especially for the Japanese civilians in Baguio who immigrated here before the war."

"It means the enemies within—agents and provocateurs who work for an enemy to undermine a government and civil order by sabotage, spying, propaganda," Barnett explained, "During the Spanish Civil War, a reporter asked the rebel General Franco how he could expect to capture the capital Madrid with only four columns. He replied, 'I have a fifth column inside the city."

"Who are the real fifth columnists?" Maria asked.

Cushing gave a resigned shrug and shake of his head. "That would be the party of Benigno Ramos, and the poor fools who follow him, the Sakdalistas. They're pro-Japanese; they think an alliance with Japan is the road to independence."

"But America has already promised us independence in 1946," Maria protested.

"Ramos's followers are primarily tenant farmers in Central Luzon who want to break up the big land estates and distribute the land to the people. They think that America will rig independence in favor of the rich landowners, but that benevolent Japs will right the system and eliminate the greedy plutocrat elites. The funny thing is the Sakdalistas, and communists are competing for support of the people for the same purpose, each promising redistribution of wealth. The major difference between the two groups, the communists are just as intent on killing plutocrats as well as traitorous Sakdalistas and Japs. But now the Japs are pressing them harder. They can deal with the elites later."

"I recall Ramos is serving time for swindling," Barnett said.

Cushing snorted, "If the Japs haven't already freed him. His Sakdalistas staged a short-lived revolt in 1935—a pathetic affair. Afterwards, Ramos fled to Japan and lived there three years in exile, soaking up Japanese propaganda before returning in 1938 to do their bidding."

"These Sakdalistas don't believe the stories about Japanese atrocities in China. The more the rich resist reform, the more the poor believe any change here would be a good thing," Ordun said.

"When they realize the Japs' true intentions, most Filipinos will figure out they ain't nobody's salvation," Cushing said.

Barnett leaned forward, his voice grave. "Hope so, otherwise we'll be up to our eyeballs in Filipino spies and informers. As conditions worsen, the only thing most people will care about is protecting themselves and their families. When it comes to choosing between us and the Japs, they will choose whichever they believe is the safest bet."

Cushing objected, "The people need to know we are on their side," which to James seemed easier said than done. James wondered, was Barnett hinting at a more Machiavellian strategy, 'better to be feared than loved.' But Machiavelli had qualified his advice, feared, yes, but not hated. The Japanese had already sown a heap of hatred in a short time.

"Most Filipinos are quickly learning the Japanese are all stick and no carrot," Cushing said. "They don't give, just take."

"Where are the rest of your men?" Barnett asked.

"At the Lagangilang Farm School, the only town with facilities to house that many. Also, we had a pleasant surprise. A footloose American officer, Air Force Lieutenant Robert Arnold, showed up in Abra with a platoon of thirty-two men. They're training our irregulars. Robert was operating an air warning radar station at Cape Bojeador, you know, the most northwesterly point on Luzon, when the war started. His platoon became cut off. He led his men into Abra through the backcountry, avoiding Japs on the coast. That's when I found him and his men, hungry and with no other options."

"Hmm, electronics technicians training guerrillas," Barnett said.

"He's versatile, knows his stuff. I am thrilled to have him in my command. You'll meet him shortly," Cushing said, with a grunt of satisfaction.

Accustomed to the moods of his mine supervisor, James thought Barnett seemed puzzled, as if perceiving a glitch in the arrangement. "What's your next move, Walter?"

"I'm glad you arrived today. Tomorrow, I'm going back to the coast. The Japs are bringing in equipment at the port of Vigan and trucking it south. Highway 2 is now a major Jap artery. So, I'm going to blow up the Abra delta bridge south of Vigan, this time without the interference of that pissant constabulary officer." Cushing's eyes gleamed with restless excitement.

"Isn't it risky driving coastal highway 2, especially near Vigan?" James asked. Maria's eyes cast a troubled look. She had been listening with a half glass of beer in front of her, now taking a big gulp. James could tell she recognized Cushing's charisma, though found it disconcerting. She knew how easily hero worship swayed the passions of young men, obvious in the way they idolized star sports athletes. But it made her wary for his sake, even though she clearly liked Cushing, flattered by his charm.

Cushing responded confidently, "There's a dirt road from Bangued that parallels Highway 2, drivable at this time of year. Spur tracks run between it and Highway 2. Any Japs that I can't handle, I can scoot back to the dirt road."

"I would sure like to go with you," Barnett said. "I work fast."

Cushing gave a crooked grin. "Sorry, I don't want anyone on this trip who looks too Caucasian."

"Well, bless your Mexican mother," Barnett said with a smirk.

"However, George your covered truck is perfect for the mission, four-wheel drive, and can hide my men under the tarp."

"Hmm my truck commandeered already," Barnett said, laughing. "Try to bring it back in one piece?"

"OK Pop! I guarantee it." Cushing said, spoofing a teenager borrowing the family car.

"Where d'ya want us?" Barnett asked.

"Just cool your heels here. Pitch in where you can. Peewee can show you the accommodations, introduce you to Robert Arnold."

CHAPTER 8

Cushing's First Strike

MIDMORNING OF DECEMBER 31, Cushing, accompanied by five armed men, left the Rainbow Mine in Barnett's truck, and turned off the main road onto a narrow, rutted dirt road, avoiding Japanese military traffic on Highway 2. He hoped to reconnoiter the bridge before sundown. Arriving in sight of the bridge before dusk, Cushing parked the truck behind a bamboo thicket hidden from sight.

"There's still enough daylight left to place the explosives," Cushing said. "Juan, Alfonso, I want you two as lookouts at opposite ends of the bridge well down the road. If anything is coming, signal and take cover behind the piers."

Cushing's men unloaded the dynamite from the truck and carried it down to the river. At the height of dry season, the water level at waist height had dropped to its seasonal low. Slogging through the water over an alternately rocky and muddy bottom with packs strapped to their backs full of charges, detonators and fasteners, the men struggled to keep their balance on the precarious substrate of the river bottom, moving cautiously to avoid spills. Working quietly, they strapped the charges to the vertical piers of the bridge.

Before the men finished their furtive work with dusk gathering, the trundling sound of a truck approaching the bridge reached them from the south with the engine hum growing louder. Cushing signaled the demolition crew with an upraised palm and a point of his finger to take cover. The truck halted at the start of the overpass. From the Japanese shouting above them, Cushing at first thought the soldiers had spotted something amiss. But then two soldiers got out of the truck and ran across the bridge. To his relief and disdain, *just a bloody useless Jap drill*. He was about to give the enemy an unequivocal lesson proving that point.

The truck then proceeded north across the bridge, he assumed returning to the Japanese military base near Vigan. Disconcertingly, this would place them close on the same side of the river when he dynamited the bridge. But for his mission, there could be no erring on the side of caution. He was going to blow the bridge regardless, confident that his men were ready to fight.

Cushing waited until the sound of the truck disappeared and darkness fell. After sending the demolition party back a safe distance beyond the riverbank, he doublechecked the leg wires at the blasting caps, ensuring proper connection—plugged, crimped, and connected securely to the lead wire. In his mining career, he had seen enough examples of sloppy wiring not to skip the last check. His men ran the spool of the lead wires to the shore. He made a final continuity check of the circuit by connecting the two wires to his prized DuPont Galvanometer. Satisfied with the closed-circuit reading, he connected the wire leads to the blasting detonator.

When his men cleared the bridge, he pushed the handle activating the high voltage magneto, generating the ignition charge. In simultaneous fireballs and deafening explosions, a large span of the bridge bowed in a concave arc, cracked in three places, and collapsed as dirty grey smoke rose skyward. The heavy concrete sections splashed into the river, sending breaker waves curling up the dark riverbank. Billowing smoke and dust merged high in the air before dissipating in the wind and gloom of nightfall, trailing a strong acrid smell.

His men hooted enthusiastically. Delighted, Cushing stomped a spontaneous jig. "Well boys, it will be a while before any more Nip traffic moves across the Abra River. Everyone back to the Truck! Let's get the hell out of here." Cushing knew from experience the sound of the explosion would carry all the way to Japanese HQ in Vigan. He waved furiously at his men. "Every Nip in the area's going to be here like flies on shit." *Including the truck that just crossed the river*, he thought. The men at a running clip vaulted into the back of the truck, as his sergeant, Juan Valasquez, commanded, "Magma Dali [hurry]."

Under cover of darkness, the team retraced their route back on Highway 2 to a turnoff onto the spur track back to the dirt road. Cushing shut off the headlights on straight sections of road. On approaching a curve, he flipped the headlights back on, as if inexplicably able to divine just when in complete darkness. "Juan, I recall there's a deeply rutted section of road on the next turn." Approaching headlights appeared behind him in the rearview mirror. "Damn! That fucking Jap truck that crossed the bridge!"

Valasquez grunted affirmatively and slipped his arm through the BAR gun sling, at the ready for the inevitable fight. The automatic rifle had a notch cut in the flash protector to lessen recoil and limit the gun rising during firing, a fix that would become a standard practice by guerrillas in possession of the coveted firearm.

"Juan, we're going to ambush the bastards. We'll get through the curve first. The sons of bitches will have to slow down or risk getting stuck in the ruts. Either way, they will be sitting ducks," he shouted to Sergeant Valasquez as the truck frame transmitted jarring jolts of the road, with his head coming short of banging against the truck ceiling. *Poor bastards in the back.*

Cushing flipped the headlights on out of necessity, slowing down gingerly, straddling the dark pits in the rutted curve. The pursuing enemy, as expected, sped up, chasing his taillights, gaining on him, their headlights growing brighter in the rearview mirror. Clearing the deep furrows and pitted holes, menacing snares in the truck headlights, he flipped them off. He simultaneously twisted the steering wheel and pulled the emergency brake, locking the front wheels and skidding the truck around in a moonshiner's turn to a stop behind bamboo thickets, tasting but not seeing the dust kick up in the dark. The enemy truck reached the curve. "Rifles ready. Move!" Cushing ordered. The men in the back flung open the tarp, leaping from the truck. "Into the cogon," he ordered. His men dived into the tall, spiky grass.

The Japanese truck reached the curve at high speed, and then suddenly slammed on the brakes, the left-front wheel skidding into a rut. Stuck with the truck almost tipped over, the rear tire spun uselessly in the air. "Fire on the cab, Juan," Cushing ordered.

In Valasquez's firm grip, the BAR blurted out a deadly burst. Seen in the truck headlight glow, two silhouettes in the cab bounced off the seat from the force of the bullets and slumped forward. Controlling the rifle with the sling tight round his arm, Valasquez raked the length of the covered truck bed with automatic fire. All the guerrilla rifles opened up in synchronous fire, dropping the Japanese troops still able to fling themselves from the back of the truck, adding to the pile of the fallen enemy beneath the tailgate.

A few surviving disoriented Japanese soldiers frantically squeezed out of the truck between the truck side panel and canvas canopy. They crouched behind the tires and truck frame, wildly returning fire. Stepping into the road breaching cover, Cushing fired his .45 pistols, one in each hand, dropping two Japanese soldiers rising to flee across the road toward the brush. His men poured .30-caliber rifle fire into every shadow that moved or appeared human. Three of the enemy sprinted out from behind the truck, vulnerable in the open upon crossing the bare track. Two collapsed headlong before reaching the shelter of the brush, their faces thudding on the ground as only dead men would do. The thrashing of leaves showed the direction of the one who made it into the brush and kept going.

Valasquez fired a burst from the BAR into the bushes after the escaped Japanese soldier. *Dead meat if he runs into any locals*, Cushing thought, considering the growing animosity of the populace to the invaders. As a final precaution, Cushing pulled the pin on a grenade and threw it into the bed of the truck. He crouched down into a duck as the explosion shredded the canopy and ignited the truck. The flames illuminated dark bodies on the road." *No one could play possum through that*, he concluded.

"Forget about the one that got away, Juan." Cushing called out, "Pick up the damn Jap rifles and get back in the truck." He then noticed in disgust a Japanese Arisaka rifle discarded at the edge of the road. "Worse than cowardly, estupido!" Valasquez exclaimed. All six men piled into the truck with a cache of scavenged Japanese arms, a guerrilla necessity in response to chronic shortages of arms and ammo. Cushing drove away at a cautious pace, now with the headlights back on. "I think we killed at least fifteen," Valasquez said, guessing by a quick count of bodies on the ground and his best guess in the truck.

"Good counting, Juan! Your night vision is better than mine," Cushing answered, self-effacingly after his dead reckoning driving in total darkness.

"The one who escaped, he have a good story to tell his CO. Yis?"

"Yes, Juan, I can just imagine. How about Highway 2 closed to Jap traffic. No damn detours available." Juan cackled with mirth. The rest of the return drive back to the Rainbow mine passed without incident. From the cab, he listened to the men in the back, the tone of their voices flush with victory, their high hoots and giddy banter relishing their success.

Cushing pondered his own nature. He had to admit to himself, today's combat topped out as the most exhilarating event of his life. He had experience with men who compulsively sought thrills, like drug addicts, always searching for highs and lows to feed their addiction.

Did he fit the profile? He recalled his early adult years, roaming the United States in the latter part of the 1920s, working at such unconventional jobs as a parachute jumper for a barnstorming pilot, rivet bucker on a skyscraper, and a hard helmet diver on a Mississippi River pier and bridge project. The shortest guy on his high-school football team, his yearbook described him as "Full of LA Fight." Maybe his choices could explain his tendency to hit the bottle when life became too staid.

The actions today had proceeded according to the strategy he and Lieutenant Arnold envisioned, hit-and-run tactics by a mobile strike force against exposed, unwieldy enemy. In Cushing's judgement, the ambush in his first test confirmed the unit's moto 'everywhere but nowhere.' He looked forward to reporting the outcome, damn sure Arnold would be over the moon delighted.

CHAPTER 9

Guerrilla Training Camp

D URING CUSHING'S ABSENCE ON HIS BRIDGE demolition
mission, Maurice Ordun drove James and Barnett west down
the dusty, dry season Abra provincial thruway, turning off to
the Farm School at Lagangilang, the only practical billet for a battalion
of men in the province. "Lieutenant Robert Arnold put out a call over
the bamboo telegraph," Ordun explained, referring to the Filipino
informal, networking method of communication, "for reservists and
volunteers to report for duty, netting over two hundred men. Because
the Japanese struck first, Arnold had figured hundreds of reservists
dispersed throughout the province never received the original call to
duty."

Ordun parked in front of a long, single-story rectangular building
set next to a landscaped patio and field with raised garden plots. The
practical tropical design of the building included a galvanized iron
peaked roof painted white with broad eves to channel the rain away and
heat vents underneath to expel heat from inside. Overhanging palm
trees, blocking the sun during the hottest period of the day, cast shade
over the building.

The school site bustled with activity. "Walter turned the training
of the men over to Robert, a wise decision since he doesn't have any
formal military training," Ordun said. Several American army and PA
non-commissioned officers moved among the men checking their rifle
handling, aim and grip. Others appeared tasked with teaching basic

military skills, hand signaling, and small group maneuvers. "With stealth tactics, us doing the teaching could learn a few lessons from the Men." He looked pensive. "Guerrilla methods aren't much different from those of common criminals, something that doesn't come natural to upstanding, pillar of the community types. It takes a devious, cunning mind to think like a guerrilla. I'm certain we have more than a few bandits and carabao rustlers in our ranks," he said, referring to the Philippine water buffalo, the lumbering longhorn, ubiquitous beast of burden. He waved to a lean American of medium height in regulation army fatigues, with a long face and extended lantern jaw, observing the proceedings. "Ah, there's Arnold."

Lt. Arnold greeted James and Barnett with firm handshakes. "Glad to meet you fellows." He ushered James and Barnett to a table under a Narra tree, when not harvested for lumber favored for its sprawling shade. "George, James, welcome. Sit down for a minute."

"You got quite a turnout here," Barnett said.

"We're up to battalion strength. The farm school has the best facilities in Abra for billeting a group of this size. It has a schoolhouse and dormitory facilities." Arnold waved toward a group of squat nipa huts completing the campus. "Originally this was a trade school established exclusively for the native Tinguians," he explained. "The Ilocono settlers of western Abra regard the hill people from the highlands tolerably as semicivilized because they adopted Christianity to a greater extent than other highland tribes. But when the Iloconos objected to what they considered favoritism in the admission policy, the student body grew." With a glum shrug of his shoulders, he said, "Unfortunately, school's out all over the Philippines. You can thank the Japs for that."

Barnett's mouth turned down in a grim frown. "What do you call this unit?"

"For now, the Abra Battalion, until we get some kind of military designation."

"A battalion. That's still small considering what were up against," James said.

93

"Small may be perfect for our objectives, creating a military diversion—raids, skirmishes, sabotage—from the battles in the south," Arnold said. "Consider a historical precedent, the depression-era manhunt for the bank robber John Dillinger. The nation mobilized the entire U.S. law enforcement system to catch seven outlaws. The FBI spent two million dollars alone trying to catch him, far more than he ever stole. That's what we want to create with our small guerrilla force, a big headache for the Japs."

"John Dillinger was killed," James said, thinking he had spotted the flaw in Arnold's reasoning.

Barnett emphasized, "The Spanish ran Napoleon out of Spain using guerrilla tactics. I get it. . . tried and true."

"What I'm training here are practical squad and company tactics, surprise and mobility against a more powerful enemy. Fighting in rough jungle terrain with limited visibility tends to break up units and isolate men. Squads and small units can easily find themselves fighting on their own before they can regroup, like what happened to my platoon before we met up with Cushing."

"Doesn't that work both ways for us and the Japs?" James asked.

"Yes, but we will be better at it. The Japs are so goddamn regimented and inflexible, they can't function without effective leadership. When they scatter, we hit them before they can form up again. And when they press us in force, we deliberately fragment and vanish. Such fighting is fluid and calls for greater initiative and independent decisions from junior officers and NCOs. On the other hand, the Jap chain of command discourages individual soldiers from thinking tactically. They place so much importance on blind obedience so when they lose superior leadership, they are rudderless, unable to make decisions."

"And knowing the lay of the land gives us the home-field advantage," Barnett said.

"That's right, and the geography makes northern Luzon a haven for guerrilla resistance. Knowing it gives our men confidence. To the Japs, it is all a disturbingly unnerving unknown. As long as the people

94

are with us, the Japs only occupy the ground under their feet. When they advance, that ground reverts at once back to guerrilla territory. We engage the enemy when we have the advantage, kill their collaborators, and make it impossible for them to govern."

"We just have to outlast them," James grumbled. "Like a bad dream." He cringed, fearing his words showed weakness. He glanced at Arnold and Barnett for any sign of censure, relieved not to receive any.

"Kind of the way I felt when we visually spotted the Jap planes at Cape Bojeador," Arnold said.

"Just curious, Robert, what happened at your air warning radar station? Malfunction?" Barnett asked.

"Are you kidding? Why'd our radar miss the incoming Jap bombers?" Arnold said, his voice stressed defensively.

Sensing a raw nerve, Barnett said, "You don't have to tell us anything."

"We had just arrived and were still tuning the radar when the Jap planes roared overhead, close enough to see the fucking red meatballs on their wings. Ironic, with all our sophisticated equipment, we spotted them the old-fashioned way. We might as well have placed spotters at the lighthouse on the hill overlooking the cape," Arnold said, referring to the old Spanish edifice and signal light high above the precarious rocky coast. "At least up there we could have heard them coming."

He shook his head fitfully; his eyes darkened like a storm brewing. "I sent a radiogram to Air Force Headquarters, '35 Jap bombers flying south,' but no one responded on the assigned radio channel. More bombers flew over. I tried several times to report the bombers but got no answer." As if reliving his suppressed frustration, Arnold's shoulders gave a fitful jerk.

"Finally, after it was too late, all we got was a lone message, an order 'Destroy your secret equipment,' the only confirmation I got to my earlier message." With a dark look of consternation gathering in his eyes, he said, "My first thought was to return to the main body of troops around Manila. When we reconnoitered coastal Highway 2 a couple days later, we discovered the Japs controlled the road south of our position. With the coastal highway crawling with Jap traffic, escape to the south was impossible. We realized we were cut off."

Barnett rolled his eyes incredulously. "All factors out of your control."

"Yeah, a FUBAR from MacArthur on down. Nobody seemed to be in control." Arnold cast a savage look at no one in particular. "The fuckups started even before Pearl Harbor, December 7. By December 5, we knew there were five hundred Jap bombers on Formosa pointing this way. One of our Manila radar stations had been reporting blips off the west coast of Luzon every night since December 1."

Barnett's brow furrowed. "Reconnaissance flights?"

"Yeah, what we suspected. General Brereton wanted to strike Formosa immediately, but General MacArthur overruled him. MacArthur may have thought he could still keep the Philippines out of a war, and we know how fucking well that worked out. No one expected a bombing attack on Pearl Harbor either. The attack on the Philippines happened too soon after the first debacle to learn any lessons from it. Up here, we realized we were cut off.

Despite all the bad judgments, obvious in retrospect, James noticed a disturbingly critical disposition in Arnold's nature. Though nobody doubted there was enough blame to go around.

"That's hindsight for you. So how did you end up here?" Barnett asked.

"We bushwhacked our way inland to skirt the enemy. That's when word of our whereabouts reached Walter Cushing."

"The bamboo telegraph again," Barnett said, forever in awe of the traditional, amazingly dependable Filipino oral method of spreading news word-of-mouth by runners, intermediaries, and sometimes plain old village gossips. "It's like the whole of Philippine society is a living switchboard."

The sound of popping reports came from a makeshift firing range. "That's .22 rifle fire!" James exclaimed.

"Yes, a good training rifle. In farming communities, .22s are common for varmint control, so .22 ammunition is plentiful. On the other hand, .30-caliber ammunition is precious. I don't want them firing .30-caliber until they've developed some basic marksmanship with .22s."

"Lucky you linked up with Cushing here."

"Very fortunate for us. For a while, we didn't know where our next meal would come from. Cushing has been of tremendous assistance. I expect he's going to be particularly useful for demolition and help with civilian officials. I'm damn pleased to have him in my command."

James cast an uneasy glance at Barnett, signaling, 'Arnold thinks he's in command!'

Barnett looked away. "We are a couple more strays Walter rounded up,"

"I'm sure we'll put you fellows to good use. As miners, you're experienced with explosives and native labor management under difficult conditions, useful skills in the struggles ahead. I'm convinced this is going to be a long war. Things are going to get worse before they get better."

"My thoughts exactly," Barnett said.

"I hope you find the training here enlightening. In leadership roles, you will need to know the capabilities of the men."

After meeting Arnold and saying goodbye, James and Barnett returned to the car for the drive back to the Rainbow mine. James asked Barnett, "How do you think Robert and Walt will get along?"

Barnett responded with a troubled shake of his head. "Both think they are in charge. I hope they can resolve that amicably."

On January 2, 1942, well after dusk, Cushing returned to the mine, the headlights of his truck signaling the sentries, who hooted enthusiastic greetings announcing his arrival. In response to a phone call, Arnold arrived soon after from Lagangilang, grousing about the lack of security on the telephone line. "It's just a damn loop. The fucking Japs can tap into that line anywhere and listen," he grumbled.

Cushing exhaled a dismissive sigh. "Our lingo confuses them." Over beers in the guest house, he related the events of the bridge demolition and the ensuing ambush of the pursuing Japanese. "I tell you, taking out Jap vehicles is easy. You can boil it down to a formula. Just ambush them at a spot where they have to slow down. When they're practically sitting ducks, open up with everything you got on the cab and rake the truck bed before they can jump out and take positions." He gave an animated version of the fight with the pursuing Japanese soldiers, swinging an imaginary BAR. "Pow, pa, pa, pow! You should have seen Juan on the BAR, popping more shadows than Japs! I kid, the actions of all our men were exemplary. Arnold, your training stood them well. They all used the hand signals you taught them." He ended his utterance his fervent, "I hope the Japs got the message, no safe passage on the highways,"

As if not willing to be flattered, Arnold favored a skeptical frown. "No safe passage applies to us as well as them. The Japanese now know there is a resistance, whether we're ready or not. It will mean larger, more frequent Jap patrols. And it won't take long for them to install makeshift repairs to the bridge where you had your dynamite party— with pontoons and girders, much better guarded next time."

"But isn't that part of the plan!" Cushing said, taken aback. "Creating a costly liability for the enemy." *Like the Dillinger gang*, James thought cynically.

"Yes, but timing is the key and so is informing me before you do these things," which to James sounded irritable, like a rebuke to a subordinate who really deserved praise.

"OK Bob, how about mixing things up? As soon as they get traffic rolling again, we'll set up a large-scale ambush in Ilocos Sur. We have the men and arms to knock off a big convoy, and the sooner we do it the better."

"Well, the cat's out of the bag now." Arnold scowled disagreeably. "I'd say it forces our hand." James judged Cushing gained the upper hand. Arnold could not object without seeming *like a milksop*. "Okay, Let's look at the map of the coastal highway."

Peering over a map spread on the table, Arnold tried to glean a sense of the area south of Vigan. "Do you know the southern part of Ilocos Sur?" Arnold tapped his finger on the area around the coastal town of Candon on the coastal highway. "I breezed through it on the way up here.

"Candon is a medium-sized coastal village. It looks like promising terrain for an ambush—sea to the west and rice paddies to the east, all open ground, poor cover for the Japs.

"We will have to evacuate the town before the ambush."

"Yeah, the buildings are the only real cover," Cushing said.

"Yes, clear the whole town!" Arnold said. "We can't have panicked civilians in the line of fire or give away our presence."

With plans underway, the men of the Abra battalion busied themselves preparing supplies for the laborious, back country journey to Candon, marshalling arms, ammunition, and rations. James approached Cushing. "Walter, I see you are boarding up the mine and guest house and we're moving out. I have a personal issue—Maria. I need to find somewhere safe for her."

"I know that's the reason you brought her out here. We both have the same concern. I have a Filipina woman of my own named Dely. I'm boarding her with friends, the Villas in Bangued. Cesar Villa owns a gravel quarry where I bought paving gravel for the road to the mine; that's how I got to know them. They are fairly well-to-do by local standards. They should have room for one more adrift Filipina." Cushing stroked his chin thoughtfully. "Thank God nobody brought an American woman with them. Frankly, I prefer the local dalagas." He poked James in the shoulder. "They're the best in the world."

"I'll take your word for that, Walter. I don't have your extensive experience."

Cushing looked at James with an amused smile that conceded touché, point scored. "Most American women out here are nothing but trouble. My wife immediately became bored, started hitting the bottle, and complained about everything. She finally went back to the States and divorced me."

"That could've been me. I almost brought a woman from back home out here, but she got cold feet. Sent me a Dear John letter. Worked out for the best."

"I can see that. Maria's a charm."

"I'd be happy to pay for her boarding in silver pesos."

"We'll see. Spreading those around in these times might attract unwanted attention." Cushing looked up at the late afternoon sky with the sun low over the coastal mountains. "We don't have time to waste. I'll drive you there."

"Thanks, if it's not inconvenient."

"Hell no! I'd like to say goodbye to my gal Dely and introduce you to Cesar and Jocelyn Villa. Tell Maria to grab her things; we'll leave in fifteen minutes."

James hustled Maria and her suitcase out the guesthouse door to Cushing's truck.

"You know nothing about these people," she said.

"The Villas? They are friends of Walter's. I doubt Walter would leave you in the care of untrustworthy people."

"Yes, Walter is a gentleman," Maria said earnestly. "He has a good heart. I can see it in his eyes, though I believe he has had bitter disappointments."

"He perseveres. He has a fire in his belly that keeps him going," James said.

Maria slowly turned her head slowly side-to-side. "I don't know! But I fear his passion makes him zealous," a word James guessed she learned from a priest. Her vocabulary sometimes surprised him.

Cushing drove west down a road through open plains punctuated by occasional clusters of thatched-roofed houses. In Bangued, he turned left off the main highway toward the south side of town. "This is the Casmata Hill neighborhood, the better part of town, for what that's worth in these parts." In place of common woven bamboo siding, the Casmata Hill homes had walls of weathertight wooden planks, favoring sliding windowpanes of translucent capiz oyster shell instead of more common wooden shutters, Spanish tile roofing in place of thatch, and more spacious yards with gardens. As sunset approached, with the glowing red sun sinking toward the cover of the coastal mountain crests, Cushing pulled up to a sprawling wooden house raised on sturdy pilings setback behind a stone wall with sharp shards of glass cemented into the top, a deterrent to intruders vaulting the wall. A short, solid man with strong shoulders and a broad, smiling face and pleasant surprise in his eyes opened the gate, motioning Cushing to drive in and park. Clapping the man on the shoulder, he made introductions. "Hello Cesar! Maria, James, I'd like to introduce Cesar Villa.

Two women emerged from the house, a handsome middle-aged woman with twinkling eyes, followed by an attractive young Filipina woman, late teens James's guessed, with alluring dark eyes, a tantalizing smile. Her round cheeks transitioned to a small, firm chin; her long dark hair contrasted strikingly against her light amber complexion. James's eyes lingered on her shapely, feminine figure, outlined in a short, flower-patterned, pastel dress, until he felt Maria's familiar grip pinching his arm.

"Dely! Jocelyn! How are you ladies?"

"Oh Walter," Dely gushed, throwing her arms around his neck. "It's been too long. The Villas are such good friends to me, but I still so lonely without you." Her voice had a tiny tinkle to it, reminding James of bells on baby shoes. I hope the house not a mess without me to clean it. But with this damn war, there is no normal anymore." She looked apprehensive. "Are you going someplace?"

"Yes dear, we are leaving early tomorrow for the coast. That's all I can say."

Hanging her head, the young woman looked downcast and pouted. "Is it dangerous?" she asked, slowly raising her eyes as if acknowledging a foregone conclusion.

"The war has made things dangerous for everyone. It can't be helped."

Dely reached for his hand, clasping it between hers. "Please come back as soon as you can. I worry so when you are gone." Her voice quavered anxiously.

When James shook hands with Dely, she allowed her hand to linger briefly in his. If Maria noticed, she did not show it. She responded, "Dely, I look forward to getting to know you," and to the Villas, "Cesar, Jocelyn, I thank you deeply for your hospitality and generosity."

Both smiling, the Villas invited them into the house living room comfortably furnished with rattan chairs and a cushioned mahogany sofa. The capiz shell windows lit the interior with the red glow of sunset. After small talk and obligatory inquiries about wellbeing, Cushing came to the point. "Cesar, I apologize for springing this on you on such short notice, but I need a favor. I was wondering if you could board Maria, James's fiancée, for a few weeks."

"Yes, of course," Cesar said without hesitation. "Difficult times have come. Friends must help each other."

Jocelyn gushed, "Engaged! I am so happy for you. You are meant for each other; I can feel it." All expression disappeared from Dely's face for a bleak instant suggestive of self-pity before resuming its sparkle.

"All our children are grown and have left home," Jocelyn said. "We have extra room. Walter, James, won't you please stay for dinner?"

"Yes, please stay," Dely implored.

Jocelyn served a typical Filipino meal of adobo chicken over white rice, fried egg plant, and string beans. "Delicious!" Cushing complimented her, working the savory adobo vinegar sauce in to the rice.

"Oomasarap [delicious]," Maria concurred. She directed James, "See how she simmers the sauce to just the right thickness, so the garlic sticks to the chicken."

Jocelyn beamed with pride.

"Umm, I could eat this every day," James said, patting his stomach.

"His stomach is truly the way to his heart," Maria teased, with James radiating a soppy smile brimming with contentment.

"Cesar, what's the Jap presence here?" Cushing asked.

"As you know, there have been patrols, but no permanent garrisons yet. How long before they occupy us is anyone's guess."

"It is only a matter of time," Cushing said, his face dour with concern.

"Things are bad enough. A patrol this week kidnapped three teenage girls. No one has seen them since," Jocelyn said, with tears affirming her sorrow and dread. "Their families are beside themselves with worry."

"Bloody hell," Cushing exclaimed. The distant cries of violated women in Vigan flooded back into his mind. In the Philippines, rape was a crime that demanded vengeance, leading to a blood feud between the perpetrator and the victim's family. But a blood feud against an army of heavily armed invaders? *Vengeance is mine because it can't wait for the Lord*, an outraged Cushing thought. Nothing infuriated Filipinos like rape. The reports of Jap violations reaching him were increasingly appalling, not just for their frequency but for their degree of sexual sadism.

Jocelyn crossed herself. "No more wearing makeup for you two!" she admonished the young women. "Dely, no more pretty dresses. You are too tempting. These Hapon are wicked men." Dely hung her head, looking at the ground.

"I have a thought—been rolling around in my mind," Cushing said, "on how to keep the bastards out of Abra. It came to me like a revelation. Block the Tangadan tunnel!" All eyes in the room widened, considering the implications of the proposal. Hewn through solid rock, the Tangadan tunnel, completed in 1934, extended seventy meters beneath a prominent ridge, providing the only reliable all-season vehicle access into Abra from the west coast. The locals referred to the tunnel as the Gateway to Abra, obsoleting an old Spanish road, a steep, washed out, landslide-prone track cresting the ridge, especially dangerous in the rainy season. Since the opening of the tunnel, the old road through neglect had crumbled into derelict disrepair.

Cesar's eyes formed an astonished 'O'. "Forgive me, but I don't think there is enough dynamite in all of northern Luzon to collapse that tunnel."

Smiling indulgently, Cushing wagged his finger. "Oh no, no! We do not have to collapse it. I said, block it. We will dynamite the hillside above the tunnel entry to create a landslide. Then we shovel all the dirt, gravel, and boulders into the tunnel to make it impassable. No, it's not the only route into Abra from the west but it's the only one fit for convoy traffic year-round. For all practical purposes, the old Spanish road is impassable."

Cesar's eyes took on the look of a sage with a vision. "I know a road contractor in San Quintin this side of the tunnel with a bulldozer. With it, you can move much earth quickly. I will approach him. He hates the Japs and guess he would take pleasure halting them in their tracks."

At the end of the meal, Jocelyn passed around a large bunch of yellow bananas followed by cups of freshly brewed coffee, with all lingering at the table, enjoying the last satisfying moments of serenity together.

At ten o'clock Cushing said, "It's about time to leave."

Cesar said, "Wait here, I'll be right back. I will go now to the mayor's house, just down the street. If there are any Jap patrols on the road, he will know."

After Cesar had left, Dely softly cooed, with a mischievous glint in her eyes, "Oh Walter, could you come with me. I have a gift for you. I put it in the storage shed." The look was as old as time. While Jocelyn rolled her eyes, Maria looked as if she was biting back a giggle. A furtive, embarrassed look flitted across Cushing's face as he allowed Dely to lead him by the hand, out the back door and through the shadows behind the house to a storage shed. Once inside, Dely dropped to her knees. Deftly, she unzipped his trousers, freeing his erection, and, sensually parting her lips, took him deep into her mouth. Ambivalent feelings gripped him, one like a stallion aroused by a mare, the other self-conscious about the ambiguity of privacy. He stifled vocalizations of pleasure, quietly stroking her hair.

A mattress leaned against the wall. She rose, flipped it onto the floor, and seductively stretched out on it pulling Cushing to her. "I don't know when we can be intimate again. I think Jocelyn will understand."

104

His qualms succumbing, Cushing pulled her skirt hemline up over her waist and her panties off. "Ain't you the temptress. I surrender."

Giggling, she guided him adroitly inside her and began thrusting her hips eagerly in unison with his ardent thrusts. Pressing her fingers into his back, she purred and cooed in the language of love. Her body shook. "Oh, Walter, you make me feel like a true woman." Less than five minutes had passed, desperate passion on borrowed time, before they spent themselves. "It is sad we can't have more time together."

When I return, we'll make a full night of it," Cushing said. She gave him a lingering kiss. After leaning the mattress back up against the wall, they returned to the house, their absence fooling no one. Jocelyn and Maria were in the kitchen doing the dishes, James lounged in the living room affecting nonchalance, all three pretending they were none the wiser.

By the time they had composed themselves, Cesar had returned with reassuring news. The mayor said that a Japanese motor patrol had entered the town late afternoon but had left, heading west out-of-town back toward the coast. "There were no known captives this time." *A good man*, Cushing judged, hoping with trepidation the mayor could hold on to his position. The Japanese military had already begun replacing elected mayors, at least in the larger towns, with their collaborator stooges.

With goodbyes said by all, Dely clung to Cushing, woozy-eyed and languid. Beside the truck, Maria leaned back in James's embrace. "Please come back to me soon," she sniffled, examining his features, as if it might be the last time that she would ever see him. Both knew that was a real possibility.

Cesar looked grave, furrowing his brow. "We must keep this a secret. I do not trust all my neighbors."

"No problem," Jocelyn said. "Maria and Dely are my nieces staying with us after their parents died."

"Forgive me. That is too true for me, though I understand we need a good story," Maria said, solemnly. "My parents died of cholera before I came to Baguio. The mine office had been my only life until I met

James. We were both strangers in a new place." James and Maria smiled at each other furtively, acknowledging a private sentiment.

Jocelyn took her hand in hers. "I am so sorry for your loss. May you and James give each other comfort. God protect you."

"Thank you, we do. I pray."

Cushing and James drove back down the side road to the main highway, returning east back to the Rainbow mine. "The sooner we block that damn tunnel the better."

"Do you think it will keep the Japs out of Abra?" James asked. "Our ambush is going to stir up the hornet's nest."

"You are right about that. Hopefully long enough," Cushing said. All hoped aid and reinforcements would arrive in time to rescue the Filipino-American military forces now fortified in Bataan after withdrawing from positions around Manila.

"The rainy season will soon make the dirt roads through the bundocs impassable and buy us time," Cesar said.

Cushing recalled that the Tagalog word 'bundoc' as far as he knew had been the only Filipino word adopted into the English language, courtesy of the first American troops of 1899, who changed the short 'u' to the long double o's of boondocks.

CHAPTER 10

The Candon Raid

J NUARY 18TH, ILOCOS SUR, ON THE MOVE TO CANDON, the Abra battalion with more men than their few vehicles could carry traveled in shifts as far as the roads allowed, then continued on foot, spread out in groups along a narrow trail into the highland forests. Because of its remoteness and challenging terrain, the southwestern area of Abra provided covert access through the back country into Ilocos Sur. The first day, the Abra Battalion reached the hill village of Tubo. In contrast to their fearsome reputation as headhunters, the local Maeng tribe proved friendly and cooperative, vacating their best homes to billet troops.

Half-naked, the men wore g-strings and breach cloths, and head wraps twisted like turbans and the women, tricolored wrap skirts sewn from vegetable fiber, a bast thread, and bare-breasted. Unlike the common bamboo walled houses of lowland Filipinos, the residents built their homes from roughhewn lumber harvested from the timber rich mountain forests. Noticing bones hanging from the eaves, James drew Barnett's attention to them. "Jaw bones of their enemies from tribal wars," he observed. "Hmm, heirlooms from a more warlike time. Same as the Bontocs."

"Kind of like the way we collect sports trophies," James said with a sarcastic smirk.

The next morning, seeing the troops preparing to leave the village, the headman rushed over. He pointed to a hand grenade on Arnold's belt and motioned with his fingers 'give.' Arnold asked one of his men familiar with the border country dialect to translate. "Why does he want a hand grenade? Does he even know what they are?"

After questioning the headman, he replied, "Their fishing nets are old. He want to throw a hand grenade in river, catch fish. Maybe he learn hand grenades from comic books." Though a believer in the power of literacy to advance the people, American adventure comics were not the means he had in mind. The old headman mumbled and lifted his sinewy arms and palms up as if to symbolize great bounty. "He say it will help them very much."

Amused, Arnold let out a rare chuckle. "This I got to see." The old man led the way to a low saddle between the hills, where the flow of the river slowed, creating a deep pool. Through the interpreter, he gave the headman basic instructions—squeeze the safety handle, pull the pin, and do not release the handle until you throw. The old man pulled the pin with glee and heaved the grenade into the deeper water. A geyser of water erupted from the underwater explosion. As stunned fish floated to the surface, he whooped heartily, stamping his feet joyfully in what looked to Cushing like an Irish jig. Excited Maeng men, hooting in response, splashed into the river to retrieve the floating fish, flinging them onto the shore. Awed, Barnett shouted, "Wow, look at 'em all! The old fellow knows where to find the big ones."

"The village will eat well tonight." Cushing said. "And as esteemed guests, we will be welcomed back."

"As long as you bring a hand grenade," Barnett kidded.

Although no pack animals were available, they hired a dozen of the village men as porters, commonly called cargadores. Two days later, tired and footsore, the men of the Abra battalion cleared the mountains on the Abra-Ilocos Sur border, descending the widening trail out of the thinning forests into the lowlands. On arrival at the high elevation town of San Emilio overlooking the China Sea, the guerrillas set up bivouac, two miles from Candon. The first thing, they most wanted was to tend to their raw, blistered feet. James grimaced. His ankles and shins felt soldered together.

Leaving the distracted troops, Cushing, as ever the ceaseless dynamo, trotted off down the road alone at a brisk pace. "Where the hell's he going?" Arnold grumbled.

Cushing returned three hours later on a motorcycle with a popping engine and sidecar. "Borrowed it from the sugar mill north of town."

Arnold stared at the machine with misgiving. "Resourceful as always, Walter, but give me a heads up when you do these things."

Ignoring Arnold's irascible tone, Cushing said, "Well, do you want to reconnoiter the town before dark? I learned from the manager of the sugar mill that a Jap convoy passes through town every day about midmorning. We can hit the Nips tomorrow morning." He motioned to the sidecar. "Hop in the bathtub. We can be in Candon in minutes. The manager is also the mayor. I asked him to pass along a warning to the people of the town to evacuate."

"God, I just hope no one gets on the phone and calls the Japs in the meantime," Arnold said, clenching his fists. "I don't think it was wise to have given them that much lead time."

Cushing gave a righteous shake of his head. "It isn't much time as is; they need to get their asses out of here before their town becomes a shooting gallery. Also, the mayor told me, "There are no traitors among the people.""

Gritting his teeth, Arnold got in the sidecar. "I thought the Japs had compromised most of the mayors of the coastal towns."

Cushing quickly covered several miles to the village on the open road. As they reached the outskirts of town, forewarned residents were already in various stages of departure. Women passing by carried babies, and older girls towed younger children by the hand. Men fortunate to own Carabaos, drove them laden with packs with the help of the boys, also shouldering what necessities they could carry. Some women cast resentful and anxious looks; a few men gave them two-fingered victory Vs. "They're going to San Emilio," Cushing shouted over the clattering engine. "A good place for them to hole up with a bird's eye view of the coast. They'll be able to see anything coming."

In Candon, others were still frantically packing their meager supplies—sleeping mats, change of clothes, foodstuffs—and shuttering windows. Cushing and Arnold made their reconnaissance for about two kilometers north and south of the town center. A line of residences, stores, and structures of various utilities abutted the east edge of the road through town, with the west side open and no good cover save for the coconut groves on the edge of the beach. "Splendid! Any Japs that flee that way we'll catch in the open with their backs to the sea," Arnold noted, with satisfaction.

Just beyond the south end of town, a bridge spanned a dry gulley over a seasonal creek. Arnold looked down in the gulley spotting a discarded calessa, a two-wheeled horse-drawn buggy, staring, his face pensive as if pondering an idea.

Cushing approached him. "Robert, there's one thing I wanted to talk to you about. Whenever I give your men an instruction, they look at me as if I'm crazy or at you to see if you give them a nod. I know I'm not regular military, but I know things they don't."

Interrupted in thought, Arnold spoke calmly, in a soothing voice out of sorts with his perturbed, down-turned mouth and lowered brows. "Walter, I understand this is awkward. Tomorrow morning before we leave for the ambush site, I will tell them you are my acting second in command and that they are to obey all orders from you without question as if they came from me."

The second-in-command designation conflicted with Cushing's perception of their relative ranks. In his opinion, he shouldn't need a proxy command sanctioned by Arnold, but for now he'd let it slide, though mentally flagged it as something that should be resolved at the proper time. He had created the Abra Battalion and had rescued Arnold and his men from starving in the Abra interior. Though Arnold's training of his men had been invaluable, and his signal corps skills were indispensable for the raid's success, Cushing had no intention of letting him hijack his command—*second fiddle, out of the question*! After his bridge bombing, he increasingly perceived their differences in priorities difficult to reconcile, straining their working relationship, though

110

hopefully, not irreversibly. "OK Robert. I've seen enough. You want to return to the men?"

"Yes, Walter, I'll tell you how I want to stage this ambush as soon as we get back."

When they returned to the bivouac, Arnold called together the company commanders and key non-comms. James and Barnett, who had yet to receive a military rank, sidled up to the edge of the group, eavesdropping as Arnold spoke. "Listen up! I will set up three telephone outposts as soon as we arrive at our destination, the middle, north and south ends of town, all spliced into the main telephone line running through town. We'll all be hooked in like a goddamn rural party line, so all three companies will know what's coming.

"Sergeant Hunter, you're in charge of Charlie Company at the telephone tap at the north end of town just before the sugar mill. I will be at the south end of town near the bridge with Able Company. Cushing will command Baker Company in the center of town, at the junction of the east road. Take up positions with your men in the buildings facing west toward the beach or any other positions of suitable cover on that side of the road."

The men began murmuring among themselves. "I'm not finished! As soon as Charlie sights a convoy heading south toward town, Hunter will alert me at my command before the south bridge. Able will stop the convoy before it reaches the bridge." Arnold paused, gazing at the men, gauging their attention, noticing confused looks.

"There is a broken-down calessa below the bridge. Able Company will pull it up onto the road. The lead truck will have to stop to move the calessa. When they do, the trucks will close gaps, bunching up. But I goddamn guarantee when they see an untended buggy in the road, they will be on heightened alert, so stay hidden. Arnold glared at Cushing. "And, after your Abra bridge demolition, they damn well know there is an armed resistance."

As soon as they stop, Able Company will fire the first shots; this is the signal for all companies to open up on the convoy with everything we got. Cushing, with Baker Company, will direct fire from the center of town. Once the return fire ceases, we'll move from our positions and mop up. A special word to my company Able, I don't want any of these Jap bastards reaching the gully at the bridge. It's the only good cover anywhere near town; I don't want to have to flush them out." He addressed the two corporals from his platoon holding BARs, "Gunn, Goldblum! You two make sure that don't happen. Put those BARs to good use!"

"What if only a few trucks show up?" Barnett asked.

Cushing waved his hand dismissively, answering for Arnold, "We'll stay out of sight. If they don't spot us, we let them through and wait for a bigger convoy. We move out at 0500 tomorrow morning. I want us to be in Candon by dawn. I'll check the positioning of troops while Arnold is setting up the telephone taps."

Before dawn, breakfast consisted of papaya, scrambled eggs, coffee, and bread. Each man received a piece of fried chicken and rice, his food wrapped in a banana leaf and a banana to add to his day's rations. "Fill your canteens with water. You won't get another chance," Arnold said. All companies moved out on time and were in Candon as planned by 0600. When Arnold had finished supervising the installation of the telephone outposts, Able Company took up position before the south bridge, while Cushing double-checked troop positions along the length of the town. The men of Charlie at the north telephone outpost hunkered down in a sugarcane field among the canes with their field telephone ready, scanning the north approach to the town.

With the evacuation of Candon complete, the deserted village resembled a ghost town except for a few intrepid young men with long bolo machetes lurking among the shadows of the building. Cushing scowled. *Out to prove their mettle in blood.* Since he could not fault or shoo them away, he passed along a warning: "Hey hotheads, stay behind the buildings. Don't let the Hapon see you or do a damn thing unless they reach the buildings." He hoped to keep them behind the line of riflemen, away from friendly fire, but most of all from exposing troop presence before they could spring the ambush. He ordered one of his fighters, "Tell them in Ilocono, "Stay hidden. I'll kill any bastard that gives us away." He bawled out his message. The young men shook their heads with emphatic 'Heaven forbid' piety. He moved about double-checking positions while waiting for a phone call from the spotter at Charlie.

James and Barnett took positions in a house behind partially shuttered windows along with several other soldiers. "Well, we're as ready as we're going to be. Let's do some good," James said, clutching his Springfield rifle. Self-conscious, he perceived his voice sounding frail, lacking the toughness of a James Cagney delivery.

"We'll have a better idea when we see what kind of cargo they're transporting to Bataan," Barnett replied.

A dark-haired young man with corporal stripes and intense eyes solemnly murmured, "The righteous cry, and the Lord hears, and delivers them out of all their troubles."

Another American soldier looked at him like a hayseed with corn for sale and snickered, his lips drawn. "Let me make introductions. I'm Corporal Ray Hanley from Billings, Montana. The biblical scholar here, one of our radar techs, is Corporal Louis Heuser from West Virginia. He got a Bible verse for every situation. We call him Apple on account of him growing up in the apple country of the western Appalachians."

Heuser grinned. "Ray's getting polite. He usually introduces me as 'that damn hillbilly.'"

"Only when you're drunk," another soldier chuckled. "What you got in your canteen? That local Luzon Port?" the American slang for sugar cane wine.

"Basi?" Heuser replied with the Filipino name. "Not while on duty."

Barnett introduced himself and James. "George Barnett and James Novak, miners from the Baguio area." The three PA Filipino soldiers, clad in blue denim uniforms of the Philippine Army, smiled self-consciously, and gave their names; one with three sergeant stripes introduced himself as Conrado Potencion, the other two, as Hector and Emilio. Potencion explained he had been rounding up scattered PA reservists for a resistance group headed by a Major Cadonia Gaerlan, though none of the Americans recognized the name.

The door flew open; Cushing stomped through the doorway. He held one .45 pistol in his right hand, and another shoved in his pants. "Ok boys, I'm in the next house. This is the last check. I want everyone positioned at the windows ready. When the fighting starts, shoot straight, and don't stop until there ain't a Nip moving in the street. Then, when I whistle, move out." With two fingers in his mouth, he demonstrated a shrill whistle. "We'll mop up the area to catch any that might have slipped away." Cushing demonstrated a shrill two-fingered-whistle before slipping out the door. When he turned his back, James noticed fused sticks of dynamite sticking out of his back pocket. Peering out the bottom of an open window, covered by a slat bamboo blind except for the last eight inches, James slid his arm through the rifle sling. His hands felt clammy clutching the smooth walnut rifle stock. He licked his lips, his mouth dry.

Arnold moved south through the town back to the bridge at the southern end, inspecting troop positions. When he reached the bridge, the telephone rang. Hunter at Charlie outpost shouted, "Sir, a big convoy's coming. I can see six vehicles and hear more."

"They're coming," Arnold yelled to the four men near the bridge. "Get that damn calesa across the road. Fast!" The men thrashed down the slope and, snorting like workhorses, dragged the calesa from the gulley onto the road before the bridge. Arnold and the men retreated to the cover of the bushes on the east side of the road near the first house. As expected, the lead vehicle came to a stop before the calesa. Two harried Japanese soldiers jumped out to clear it from the road. The trucks behind slowed, closing the gap between the vehicles. The whole convoy of fifteen trucks came to a simultaneous, near bumper-to-bumper stop.

On Arnold's order "fire!," sudden bursts from Benedict and Gunn's BARs blasted through the windshield of the first truck. The driver bounced off the seat and slumped over the wheel. Rifle fire caught the two soldiers in the open as they tugged at the calesa, dropping them like scattered bricks. As arranged upon the first signal volley, .30 caliber rifle fire belched from the houses lining the east side of the road from one end of town to the other. The Japanese soldier in the passenger seat tried to duck below the dashboard, the bullets punching through the sheet metal like a can opener through tin, killing him instantly.

The second truck tried to pull out of line past the first truck but riddled by rifle fire, veered left too slowly. It collided lengthwise against the first truck in a crunching, screeching protest of metal grating on metal. The panicked driver of the third truck tried, unsuccessfully, to ram his way through, creating an impassible congestion of vehicles with mounting casualties from the piercing bullets along the length of the convoy.

Japanese soldiers still able poured out of the blocked, bullet-riddled trucks dropping in twisted contortions struck down by the hail of bullets from the gunfire erupting from the buildings. The more mobile Japanese who escaped the first volley tried to return futile fire from poorly covered prone positions underneath the trucks, unable accurately to sight their rifle fire from the restricted angle of fire. Their bullets zipped wildly through the air, ripping through the flimsy walls of the houses.

James crouched down at the window as a bullet hissed past his ear. "Fucking A," he howled. Barnett steadied his rifle in the crook of his shoulder, ignoring the snapping of bullets, leading his rifle sights on an enemy soldier running parallel to the road. He squeezed the trigger; the soldier crumpled to the ground. Humbled by Barnett's example, James rose from his cringing crouch, pulling the rifle into his shoulder, and blazed away through the window, chambering rounds and inserting clips as fast as he could operate the bolt on his Springfield. He could not credit for sure whose shots felled the enemy, but he knew with morbid certainty he had contributed to the overall slaughter. His worst fear eased; he had not shirked at the critical moment.

Uptown near Charlie Company, a Japanese officer with a sword attempted to lead a faltering banzai attack of soldiers across the road into the fray. Rifle fire erupted from multiple positions on the east side of the road, mowing down the dismal suicide attack faster than the enemy could rally an offense. Peering from his vantage at the window, James saw Cushing running down the street, a .45 pistol in each hand, shouting, "Get 'em boys, they'd do the same to you." The sputtering blast of BARs mopping up came from Charlie Company down the road and from Able Company catching the remaining Japanese in the center of town.

A few enemy soldiers quicker to react made it across the road amongst the buildings where the waiting Filipino bolo men intent on settling scores against the hated invaders, dispatched them with vicious strikes of their long, heavy knives. Like looters, they snatched up the long rifles with lethal bayonets, along with the ammunition pouches of the fallen enemy, emerging from the houses as formidably armed guerrilla fighters.

The last holdouts at the road, a dozen Japanese in a steel-sided dump truck, alternately fired and ducked to reload. Along with the soldiers, Barnett and James charged from the building onto the street trying to sight their rifles on the return fire and bobbing heads popping up in random order from the truck bed. A helmet flew off one of the bobbing heads, which disappeared in response to Heuser's quick shooting. Out of the settling smoke, Cushing came running down the street brandishing his .45 pistols. "What the fuck's going on?" he hollered.

"Damn Japs in the dump truck. Hard to get a bead on them," Heuser shouted back. "It's durned like fucking pop goes the weasel."

"Hell!" Cushing shouted. "Enough of this damn Nip-In-The-Box! Cover me." Thrusting his .45s into his belt, he strapped three fused sticks of dynamite together in a bundle with a looped cord. "Shoot at the rim of the bed! Keep them pinned down!" he hollered. As all poured fire on the truck, he lit a fuse from a cheroot and charged the truck. Simultaneously, a prostrate wounded Japanese soldier in the street raised himself off the ground and directed his rifle at Cushing. Reacting quickly, Barnett fired from the hip into the torso of the soldier, who collapsed face down on the road. Cushing gave Barnett a split-second glance of comprehension before hurling the dynamite into the truck.

A hand in the truck bed snatched up the deadly package, attempting to hurl it back. But the dynamite exploded a foot above the truck, shredding the steel sides into metal strips, revealing the concussion-mangled truck frame and shrapnel-riddled bodies. Taking no chances, the guerrilla fighters shot the dead Japanese bodies to ensure none resurrected from the dead armed with a live hand grenade.

When the last of the return fire from the Japanese ceased, more Filipinos with torches rushed into the street toward the trucks. Filipino guerrillas ran to the rear of a truck loaded with fuel barrels and tossed the torches into the back, which burned harmlessly around the barrels. "Ah hell," growled an American soldier who stepped forward with a BAR, riddling the barrels. When the torches ignited the leaking fuel, the fire engulfed the truck with a whoosh like a low rumble of thunder. Everyone close by leaped back as a fireball and greasy black smoke rose high above the nearby buildings.

"It's a goddamn signal flare to every Jap in the whole damn province," a soldier yelled. "We got to get the hell out of here. Damn quick!"

As grenades and dynamite hurled into the trucks were exploding along the length of the Japanese convoy, Cushing began shouting orders, "Hey unload them of anything useful first, damn it…Save those three Nip troop trucks over there for me," he pointed. "Pull 'em out. I want them." The rest of the trucks erupted in fire one after another down the length of the column.

Arnold arrived in the center of town greeted by the sight of a pumped-up Cushing running in a frenzy up and down the street, waving his .45s, "Whoo…we got 'em boys, we got 'em," skipping over pooling blood oozing from enemy bodies on the road. He ran over to Arnold, drawing his attention to a load of artillery shells that had not detonated in the back of a burnt-out truck. "Look what they were hauling, shells that ain't going to be used against our troops."

"Right, but first we have to dispose of them," Arnold acknowledged. "Check all the trucks for ordnance."

In a desperate attempt to escape, a few Japanese fled toward the shore. The guerrillas quickly dispatched them in a lethal hunt among the palm trees. A few more fled into the rice paddies. The young bolo men raced out from among the buildings, eager to try out their captured arms. Running along the paddy dikes, they easily hunted down the enemy wallowing through the thick rice paddy mud. Listening to the sharp cracks of .25-caliber Arisaka rifles popping, Arnold stood with his hands on his hips and a frown on his face, as he and Cushing watched a young man jabbing a bayonet at a prone body in the mud. "Unless they are with the recognized guerrillas, they should relinquish the captured arms."

Cushing waved his hand dismissively, "They earned it, let them blow off some steam."

"I don't want any independents," Arnold barked.

"I'll see what we can do about enlisting them in a legitimate local group. That would be Major Candonia Gaerlan's La Union Regiment. Some of his boys were near your Able company."

Arnold recalled, "Oh right, Walter. How do you recommend disposing of the artillery shells? We can't just leave them for the Japs to come back and collect."

"I thought about that too. The safest way to destroy explosive ordinances is open pit demolition. The pit absorbs the shock wave. I've done it before. I once had to destroy negligently stored dynamite sweating nitroglycerin. Instead of a pit, we can throw the munitions in the gully on the south side of town and blow the whole load."

"How effective is that?" Arnold asked.

"It will have to do," Cushing said. "Artillery shells are mostly TNT, which is more stable than dynamite so harder to detonate. Otherwise, the rounds would blow up the artillery piece when fired. That's why the shells didn't detonate when the boys burnt the truck." Cushing chose not to take notice of the impatience building in Arnold's face. "We'll place dynamite among the shells, which should provide an adequate pre-charge."

Working frantically, the guerrillas dumped the captured artillery shells from the trucks in a large pile at the bottom of the gulley, all conscious of the time passing. The miners Cushing, Barnett, and James placed dynamite sticks among the shells, connecting their short leg fuses to a single slow-burning ten-foot leader fuse. "I'm guessing the burn rate at three seconds an inch."

"Sounds about right," Barnett said. "That gives you six minutes to take cover."

On Cushing's order, men dug a slit trench with an earth berm facing south toward the gulley while the miners rigged the explosives. "That should do it," Cushing hollered. "Everyone move to the north end of town!"

Cushing pushed twisted pieces of cloth into his ears. With his cheroot, he lit the fuse, committing himself. Clambering out of the gulley, he ran flat out to the trench, hurling himself bodily into it. Despite his efforts to create a synchronized explosion, the shells exploded in a series of deafening blasts that shook the ground, sending up fireballs, dark plumes of smoke, and gritty, grey dust from the gully. One blast wave after another rolled over him as he lay flat on the bottom with his face in the dirt, with earth and debris raining down and projectiles whipping through the air above him. When the explosions stopped, he rose from the trench wobbly, covered in dust, and a look of awe from the shock of the concussions. Arnold came running up. "Holy cow! You look like you took a dirt bath."

"Yeah, it's cleansing for the soul," Cushing rasped, spitting dust, looking at the shrapnel-riddled buildings on the south end of town. He twisted his head with his hands, massaging his ears.

Arnold looked hard at him for an instant, then responded with a dry, affected laugh. "Very good. Fifteen enemy trucks destroyed or captured, all the munitions destroyed, sixty-seven enemy soldiers killed with only one casualty on our side, a soldier with a flesh wound to the thigh." As they carried the wounded soldier away on a stretcher, he insisted on holding on to his rifle in case fighting resumed.

As the reality of their situation sank in, Arnold called out, "Hell bells! The Japs will hear that all the way from Lingayen Gulf. Bottom line, enemy reinforcements are headed this way. Now!" At that moment, the racket of an airplane grew from the south. A Japanese twin-engine light reconnaissance bomber, a type called Betty, heading home to the Japanese air base outside of Vigan twenty-five miles to the north, dipped low over the town.

"Crap! Sure as hell, it's radioing the whole goddamn scene to Jap HQ," Arnold growled, "Move out. Now! Eat your lunch on the move." The order passed down the line of men. The retreating men strung out on the trail so as not to bunch up in vulnerable groups. On their arrival at the inland village of Galiyod, Arnold looked around for Cushing. "Anyone seen Walter?"

"Sir, he rushed on ahead," a soldier responded. When they arrived at the arranged rendezvous, a messenger delivered a note:

Dear Robert,
  Am going to the Mt. Province for
  A few days. Will join you later
Best regards.
Walter

Arnold showed the letter to Sergeant Joe Hunter. "Damn! If Mr. Cushing were in the service, I'd charge him with going AWOL. But since he's not, I guess I'm lucky to have his services whenever he wants to offer them. No telling what kind of quixotic mission he's off on now."

Incensed, he fumed, "His damn schemes completely lack sound military tactics. I give him credit due, he's a fighter, but his damned impulsive behavior totally lacks military discipline. It has got to stop."

Sergeant Hunter shook his lanky frame, bobbing his head mechanically. "Yes sir! How the hell would he get there?"

That damn motorcycle he borrowed, more likely stole. A skilled rider might be able to handle the trails south to the Cervantes Road. Though he's in for one ball busting ride." Arnold grumbled, "Serves him right!"

"He's one tough buzzard. Doubt that would deter him."

"Yeah, you're probably right Joe," Arnold said in a resigned huff.

CHAPTER 11

Lagben River Ambush

AS. ARNOLD MULLED OVER RECENT ACTIONS, feeling a deep foreboding. The accrual of events swayed his decision, to leave Galiyod at once. "We're moving out, heading inland. Now!" he shouted, to the relief of all. The day's incidents confirmed his instincts. Looking west from Galion, smoke rose from Candon. "Jap reprisal! The bastards are burning the town," Arnold bawled, his face a mask of anger, though he knew in his core reprisals were inevitable, no matter how much the guerrillas wished otherwise. Most disheartening, they could do little about it. The guerrillas knew the backcountry where refugees would hide. He resolved they would give the displaced residents what support they could.

With 500 Japanese troops devastating Candon two miles away, the Abra Battalion moved east toward their final destination, the mountain town of Del Pilar. Arnold advised the mayor of Galiyod, "When the Japanese come, tell them you did not like the Americans and told them to leave your town. If they come today, tell them we just left and moved east.

"Sir, just left?" Sergeant Joe Hunter asked with a bewildered shake of his head. "Obvious, ain't it?"

"I want them to think they're hot on our tail, no need for probing, forward scouting. I'm leaving a rearguard of twelve men to set an ambush at the Lagben River bridge, a delaying action to give the main column time to make an escape," he said. His body quivered, betraying accumulated tension. "Joe, you're in charge. I want our four best BAR men, including you, for the ambush."

His other three choices included Sergeants Lou Goldblum, Jim Gunn, and Bill Benedict. "I want each BAR man accompanied by a Filipino rifleman and an assistant to carry the ammunition and keep the twenty-round magazines filled. He will pick up the BAR if the gunner becomes a casualty."

Arnold unfolded a map. "Look! Immediately after this bridge, the road takes a turn sharp right and runs parallel to the Lagben river. Take up positions on the steep hillside on the east side of the river overlooking the road above the ravine." He jabbed his finger at the tight topographical lines on the map. "The Japs won't be able to flank you with the BARs holding the high ground. If they rush on to the bridge, wait until they're halfway across, then pour fire down on them from above. I will leave a picket two miles up the road to fire signal shots in case the Japs make it past you. If you encounter him, then it's safe to make your way to Del Pilar."

A mile outside of Galiyod, the road reached the narrow, wooden bridge spanning a sluggish stream at the bottom of a rocky ravine with jagged rocks breaking the shallow dry season water surface. Just wide enough for a truck to cross, the narrow bridge lacked guard rails, the absence making the crossing precarious. As each of the captured trucks crawled across the span, one man walked ahead, observing the wheel clearance and motioning to the driver left or right.

After the Abra Battalion had completed the river crossing, Arnold instructed the main body with the trucks to head toward Del Pilar about twenty miles inland at the base of the Tirad Pass. Allegorically, the Filipinos referred to the historical battle fought there in the Philippine–American War in 1899 as their Thermopylae, so venerating the memory, comparing it to the ancient battle fought between the invading Persians and Greek defenders. Stories embellished the Filipino heroes holding the mountain pass like ancient Spartan warriors in their doomed stand against overwhelming Persian forces. In the popular Filipino narrative, their martyr Rebel General Del Pilar died in a delaying action

123

covering the retreat of the main body of the rebel army through the pass into the wilds of the Cordillera Mountains, pursued by American forces. As for any similarity to the outnumbered Spartans, Hunter wondered fretfully if he and his men were about to become the modern version of that famous last stand.

From the west bank, Hunter assessed the steep, rocky terrain of the low mountain behind him, as his men prepared to fight the second battle in this vicinity in 42 years. Thick brush and boulders enveloped the slope. "Sir, the map don't lie, steep defensive terrain. Lots of natural cover from bottom to top. If the Japs charge across bridge, it'll be a damn turkey shoot."

"Exactly, Joe, that's what I'm hoping." Arnold led the men one hundred yards uphill, and with Sgt. Hunter, picking out four firing positions about twelve to fifteen yards apart among the brush and rocks. "Bill, Joe, man the center positions and take cover behind those rocks. You'll have direct fire positions on the bridge." Arnold then placed Gunn and Goldblum in the two flanking positions higher up the slopes, fifteen yards on each side of Hunter and Benedict's center positions, giving all positions interlocking machine gun sweep of the attack zone.

Arnold addressed the men before moving down the hill. "You each have a canteen of water, emergency rations, lots of ammunition and hand grenades. Sure as hell, the Japs will show up, damn soon. The bridge will create a bottleneck, stall their forward rush, like sand through the stem of an hourglass. I am betting they'll try to storm it. Stupid bastards!" He spat, "Give them everything you got. When you run low on ammunition or the action gets too hot, wait for Sergeant Hunter to order a retreat. Cover each other and move straight up over this hill.

When satisfied, Arnold left the BAR gunners, their Filipino riflemen and gunner assistants in the selected defensive positions. He hurried up the road away from site at double time after his departing column. The road narrowed to little more than a track. Hacked vegetation and dislodged boulders gave evidence of the effort needed to move the trucks he had sent ahead through the overgrown, neglected route.

Arnold heard behind him a great cacophony of steady .30-caliber rifle reports and the rapid bursts of the BARs, answered by the crackling zings of the light .25 caliber ammunition from Japanese Arisaka rifles.

Sair, sounds like dey give Japs hell," said his aid, a PA army corporal Odah Mawangga, by heritage a native of the northern Isneg tribes. Before finding his way to the Abra Battalion, he had become one of the displaced PA troops stranded in northern Luzon."

Lucky to have men like him, Arnold thought, with confidence growing in his men's resolve.

With grenade and mortar explosions joining the fray of battle, Arnold stretched his shoulders in a resigned shrug. "All we can do now is pray and hope for the best."

Mawangga mouthed the Filipino fatalistic saying, "Bahalana [Come what may]."

"Odan, I must go to Del Pilar to check on the troops at the rendezvous to make sure we didn't lose any. Wait here until dusk for relief," Arnold explained unnecessarily to the astute corporal. Mawangga, damn well knew, as forward picket, he was the first point of contact with any enemy coming up the road. Arnold instructed Mawangga to fire a few signal shots from his rifle if he sighted oncoming Japanese and make haste back to Del Pilar to report the enemy strength. "Make your best guess, no unnecessary risk, and beat it back as fast as you can."

As the rearguard had waited, readied for the approaching enemy, the day transitioned from cool to the scorch of the midday sun; the jungle shimmered in the hot, sticky air. Bill Benedict clambered fifty feet down the ravine to the stream below the bridge to wash up. While Bill was splashing water on his face, Joe Hunter heard the engines of a Japanese motor column moving east toward the bridge. He shouted down at him, "Damn it Bill! Get the hell out of there."

Benedict scrambled back up the steep bank and resumed his center position, as the first truck appeared before the bridge. Hunter fired a burst of his BAR through the windshield of the lead vehicle just before it reached the bridge. The truck careened off the road with a jarring thud into the trees alongside the road, with the two soldiers in the bullet-riddled cab slumped over dead. Enemy soldiers spilled out the back. A Japanese officer rushed forward waving a sword. He cried out "Banzai," the command for a human wave attack, signaling the soldiers gathered before the bridge onto the span in clear range of the ambush party waiting across the river.

The BAR and riflemen held their fire until the Japanese troops had concentrated in the middle of the bridge, jamming up the crossing, like sand through an hourglass. Upon Sergeant Hunter opening fire with his BAR, all his gunners fired at will on the mob of Japanese soldiers massed on the bridge. The appalling folly of the attack astounded him. *Like shooting fish in a barrel!* Strafing the bridge, he thought, *make your bloody sacrifice, for your bloody emperor, the sun god, whoever the fuck you think's worth dying for.* The .30-06 rounds from his light machine gun ripped through the officer's torso, with a red mist blossoming from his back. The advancing troops behind him fell to the fusillade of automatic fire, as fast as the gunner's assistants could reload the magazines. The riflemen fired at the enemy, easily scoring precision kill shots. Disgusted, Hunter wondered what the hell the Japs thought their exposed, head-on attack on the open bridge would accomplish tactically?

As the layer of fallen bodies on the bridge grew thicker, men scrambling forward stepped on and tripped over the bloody clutter, slipping on the blood slicks, losing their footing. Wounded and disoriented soldiers tumbled off the bridge into the river screaming, proving another way to die on the bone-shattering boulders below. Grasping the grizzly reality, another officer waved off further attack via the exposed bridge. The enemy halted and hunched down on the west side of the river. *Deadly obvious assholes, huh*! Hunter concluded.

More trucks of Japanese troops arrived. They split into two groups, one before the bridge returning fire that went wildly astray. So far, Hunter's squad had escaped casualties from the haphazard attack and halted the enemy on the other side of the river. Just then, another Japanese officer rushed to the head of the troops, waving his sword, signaling the second group to flank right along the top of the ravine, forewarning Hunter that the next attack would not be just another repeat of the earlier suicidal folly. Having wised up, the Japanese officer directed the mass of the troops from the upstream side of the bridge and into the ravine, launching a counterattack from the shelter of its steep, rugged banks.

The men of the ambush party fired at will against the shielded enemy with little effect. Hunter yelled to the Filipino riflemen, "Throw half your grenades into the ravine." He waved the eight guerrilla fighters down the grade. Moving from the BAR positions, they hunched low, advancing in a zigzag approach to within throwing range. The BAR gunners directed their fire at the top of the east bank to pin down the enemy congregating below. Pulling the pins, the grenadiers hurled their fragmentation grenades in long arcing lobs into the ravine, the shattering blasts overcoming the enemy's cover advantage. The shrapnel shredded through the mass of Japanese soldiers huddled beneath the bank. The greeting salutation of BAR fire mowed down the few Japanese who made it out of the ravine. *Hunker down or come out? Dead either way,* Hunter thought contemptuously; his mounting confidence proved premature.

As the riflemen resumed their positions, telltale pops announced Japanese light 50-caliber versatile infantry mortars joining the fray. The close-quarter shell launchers hurled fragmentation and concussive shells out of the ravine and up the slope. The rain of mortar explosions marched uphill toward the squads' positions as they ducked behind the cover of the rocks. A mortar round hit higher ground behind Hunter, too close for comfort.

With a lung-bursting shout, Hunter commanded the retreat. "Move out! Up the damn hill." He called to Gunn, "Cover us." Again, with the same bloody recklessness, the Japanese, though diminished in numbers, charged out of the ravine onto the open road. Hunter's men below heaved the last of their grenades toward the road before racing up toward the defending covering fire. They scrambled up the mountainside leapfrogging past the men above, taking shelter behind rocks and shrub to cover the retreat of the men now behind them. As the guerrillas scrambled up the mountainside, mortar shells fell increasingly farther out of effective range behind them.

Not letting up their pace, all scrambled away from the furious but fading Japanese shouts and fire from below. The hard panting, grunting men of the ambush party reached the top of the low mountain. Perspiring profusely, they paused at the top to guzzle water in insatiable gulps from their canteens and catch their collective breath.

Bent over, hyperventilating, supporting himself with his hands on his knees, Sergeant Hunter gasped, "We'll lose them on the descent. We can catch our breath while they're slogging up the mountain after us." Descending on the other side of the mountain, the squad gained distance from their pursuers. Revived upon reaching the bottom, the ambush party continued at double time to the east, not stopping until dusk upon reaching a barrio on the outskirts of Del Pilar, exhausted.

When Hunter reported to Lt. Arnold, he looked back at him like an apparition. "Thank God Joe am I glad to see you! From the trail, it sounded like a hell of a fight. How'd you get here?"

"Sir, we found the back door." Having feared the worst, Arnold gazed at his men in amazement, wanting to drop all formality, but unable to, owing to the years of military protocol drilled into him.

The next day, two messengers from Galiyod arrived in Del Pilar and told Arnold what the villagers had seen, the Japanese trucks returning full of wounded and dead soldiers. "We count best we can, but careful so Japs not know. Then we all talk what we see. We think two hundred Japs dead, many wounded."

"Casualty report by committee," Arnold mused.

"Dey leave in evening."

"Did they harm anyone in Galiyod?"

"No! Dey hardly look at us. No want to meet our eyes. I think dey too ashamed, just want to go back to their garrison, get drunk, fuck whores, lick their wounds."

Arnold took in his surroundings. At the foot of the historic Tirad Pass, Del Pilar in the western foothill of the Cordilleras offered sweeping views of the Ilocos Sur plains to the west and a path to the northeast, the Old Spanish Trail, fit for a hasty retreat, upon the day of the inevitable. "From here we can see anything coming. The road provides plenty of zigzags and good cover for ambushes. If anything comes that we can't handle, we scram out of here through the Tirad Pass, like ol' General Aguinaldo."

Pleased, Arnold lifted his shoulders and pointed his chin in the direction of the pass. "Amazing work men! This time, nobody had to martyr themselves." For now, they had stopped the Japanese advance on Del Pilar. As for the people, Arnold could offer no consolation to the populace of Del Pilar, in the path of Japanese rage, short of the Abra battalion abandoning the area, hopefully drawing the enemy away.

After delivering his message to Arnold, Cushing had gained a day's head start before Arnold reached Del Pilar. After crossing the bridge, he took the right fork in the road instead of the left to Del Pilar, his destination the Lepanto Consolidated Mine in Benquet. Colonel Horan had chosen the mine as his command headquarters. Cushing hoped to make his case with Horan and put to rest any question about his rightful command of the Abra Battalion.

The path of the road followed the river valley south. To the east rose the green, pine tree crests of the Cordilleras and to the west the lower ridge lines of the coastal foothills. Past the remote barrio of Sigay, where the eastern highlands of Ilocos Sur and the Mountain Province converged, over sixty miles of hard riding on horse paths and rugged mountain roads lay ahead of him. He gunned the motorcycle, with the sidecar bouncing, at reckless speeds down narrow paths in places barely three feet wide, bouncing over exposed roots and straddling ruts and rocks that could bottom out the motorcycle frame in a nasty skid. Cushing hooted in elation as the sidecar wheel lifted into the air on sharp right turns, when sliding the motorcycle around corners and obstacles, throttling the engine and braking in quick succession in controlled skids. When his control of the rig became precarious on the rougher ground, he stopped and weighed down the sidecar with rocks in the compartment and rode on, still pushing its limits.

After sixteen miles, the path terminated at a T-junction with a single lane road, on which Cushing turned east to Cervantes, the easternmost town of Ilocos Sur province before entering the Cordillera Mountains. The road rose out of the valleys of the bottom lands of encroaching jungle, up a concave gradient of spiny mountain ridges on a steep, winding course, past mountain meadows, scattered pines, and a boulder-strewn landscape. Cliff edges overlooked gorges into which waterfalls from opposing mountainsides flowed.

At the imposing Bessang Pass, where the road reached a maximum elevation at 4,600 feet, Cushing throttled the motorcycle into a deep cut through the craggy cliffs of two opposite steep rock precipices towering over 1,000 feet above the pass. Amid this natural splendor, Cushing realized with rising foreboding that the cliffs of the pass formed a natural blockade to the mountain province by whomever controlled the heights. Beyond Bessang Pass lay the prize, the vast mineral riches of Luzon. With a sinking feeling, he realized that nothing, but a rapid return of American forces would prevent the rising sun flag from flying from the precipice. Dislodging the Japanese from such a natural fortification would amount to a horrendous military undertaking.

Bessang Pass remained the only access into the mountain province not yet controlled by the Japanese military. They had already closed off Halsema's Highway from Baguio. Of the other routes, the Villa Verde trail from the south was no more than a horse trail in places. Route 11 between the eastern Cagayan valley and Bontoc was one of the roughest thoroughfares in Luzon, loosely called a road.

Coming out of the pass, Cushing descended from the mountains into a valley of open rice-paddy country at the headwaters of the Abra River. Cervantes had benefited commercially as a road junction between the coastal lowlands and mountain regions, an important hub and settlement for mining operations in the nearby mountains. In a blur, the town noted for its handsome American houses, brick municipal buildings, a tall church, and even motels receded behind him with the twist of the motorcycle throttle. A one-lane dirt and gravel road ascended a spur of the Cordillera Central in a near straight-line southeast to about 5,800 feet in fourteen miles to the mining outpost of Mankayan. The motorcycle responded sluggishly to the changing altitude.

Body sore and groin tender, Cushing arrived at the Consolidated Lepanto copper mine late that afternoon. A collection of mining buildings sat on the flattened butte top above pine-covered ridges. Spread out below lay the small mining village of Mankayan. He slowed to a putter up to a long, rectangular clapboard building with men in work khakis outside lounging and smoking. Attracting their curious gazes, his khakis still bearing dust and grime from the Candon action, he announced, "I am looking for Colonel Horan."

The men looked at him in amazement. One said, "In there," he directed him, pointing toward a building. pointing toward a building. Cushing entered a spacious office where several men congregated. As the only person of any regular military dress, a hefty, jowl-faced man in olive drab, with the eagle insignias of a colonel on the lapels of his half-buttoned shirt, rose from a desk. Behind him against the wall, a shortwave radio transceiver at ready hummed with Morse code over the crackling speaker. Cushing saluted him. "Sir, I am Walter Cushing, commander of the Abra Battalion, an irregular, guerrilla militia as the name suggests out of Abra. Before that, I was a gold prospector, co-owner of the Rainbow Mine in Abra until the Jap invasion shut me down. I heard I might find you here."

131

Horan looked at him dubiously but answered politely, "How do you do, Mr. Cushing. And how did you hear that?"

"Call me Walter. Bamboo telegraph, sir."

Horan chuckled at the cliché. "What can I do for you, Walter?" he asked, with an unctuous civil servant demeanor and smile.

"After the Jap invasion shut me down, I formed a battalion-size group of two hundred irregular soldiers. As a welcome addition, I linked up with a cutoff U.S. Army Signal Officer, Lieutenant Robert Arnold and thirty of his men who had been operating a radar station at Cape Bojeador. They have been training my men. Sir, I'd like to report that the Abra Battalion has already conducted actions against the enemy in Ilocos Sur."

Horan's eyes widened. All present in the office gave Cushing their full attention. "A private guerrilla army? What actions, Walter?"

"On December 31, we destroyed the bridge over the Abra river on Highway 2 south of Vigan and attacked a troop truck, killing fifteen enemy soldiers. Two weeks later, just yesterday, we ambushed and destroyed a Jap convoy of 15 trucks moving men and military cargo south on Highway 2 through Candon. We killed 67 Nip troops, destroyed their trucks, and the fuel and artillery ordnances they were carrying. None escaped." Cushing received audible gasps and murmurs from all present. "Sir, I would consider it an honor to place myself and my outfit under your command."

For an instant, Horan looked dumbfounded. His eyes narrowed, "This is astonishing news, Walter. Do you have any evidence to back up your claim?"

Cushing reached into his breast pocket and flicked a brown slice of cloth with three white stars stamped over three red and two yellow stripes. "This is the collar emblem of a Japanese Colonel. You can still make it out despite the bloodstains. This guy was in the lead truck and caught a burst of BAR fire."

One of the other men in the office spoke up excitedly, "Sir, that's right! I heard about that on Radio Tokyo last night—listening for kicks. The fucking Nips were howling bloody murder about the hit and run tactics of some sons of bitches on the coast, like they cheated them in a damn sporting event."

"That would be us," Cushing responded earnestly, his expression solemn.

Horan stared back at him in amazement. "Impressive! But unfortunately, we can expect reprisals from your attacks."

"Why do you say that?"

"A Jap colonel from the Vigan base has been exacting brutal treatment, torture and execution of the locals. His name is Colonel Hidemi Watanabe. Reports are that he's a ruthless sadist with an insatiable appetite for murder and depravity."

Cushing swallowed hard. Though he had hoped otherwise, he feared reprisals against civilians would prove unavoidable, hating the thought, the consequence of guerrilla operations against a merciless enemy.

"Sounds like you have a hell of a story to tell," said Horan. "I want to hear it from start to finish. But first, I imagine you're tired. Would you like to rest up?"

"Sure would."

Horan addressed one of the men. "Ted, take Walter to the guesthouse. Get him some grub, a beer, and a cot."

As Cushing turned to follow Ted, Colonel Horan asked "Walt, where are your men now?"

"They're with Lieutenant Robert Arnold, acting commander, setting up headquarters in Del Pilar just west of the Tirad Pass. Key country for guerrilla operations—close to the main Jap routes in Ilocos Sur but rough, defensible terrain with tried-and-true escape routes."

Colonel Horan gave him an indulgent smile. "Ah yes, the rebel General Aguinaldo's mountain pass."

After Cushing left the office, Horan said to the other men in the office, "If he's legit, Mr. Cushing may be just what we need. MacArthur will be pleased as a preacher with a new convert—something to confirm his faith in guerrilla warfare."

After a night's rest and a breakfast of eggs, rice and canned fruit cocktail, Cushing resumed his conversation with Horan with his immediate staff present. He began his narrative starting on December 10, his first encounter with Japanese troops, eliminating two enemy scouts, after witnessing enemy atrocities during the invasion of Vigan. Horan stared back with keen interest. He informed Cushing that Vigan had been one of four such Japanese incursions that had occurred. The other invasions included the port town of Aparri on the north coast, Legazpi at the narrow southern end of Luzon, and in Mindanao, the second largest island of the Philippine archipelago, the city of Davao. "Enemy capture of these towns has ominous portent. All these towns have airstrips suitable for enemy fighter planes that can now strike anywhere on the island at will."

After absorbing the significance, Cushing continued relating how he recruited his men, first from the local miners, then overlooked Filipino reserve troops in remote Abra who never received the call to active service, and how later he collected arms, ammunition, and more men from a Philippine Constabulary camp. He recounted how he had brought men and materiel to his mine, his dynamite demolition of the Abra River delta bridge, and his successful skirmish against a squad of Jap pursuers. He related how he found Lt. Robert Arnold and his thirty-two hungry, bedraggled men of the U.S. Army Air Warning Station from Cape Bojeador, recruited and put them to work training his men. Now his force amounted to over 230 men. "We call our outfit the Abra Battalion after the province of our origin," he said, proudly.

He elaborated blow-by-blow the details of the January 20 ambush at Candon and the destruction of a 15-truck convoy, its cargo of fuel, munitions, and the annihilation of all 67 enemy troops. Despite his notable quality, fearless to a fault, Cushing would notably succumb to unabashed vanity, and this was one such time. He took full credit for positioning of the men along the main road through Candon. At his instruction he claimed, Lieutenant Arnold had set up the phone taps to his specifications to coordinate the attack.

However, Cushing concluded, graciously complimenting Arnold's role. "He performed flawlessly, anticipated my plans to the letter. lucky to have him and his men in my command—he's a fine executive officer."

Horan's eyebrows raised for an instant as if Cushing had piqued his sense of audacity, then looked pensive. "Walter, do you have any military experience?"

"I was in pilot training in the U.S. Army Air Corps in 1928."

"But you didn't become a pilot."

"No, I washed out because I secretly got married."

Horan mulled over his answer. "General MacArthur on Corregidor wants an organized guerrilla resistance in Northern Luzon under my command, now attached to the Thirty-first Infantry Regiment of the PA. The goal is to take pressure off our forces fighting in Bataan by creating diversions and making conditions difficult for the Japs in northern Luzon. To date, I have rounded up some miners with no formal military training, constabulary in Bontoc and Ifugao, and soldiers of the 43rd PA, formerly under the command of Major Leo Giitter out of Baguio." Horan snorted, "The bastard seems to have just disappeared, his whereabouts unknown." Cushing had heard the scuttlebutt from Barnett about Giitter's cowardly flight and failure to seize the advantage on Naguilian road into Baguio. *Good riddance*, he concluded.

"Without a professional officer core, I'm improvising. I have a sizeable number of American mining personnel who did not want to surrender." *But do they want to fight*, Cushing wondered. *Or just remain free, day to day?* "So, I have adopted the mining management hierarchy, something familiar to them. Thus, a mine superintendent becomes a major, a graduate engineer, a captain, a foreman a lieutenant. Platoons consist of mine laborers, Igorot tribesmen, and PA enlisted soldiers. From these I have created three companies, one based out of my HQ here at the Lepanto copper mine, another at the Suyoc copper mine, and the third near the Batong Buhay copper mine in remote Lubuagan, Kalinga. I see the Batong Buhay mine as an evacuation camp of last resort, perish the thought. Now with your Abra battalion, we can extend guerrilla operations all the way across north Luzon from the west to the east coast.

Yes sir, the Japs are fighting the Fil-American troops in Bataan with their backs exposed to us."

"Exactly, strike from behind, easier to kick them in the ass. Guerrilla warfare is so damn unconventional, the regular military aren't trained for it. It takes a certain type of imagination and cunning, more likely found in hardened bandits than gentlemen with moral boundaries. You and Arnold have shown that it can work." Horan chuckled, "No slight intended."

Cushing laughed, "I've been called a gentleman before."

"I need officers under my command who are resourceful, intrepid, and know the country. So, I envisage promoting both you and Arnold to captains."

Cushing frowned visibly. "Sir, I really appreciate it. But I don't believe I could be an effective commander unless I am the ranking officer in the battalion. After all, you are promoting mine superintendents to major."

After a significant pause, Horan responded, "Yes, I see your point. It doesn't make sense to have two commanding officers. And you created the 121st. Then Arnold should be the executive officer."

"He responded with the conviction of a revelation. Cushing kept a straight face, wondering uneasily how as a career military officer he could overlook so much. "So, I concur it's fitting that you be promoted to major. Also, I've decided to create a new organization from the Abra battalion, the 121st Infantry."

"Thank you, sir, for your confidence," Cushing said, affecting deference.

"Central command on Corregidor suggested the 121st if my organization grew. I gather, it has some WW1 significance to General MacArthur. He won a heap of medals in that war. I digress, the fact is the Abra Battalion no longer sums up the organization's full potential for growth, area of operation, and importance. Your promotion to major rates as brevet, but as far as I'm concerned gives you full command of the 121ˢᵗ. Congratulations!" Cushing shook Horan's proffered hand. But Horan looked pensive. "Before the war, I would never have considered giving officer commissions to civilians. But in the extreme conditions in which we find ourselves, regular military protocol does not apply, but merit does. You've proved that."

Confident that he had Horan's interest, Cushing said, "Sir, may I also point out I've got a couple of good men who match these qualifications and was wondering if you could see fit to commission them as well. Threre's a mining supervisor George Barnett who performed exceptionally at Candon. Saved my damn bacon, shot a Nip that had me in his sights. He showed up with a young sidekick, an equipment engineer, James Novak, who also showed grit during the fight."

"Hmm, battle-tested! That's something none of these American volunteers from the mines have." Horan admitted, "Our peace-time army had become more of a bureaucratic institution than a fighting machine. Believe me, I was part of that system, managing Camp John Hay in Baguio, biding my time till retirement." *A twilight tour*, Cushing thought uneasily. Horan transitioned without pause. "There was another noteworthy guerrilla action in northern Luzon this January besides yours."

"What did I miss?" Cushing asked.

"A Captain Ralph Praeger, a cavalry officer, attacked a Japanese airfield in Tuguegarao, a major Cagayan River town in Cagayan province, with a force of 150 men, a mixture of Philippine scouts and Constabulary. He estimates they killed two hundred Japs and destroyed about a dozen parked airplanes. If the Japs believe there's coordinated guerrilla action, they may send more troops to northern Luzon to root out this phantom unified command."

"Yes sir, hopefully that will divert Jap forces from Bataan."

"By their code, saving face demands it, but it's a strategy raising hell with the people. The word is, after Praeger's, raid the Japs burned half of Tuguegarao, the provincial capital of Cagayan, and killed civilians who could not evacuate." Horan paused, his face grave.

"That's how this son of a bitch commander, Colonel Hidemi Watanabe, first came to our attention. He gave the scorched-earth order and damn well wants the credit."

"Yeah, so all fear his name." Cushing exclaimed. "They burned Candon after our raid."

"The Japs are predictable in that way if their six years in Manchuria and China is any measure. The word from Tuguegarao is that the Japs claimed the locals gave support and cheered the guerrilla victory. Apparently, some guerrillas posed as locals, welcoming the Japs to Tuguegarao with gifts of squawking chickens, which they used as a diversion to case the base before the attack. Well, a dirty business landed in our laps. Walter, now that we've seen the cream rise to the top, how's captain for George Barnett and second lieutenant for James Novak sound?"

"Very good, sir," Cushing nodded. "It's been a pleasure meeting you," Cushing said, happy with his new leverage over Arnold. "Sir, I swear I'll raise hell with the Nips."

Colonel Horan gazed at Cushing with the look of a newfound believer. "I'll have the letters stating the commissions ready for you first thing in the morning." Horan rose, hoisting his bulk out of his chair, and shook hands enthusiastically with Cushing.

The next morning, with the letters in his canvas musette bag, Cushing retraced his route back to Del Pilar along the same punishing roads and tracks, across the mountains through Bessang Pass, with a hard ride ahead of him back to Del Pilar. Obscuring the mountain summits, misty clouds descended the stark cliffs of the pass, reducing visibility on the road through the cut. *A hell of place for a fight*, Cushing thought. *A battle in the clouds*.

CHAPTER 12

Captain Arnold Usurped

ON HIS RETURN TO DEL PILAR, Cushing briefed Arnold on his visit with Horan at Mankayan, or at least the version he wanted to convey. Taking Arnold aside, Cushing produced the letter drafted by Colonel Horan and handed it to Arnold, who read it with reticence. "Robert, I'd like to congratulate you on your promotion to captain. Your leadership at Candon and delaying action on the road to Del Pilar were outstanding, to say the least. I didn't know about the ambush near Del Pilar at the time, but I emphasized favorably to Colonel Horan of your support in training the Abra Battalion and actions at Candon." Arnold appeared puzzled by Cushing's recommendation for promotion, by a subordinate he had assumed, now talking to him like a superior. Cushing proffered a firm handshake, which Arnold accepted guardedly.

Cushing held up the second letter. "Colonel Horan also extended a commission to me for the field rank of major in a new organization, the 121st Infantry. The Abra battalion is now defunct."

Arnold looked flabbergasted, usurped, and by a civilian without formal military training. "Bamboo grade," he murmured in a bare whisper, his brow knotted like the face of one who had just received a consolation prize.

"What?" Cushing asked, his tone defensive.

Arnold composed himself sufficiently to salute. "Congratulations, Walter," he stammered.

"Robert, I think you and I are going to make a great team. Now's the time to tell you about a plan I've been contemplating. The Jap situation around Baguio got me thinking. I'd like you to make a reconnaissance trip there. If we can beef up our forces a bit, we could capture Baguio and control northern Luzon until American reinforcements arrive."

"Sounds terrific, Walter," Arnold said, with an obvious lack of enthusiasm in his voice. Guardedly, he asked, "How many Americans from my platoon would you be willing to let me take on this reconnaissance? The better-trained men I have with me, the more damage I can do in the Baguio area."

"Aw, Robert," Cushing replied, ignoring the appeal in his eyes, "I couldn't give you any of the Americans. I'll need them for the operations along the coast, but you can take your pick of the Filipinos, whichever ones you want. The Igorots are native to the area, good at climbing hills and mountains, and know the most circuitous routes to avoid detection and lose pursuers."

"A couple with those skills would be nice, but I don't need an entire squad of scouts," Arnold growled, his eyes narrowing and his nostrils beginning to flare. Cushing assumed he could discern his thoughts from his comportment, all distrust and resentment. *He can think whatever he wants.* Their differences, he concluded, were irreconcilable. He was not going to tolerate Arnold countermanding or requiring his sanction of orders, especially with the American soldiers. As far as Cushing was concerned, they were no longer Arnold's platoon. Although Cushing wanted Bob gone, he did not want to send him to his death either. *Perhaps he'll link up with Colonel Horan,* he thought. Horan could use an executive officer with combat experience.

"I'd like to have a BAR to give us a little more firepower, and preferably have someone who knows how to use it."

Cushing shook his head and smiled sardonically as if dismissing a foolish request. "We'll need the BARs here. Take one of the pump shotguns; they're light to carry and good ambush weapons. 12-gauge buckshot is as deadly as grenade shrapnel."

140

"At close range. I get it, Walter," Arnold said, his voice hard but quiet, which failed to disguise his outrage. His face flushed, and his eyes narrowed. "I'll pick my men this afternoon so I can leave tomorrow morning."

Cushing concluded the obvious, that Arnold would head straight for Colonel Horan's HQ to complain about the promotion of a civilian no less above him. Why else would he play coy now when total outrage would be more in keeping with the outcome? He expected Arnold would protest to Horan that it was a wrong that should be righted, for whatever good that would do him. He trusted in the loyalty of all the Filipino guerrillas but expected resentment among the American soldiers, with a strong potential to impact morale. Fortuitously, a solution came to him before meeting with his officers and noncoms.

Later, alone with the men of his platoon, Cpt. Arnold delivered the news. "I want to be the one to tell you, Colonel Horan promoted Walter to major, making him CO of the newly designated 121st Infantry and me captain." His men looked back at him with astonishment. "Walter has ordered me to leave tomorrow morning on a recon mission to assess Japanese strength around Baguio."

"I can tell their strength from right here," Sergeant Goldblum snarled. "Baguio is lousy with Japs!"

"He says he wants to determine if a united guerrilla resistance could capture Baguio and Northern Luzon and hold it until American forces arrive," Arnold said.

"No, it ain't possible. Besides, guerrillas hold nothing. They hit and run."

"Well, that was my first thought too when I heard his plan—sheer lunacy!"

"But now it's clear, Cushing is not off his rocker at all," Goldblum said. "It's what they call in the military a transfer, when you want to get rid of someone you can't court-martial."

Arnold's face pinched with tension, his eyebrows drawing together, though he spoke calmly. "So, I'll just go up the mountain, take a circumspect look around, won't take unnecessary risks, and recommend to Colonel Horan against a major action. Horan can sort out reality from fantasy with Cushing. The alleged mission may be a blessing in disguise, which is why I'm not cussing up Cushing and his mother, yet! And Baguio is just a short dogleg on the way to Horan's HQ."

"His voice deeply earnest, Arnold said, "I hope to see all of you again before too long. In the meantime, I wish all of you the best of luck. Do your duty regardless of the circumstances. There is no conventional wisdom to fall back on. The regular military never taught us Shinola about guerrilla warfare. What I know, I picked up from reading special clearance memos. A small cadre of officers were intently studying it before the outbreak of war."

Rolling his eyes, Sergeant Hunter exclaimed, "I can't wait for the report!" Then with less sarcasm, "Glad you explained your intentions, sir. Otherwise, your leaving would look like Cushing got the better of you. The ambush at the Lagben River was your idea. Without it the Japs would have followed us all the way to Del Pilar. Horan needs to know the facts?"

Sgt. Goldblum spat on the ground. "And this reconnaissance mission—what a dodgy trick. You never had a chance to make your case with Horan."

"He will now," Sergeant Hunter glowered. "Colonel Horan can't just sweep this under the rug."

Putting the best face on the outcome, Arnold said, "So I'm off on a new adventure, a new opportunity. I have a premonition about it. Time will tell."

He turned away quickly, as if hiding the pain on his face. As he walked away, one of his men called, "Sir, adventures ain't necessarily fun."

Muttering, Hunter summed up the situation. "We all knew there was tension between Cushing and Arnold. This is Cushing's way of showing us who's running this outfit. Don't worry. Bob will straighten it out with Colonel Horan."

Goldblum added, "We just thought Bob and Walter would work it out, but not like this. Cushing is betting that Arnold don't come back. Dishonest but not crazy; Arnold knows it."

Corporal Heuser shook his head, speaking up. "What's botherin' me about the Lagben River ambush, Cap'n Arnold left twelve men to face hundreds of Japs and skedaddled up the road. Seems to me he asked you to do somethin' he weren't willin' to do himself."

Astounded, Sergeant Hunter locked eyes angrily with Heuser. "Dammit, Louis, that's what commanders do. Otherwise, the army would be decapitated in combat. Leaderless, with the men running round like chickens with their heads cut off."

"Maybe, but I was with Cushing at Candon. He was clearheaded, out front of us the whole time."

"Oh, yeah!" Hunter said sneering. "Grandstanding! Waving his .45s and yelling like an Apache Indian."

"What about when he took out that damn dump truck full of Japs? Did you miss that?" Heuser countered disagreeably.

Bill Benedict frowned. "Sure, Cushing has guts, but as far as leadership, I'd rather be with someone on the up and up."

Conferring aside from the other men, Barnett and James took stock of recent events. "Quite a fight at Candon," James said. "It hardly seems real. When you shot that Nip with a bead on Walter, he noticed. He knew in that instant you saved his life."

"I was in the right place," Barnett muttered self-consciously.

James's shoulders slumped. "Arnold's squad gave the Japs an ass-whooping' at the bridge but doubt it will stall them for long. The Japs will come after us soon. Pity! I wouldn't mind staying here for a while."

"Except for Maria, I suppose. She's best off where she is for now. But you're right. It's only a brief lull. We had better use it wisely."

"I'm sure Cushing intends to give them a good run. Too bad about Arnold! Nobody buys this reconnaissance mission. Is this what you meant by resolving differences amicably?"

143

Barnett looked flummoxed; his mouth formed a troubled grimace. "No! A slow burn was building between them. But Cushing has placed himself in a spot. He's going to have to prove he's the right leader to everyone, and especially to the Americans from Arnold's platoon. They'll be watching and judging his every move."

While the 121st Infantry headquartered at Del Pilar, in Abra, at the Villas house, Maria and Dely shared a bedroom. Cesar and Jocelyn addressed them together. "We have to create a story to explain your presence here," Jocelyn said, hiding her worry behind a thin veneer of outward calm. "Guerrillas have attacked the Hapon. They believe the guerrillas came from Abra and are asking questions, with harsh treatment. The Hapon slap and sometimes beat people who say they do not know, or much worse if they do not believe you, which is most everyone they interrogate. Ignorance will not protect you."

"Because they are evil. I hear they laugh when they hurt people," Dely said.

"I don't doubt it," Jocelyn said. "While I trust most of my neighbors, there are traitors among the people who spy and inform; they will sell their souls to the Jap devils."

"They do it for money or fear. No one believes the Jap propaganda about the new Asian coprosperity sphere, Asia for Asians," Cesar snarled.

"If the Hapon come here, we will tell them that there is illness in this house," Jocelyn said. "To frighten them away it has to be a very infectious respiratory disease. Dely, Maria, say you have influenza. Just breathing can spread it."

"Oh, trangkaso [flu]. How clever!" Dely exclaimed. "Uh huh!" she coughed, covering her mouth while performing a satirical bow. "Oh, I very sick with influenza. So sorry, Major-san, many pardons. I did not mean to cough on you," she spoofed, her mouth wide agape with exaggerated dismay, evoking laughter from all.

"Not so silly, Dely, or they will see the lie," Jocelyn said.

Later that night, lying in bed in their shared bedroom, Maria and Dely talked about men. "Dely, how is it with you and Walter?"

"He hired me as his dispensera [housekeeper]. But as you can see, I am more than an employee. I do not just hold the keys. We are also good friends. I listen to him, ask him questions, and give him comfort that only a woman can. He says I am extremely helpful. When he has a difficult decision, it seems to help him think."

"I can see he is very pleased with you."

"I consider myself lucky to be with him. The intimacy came naturally."

"As it should. Is he your first man?"

"You mean, was I a virgin when I met Walter? No! So, no respectable man will marry me if he believes I am soiled, the fate of poor girls who make a mistake, whether seduced or raped. Maybe the war will change how people think. The old rules do not fit during such madness. But he is good to me. I give him what happiness I can."

"Your first time, was it with a lover?"

"I wish. At seventeen, I entered a beauty contest. The promoter raped me. He used lies and trickery. He told me I was more than just beautiful, and with his help I would go far, modeling, even movies, and we should talk over dinner. I drank too much wine; he kept filling my glass and raising it to my lips to drink. I became very dizzy, remember little. He might have put a drug into the wine. When I woke up, I no longer a virgin, and he no longer wanted me. I was ashamed; I believed everyone knew. I thought they were looking at me with scorn. I quit the contest before the judging and accepted the dispensera job from Walter."

"No regrets?"

"None. He is a good man, even if he does not marry me. Walter is also generous to my family. He gives money to my parents, not too much, but enough to make things easier for them."

"And they accept his money?" Maria said, the presumption obvious in her voice.

145

"Oh no, it's not like that. My father is no bugaw [pimp]."

There followed an awkward silence. When it passed, Dely asked, "And how about you and James?"

"We both worked at the Itogon gold mine. I was an office clerk and he an engineer. Both of us were lonely, strangers in Baguio. I am from Legazpi, he from a place called Minnesota, a very strange, cold place, colder than the ice factory we had in Legazpi. When he came into the office, we talked. I learned his fiancé from Minnesota refused to join him here and broke off their engagement. I read her breakup letter. He left it open on his desk."

"No, you did not!" Dely said in mock scorn but then broke out laughing. "Please, what did it say?"

"Just a lot of satsat [palaver]—irreconcilable directions in life, never forget what we shared, and how dearly she would cherish the memory of their time together. But I felt what I did was not right. I told the priest at confession."

"And what great wisdom did the priest have?"

"He said my prying stemmed from the sin of envy; said 'not let thine heart envy sinners.' He absolved me of sin and prescribed twelve Hail Mary's."

"Then, like you say, the two of you became good friends."

"Yes! Very good!"

"Stupid priest! And her loss is your gain, so let her envy you."

"And he is my first and only love. Now we are engaged."

"But you do not have a ring!" Dely said in dismay.

"He proposed on the trip here, from Baguio along the road they call the Mountain Trail. The country was beautiful, but the trip was very frightening and dangerous. A Japanese warplane attacked us, nearly killing us! We escaped only because a cloud bank hid us the instant before the plane attacked. There has not been the time or place to buy a ring."

"How awful, I'm sorry!" Dely hesitated.

"I fear we can't hide forever, so we must run," Maria sighed. "The odd lot of guerrillas."

"Yes, a sad way to live. But for now, we must get you a ring," she said with earnest concern. "It will remind you that a good man loves you and lessen your worries."

"Thank you, Dely, but a ring might make me worry more." She said with an exasperated sigh. "And invite unwanted questions. You know, Dely, run or hide, I think I should be with him."

"But you don't know where he is, and even if you did, how would you get there?"

"Well, if I knew where he was, that would be a start."

CHAPTER 13

Cushing Splits Force

BARNETT AND JAMES ARRIVED AS SUMMONED at Cushing's Nipa thatched roof headquarters off the narrow lane that passed for the main street through Del Pilar. "Come on up boys," Cushing invited them onto a raised shaded veranda facing the street in the front of the house. He greeted each man with a firm handshake and ushered them to table with several chairs. Taking in the sight of the warrior hero fast becoming a legend, people passing glanced up and nodded reverently, doffed their hats, and sometimes saluted him. He acknowledged each with a nod and a benevolent smile. Slapping Barnett on the shoulder, he said, "Hello, deadeye. That was quick shooting back in Candon when it counted. Thank you."

Barnett shrugged modestly. "You're welcome, sir. Just happened to be in the right place."

Cushing motioned to the chairs. "Sit down, boys. I have a proposition for you." Barnett and James sat across from him at attention. "You know about my visit with Colonel Horan in Mountain province at the Consolidated Mines, where he's holed up. The gist is General MacArthur has ordered Horan to conduct guerrilla operations here in Northern Luzon, the only way our peewee force can fight an overwhelming Nip army. Horan's problem, he has precious few regular military personnel at his disposal and a bunch of miners without military experience. Just between us, I doubt he even has a clue on how to conduct guerrilla warfare. As of this week, you two have experience, which in Horan's organization makes you two prime officer material."

Cushing handed them each a letter of promotion. "Congratulations George, as of now you are a captain attached to the 35th PA—fully under the auspices of the USAFFE," he said, using the abbreviation of General MacArthur's command, United States Army Forces in the Far East. Barnett reciprocated in a firm handshake. "And James, you've been commissioned Second Lieutenant." James looked bowled over but managed a crisp salute.

"At ease, soldier." Cushing smirked. "I'm not quite comfortable with formal military protocol, yet."

Cushing stretched and looked with awe west from the hillside town across the green valley to a sliver of blue sea beyond. His range of operations now extended all the way from the coast to the mountainous interior. "Gentlemen, we're off to an auspicious start. Tomorrow at 0800 I am holding a meeting with all officers and noncoms in attendance to discuss my immediate plans. See you then. As they say in the regular military, dismissed."

James and Barnett returned Cushing's bare flick of the hand to the forehead with full salutes, receiving a facetious look in return insinuating 'cut it out.'

At 8:00 a.m. the next morning, Cushing convened a meeting of his command in the main room. With few chairs available, most of the men stood. "Gentlemen I would like to start off by congratulating each one of you for commendable service to date. We are off to a promising start. Between the Candon raid and the delaying action on the road here, we have intercepted and destroyed fifteen truckloads of supplies heading south to Bataan. With other assorted actions, I estimate we have killed over three hundred Nips, and it's still early in the war. Still plenty of time to improve our score." Mirthful laughter rose from the men.

"With all this, we've only suffered one wounded. Not bad for two hundred country boys from Abra and signal platoon of thirty-two footloose Americans troops." While cheerful grins and utterances spread contagiously among the men in the room, Arnold's former men waited subdued, blank faced. "Next the Abra Battalion has had a change in designation. As of now, it is no longer a freelance operation. We have

149

been incorporated into the PA 35th regiment as the 121st Infantry under Colonel Horan's command. We report directly to him."

"Yeah, when he's not chasing after his men," someone murmured, alluding to his role in the well-known Baguio debacle when the city had fallen to the Japanese without a fight. James worried how the civilian prisoners, enemy aliens in the eyes of the Japanese and now interned at the former PA Camp Holmes, were faring. How true were the rumors? Reportedly, whole families were incarcerated in cramped, squalid conditions, short of basic necessities—food, water, sanitation, medicine. Cushing cast a critical look about the room. James guessed flippant criticism ran counter to his view of decorum, more important than crisp salutes.

"The bottom line, we need to grow in order to better control the territory in which we operate and monitor the disposition of the people, to better know our friends from foes," Cushing forewarned. "So, I am splitting the 121st into three companies, plant them like seeds, one in each of the three provinces La Union, Ilocos Sur, and Abra. Hopefully, grow them into three larger, self-sustaining, mutually supporting forces." With prescience of conviction, he stressed, "In three locations, the 121st can survive, even if, God forbid, two units are annihilated."

Before their split, Cushing had argued with Arnold about his plans to divide the force, worsening their increasingly irreconcilable differences. "We need to stay close together; not bunch up, but close enough to reform quickly after a fight. We're not big enough for three, separately operating companies, pretending they control large areas," Arnold had argued.

Grimacing, Cushing had told Arnold, "Your way we are just one unit caught behind lines. My way the Japs can't decapitate our entire command."

Arnold leaned forward, locking eyes, "Walter, you are a damn good fighter, but I believe some of your ideas lack sound military principle. Don't divide your forces if they can't operate together, as parts of a coordinated plan.

150

Glaring back, Cushing growled, "Bullshit! I think what you really want is to keep close tabs on me so you can limit my actions and countermand my decisions."

Arnold had replied acerbically, "That's all very convenient, Walter. Splitting my platoon apart to lessen the likelihood of dissension. Are you afraid they'll plot against you as a group?" He gazed coldly at Cushing from beneath compressed eyelids. "Also, I'm letting you know that I intend to produce a counter report to submit to Colonel Horan." Arnold turned and strode away, sealing Cushing's decision to separate him from his command, though it would undoubtedly require mending fences with Arnold's men. *They're not your men anymore*, he thought. But Arnold's accusation that he was splitting the 121st to prevent mutiny by the disgruntled American soldiers, in spite of a grain of truth, was one that he could not abide.

Continuing his briefing, Cushing asserted, "Our ragtag militia needs to grow in order to better control the territory in which we operate. We need underground networks, spies, couriers, and medical personnel. We need an organization able to hit anywhere on the coast or inland." Cushing paused, gauging the attention of his men, scanning their eyes and posture. Most stared wide eyed with mounting excitement while some of Arnold's former men looked back with raised-eyebrow skepticism or stolid detachment.

Barnett nodded enthusiastically as if Cushing channeled his thoughts. "Yes sir! And keep an eye out for traitor bastards collaborating with the Japs," a vow that would shape his strategy in the coming struggles, as harm to the resistance from spies and informants became deadly obvious.

"Here's how I want to divide up the 121st. Captain Barnett…" He paused to let the recognition of his promotion sink in. "I'm assigning you one company of men to work with Major Gaerlan, the guerrilla commander of the group called the La Union Regiment. Their territory covers La Union and southern Ilocos Sur. He's keen on an alliance with us. You can't miss him, a dashing good-looking fellow with a patch over his left eye. He and some of his boys were at the south end of

Candon with Arnold. He had plans for an ambush there even before us and had even set up a phone tap from the town cemetery."

"I recall seeing someone like that from a distance," Barnett said. "Wore a broad sombrero and bandolier, looked like the Mexican revolutionary Zapata."

That's him, in civilian life before the war, he was actually an electrical engineer. He managed the electricity utility serving La Union and southern Ilocos Sur

"How did you hook up with him?" Barnett asked.

"Before Candon, I received a tip from Governor Rogue Ablan of Ilocos Norte, who is also organizing a guerrilla outfit, another potential ally. He referred me to Gaerlan, as a man of 'many fine qualities.' I met him in the town of Salcedo." Cushing tapped at points on the commonwealth map on the table. "I am convinced you and Gaerlan will work well together."

Cushing continued, "Next, the Nips damn well know we are holed up here in Del Pilar. We got to move out, pronto. As usual, we're in a race against time. So, tomorrow I'm moving my HQ with the second company to the municipality of Banayoyo, sixteen kilometers north of here. Strategically, it has great geographic advantages, a valley of farmland hemmed in north and south by rugged hill country that favors defense. It's within close striking distance of coastal Highway 2 and has a couple backdoor roads to the east suitable for a hasty retreat inland, south to the Tirad pass and the other north to Santa Maria, in another remote mountain valley." Barnett nodded in agreement.

"Next, I want to locate the third company, actually more of a squad to begin with, in the highland country of northeastern Abra to establish a rear evacuation camp in the municipality of Tineg. It is home to a remote tribal group of Tinguians called the Adesens. There're some good camp possibilities on a mountain the natives call Bawao, south of their main village Acsimao. The camp will be a refuge of last resort if retreat from the coast becomes necessary or a base from which we can strike the Japs from the rear. It's rough mountain country with natural defenses, steep mountains, raging rivers in the rainy season, and no roads. So, we will need to bring all supplies in by cargodores and pack animals."

"The guerrilla way," said a wiry-muscled PA officer with a lean, serious face and steady eyes, leaning against the wall, dressed in military kakis with lieutenant bars. When the officer lifted his head high, his sharp black eyes exuded a suggestion of challenge.

Cushing said, "Excuse me, let me introduce Lieutenant Carlos Ruiz. Carlos served with the PA 41st Infantry at Lingayen Gulf. When the Japs invaded, Carlos got separated from his unit in the confusion and is now with us."

With a mixture of awe and admiration, James studied the veteran of the hopeless fiasco at Lingayen Gulf, in which the Japanese invasion forces overwhelmed the severely undermanned PA defenses. Recognition kicked in. "Carlos, you were with Gaerlan at Candon," he said.

"That's right, now Carlos is with us," Cushing said. "James, you and Carlos will take the lead on this project." Ruiz nodded his agreement. "Carlos knows the province, which is why Gaerlan approved his transfer to us. As a first lieutenant, he has a grade in rank above you James, but I see the two of you as coleaders."

Startled, James locked eyes with Barnett, betraying himself; Cushing noticed. "I know you and George have been partners. I'm not making this decision lightly to separate you. James, I believe you have the right temperament for this assignment, considering we absolutely need good relations with the Adesens, the only source of food provisions in the whole damn area."

"Take one of the trucks we captured in Candon back to the mine," Cushing continued. "It'll haul your crew. I hid more gasoline in a gulch behind the mine. Drive it northeast into Tineg as far as you can, either until you run out of gas or road. Hide it." He gave Ruiz a purse with silver pesos. "You're the treasurer," he said. The arrangement suited James fine, figuring Ruiz could drive a harder bargain with the natives than he could. "From there, hire caribous and native cargadores, buy what supplies you can find, and pack them into the back country."

153

With a look of confusion, James eyed the Philippine commonwealth map spread on the table, trying to judge the roads. "There ain't no straight line as the crow flies," Cushing said.

"True," Ruiz agreed. "After crossing the Tirguyau River at San Juan, you come to a jumble of dirt tracks, drivable at least in the dry season. A few head in the general direction of Tineg municipality and then veer off. They end about fifteen miles southeast of the village of Acsimao."

Cushing nodded in agreement. "What you are looking for, can't miss it, is a broad, sweeping mountain the natives call Bawao, south of Acsimao. There are small barangays scattered about near the trailhead, where you should be able to obtain some basic supplies. From there, you are going to have to hike. I've seen Mt. Bawao from a distance, though clouded over," he recalled. "I prospected the area before I found the site for a mine in central Abra. The highlands of Bawao looked promising for a campsite, just not for gold."

After the meeting concluded, James motioned Barnett aside. "You think Cushing's assignments are appropriate?"

"From each according to his ability, to each according to his needs," Barnett said with a wink.

Jutting his chin, James said facetiously, "I knew you were a red."

Barnett exhaled a good-natured chuckle. "So, James, how do you feel about separating?"

"A bit like breaking up the movie duo Hopalong Cassidy and cowboy Lucky Jenkins. Hopalong Cassidy was never the same after," James said with a facetious grin and mock credit to the 1930s cowboy matinee idol of his youth.

Barnett stuck his thumbs into his belt, in caricature cowboy swagger, "Well pard'ner, I got a hunch we'll ride trails again. Hopefully under better circumstances."

James gave a lopsided grin. "Yeah, sure as shoot'n."

"Mt. Bawao may be the safest of the three assignments." For an instant, James sensed insinuation, doubt of his mettle, but dismissed it as unintended. "How do you think Walter handled the issue of Arnold's men?"

"Cagey," Barnett said. "Dividing them up, they won't be able to conspire against him as a group."

"Another matter, what do you think I should do about Maria?"

"Ah those pros and cons! She's with good people who will do their best to care for and protect her. But if the Japanese think she and Dely ain't Villa's family, that could be bad, and I don't want that worry on your mind. There are informers and spies who'd sell them out for a can of kerosene if they knew the truth—a problem we're going to have to deal with sooner than later."

"Well, that settles it for now. She's coming with me."

"Just one issue, an unmarried woman in a guerrilla camp might give some men ideas and create resentment. Consider marrying her first, so she's not seen as a camp follower."

James shook his head, working through the cobweb of questions in his mind. "Damn George, you see the practical side in everything. What about Cushing's woman, Dely?"

Barnett smiled as if he had been asked a foolish question. "Believe me, no one will dare lay a hand on her."

The two men clasped hands in an emotional farewell handshake delivered with supportive left-handed backslaps, both alarmingly aware how little they knew about the dangers ahead.

CHAPTER 14

A Wedding and an Impasse

AFTER NIGHTFALL, A DOZEN OF CUSHING'S 121ST guerrillas hunkered down inside a captured Japanese truck traversing the dark back roads near the border of Ilocos Sur and Abra province to evade detection. Lts. Carlos Ruiz driving and James Novak occupied the cab. "Cushing wants the evacuation camp ready before the rainy season," James said.

"It is fortunate we are doing this now. In another two months, when the rains come, these tracks won't be good for nothing but Carabao wallows. Impassible!"

"Both for us and the Japs."

Ruiz nodded affirmatively. "The rainy season will buy us time but make it difficult to move supplies. We need to stockpile while we can. Absolutely necessary!"

Troubled, James wondered where these stockpiles would come from if the Adesens proved unreliable. Under cover of darkness, Ruiz drove with lights off on the straight sections of the road, flipping them back on when he drove into Cushing's mine encampment. In the glare of the headlights, the front door of the staff house hung open. Boards that had been nailed over the door and glass of smashed window lay strewn on the ground. In the light beams, Japanese hobnailed boot prints in the dirt headed to and from Cushing's staff house. "God damn it, fucking Jap bastards!" James shouted, both he and Ruiz jumping out clutching .45 pistols in hand.

"Ruiz shouted epithets in Tagalog to the men in the truck, "Tangas," as James remembered 'Fools.' He commanded "Sige na! [move out]"

James leaped to the back of the truck and, whirling around, yanked open the rear tarp. "Weapons ready," he ordered. The men spilled out the back in a mass. Holding their flashlights away from their bodies at arm's length to evade the possibility of fire targeted on the lights, James and Ruiz moved cautiously into the staff house. "The Japs are long gone," James hissed to Ruiz behind him. In the illuminated interior, the flashlights revealed a thoroughly ransacked building, furniture overturned, effects littering the floor.

"Well, the Japs know who to pin the Candon raid on," James said. Ruiz grunted in agreement.

A check of the rest of the debris-strewn staff house exposed the extent of the Japanese search. James and Ruiz looked in Cushing's bedroom. Among the clothing tossed about the room were a woman's bathrobe and apparel. "Now the Japs know he has a woman," Ruiz said. "A messy situation that could have been avoided. The Japs will be looking for her. If they catch her, they will hold her as a hostage and torture her to cause Walter much distress." Distraught, James felt like telling Ruiz where to stick his insinuations. Ruiz continued, "I heard that the Japs captured the girlfriend of a PA soldier in Ilocos Norte and paraded her naked through the town. He waited in ambush, shot her through the heart while she was in their custody, to save her from a much worse fate."

Before he could tell Ruiz to clam up, a shouting commotion came from outside the house, requiring their attention. They exited the house. The men had apprehended an elderly Filipino man with graying hair. "He say he is Cushing's caretaker; he hire him to look after the place when Cushing gone," a sergeant explained.

The caretaker said fervently, "Yis, I am Felix Albio; I work for Meester Cushing. I caretaker."

"What happened here?" James asked him.

157

"Hapon come. I hide, I see one truck. After they search, they leave, go norte!"

"No time to waste." James said. "Felix, you come with me. We are going to Bangued. I will send you to a house; you will deliver a message. Do you know where Cushing hid his pickup truck?"

"Yis! I help him hide it, full of gas. I take you there."

Felix led James to a gulch in the hills, a short walk from the mine, and pointed to a pile of brush pushed against the cliff. In the flashlights glow, light reflected off the windshield underneath the brush. He began pulling the brush aside with Albio's help. Upon freeing the truck, James said, "I have an errand to run."

"What errand?" Ruiz asked.

"I think I'm going to get married," James answered.

Ruiz stared at him quizzically. "To a Filipina?"

James wanted to shout, 'In Abra what else for hell's sake?' followed by a caustic remark, 'Do you have a problem with that?' Instead, he said as impassively as he could, "My fiancée Maria Lopez. She was a clerk at the mine office, where I met her. If I am not back in twenty-four hours, leave for Tineg without me."

Ruiz frowned. "If the Japs catch you, that's more than enough time to get information out of you. A very great risk!" Though James knew Ruiz was right, he resented his counsel, a mix of realism and condescension that stuck in his craw. Determined to have his say, Ruiz continued, "Already there are informers, men of low character, spying for the Japs. They could be anyone. The damage may already be done. It would be best to leave the women where they are than put us all at risk, the greater good. You can have your way with Filipina women some other time."

This last remark stung to the core. Clenching his fists, James advanced to within two feet of Ruiz, who shifted his weight to the balls of his feet in a street fighter's stance. With his right hand in a fist and his left open, James recognized the ploy, grapple and strike, pull down blocking arm, and deliver a right cross or uppercut.

The face-off passed almost as immediately as it had started. For not quite a minute, they had taken measure of each other, readying to fight. Now Ruiz's eyes became hard and cold, no longer glaring anger. The moment for fighting passed.

James suspected that Ruiz provoked him for reasons other than the potential risks. He had accepted that a mixed Filipino American relationship and marriage might at times prove awkward. But considering the prejudice such a relationship would receive in the U.S., then why should he be surprised to experience it here? But such rationalization failed to still his disappointment. James kept the thought to himself but registered it among his growing grievances against Ruiz. "The women are coming with us. I am not prepared to explain to Cushing why I couldn't rescue them. Are you? And I will not desert Maria."

Ruiz glowered, as if realizing he had no justifiable counter-argument. "Enough! I have work to do," he growled, stalking away.

"Felix, you come with me," James said. "You will be my messenger."

James explained the plan as they drove to Bangued. "We are going to pick up two women, Felix. I cannot go to the house where they stay. The Japs are looking for us; there are informers. You know Casmata Hill neighborhood?"

"Yis sair, I do."

"I will park the car somewhere unseen and wait, then you go to the house. Speak to Cesar and Jocelyn Villa. Bring the girls back here. Tell Cesar to bring a padre if he can find one."

"A padre?" Felix asked, surprised.

"If one is available, we'll have a wedding in a secret place by kerosene lamp."

Felix just shook his head, understanding. "My, oh my."

"Do you know a secret place near Casmata Hill?"

"Yis! Behind the public market. Two blocks ahead."

James turned off the headlights with the car still in motion as Felix directed him into an alley behind the market square, stating the obvious, "No one shop at night."

"Great, I'll be waiting right here."

Felix exited the car and disappeared into the shadows. As anxious as he felt, James realized he could do nothing further, trusting Felix. He hoped the truck would escape notice by any drifters moving through town. Fortunately, the overcast night sky shrouded the still town in deep darkness.

An hour and a half had passed when dark shadows cast by a kerosene lamp moved down the alley toward him. In the light's glow, Maria and Dely appeared, accompanied by Cesar and Jocelyn Villa, with Felix in the lead and a padre in a black cassock. Maria wore a formfitting, white linen dress, open at the throat, revealing her graceful neck. From a silhouette in the dim lamplight, she materialized in James's eyes like an apparition of ethereal beauty.

"It's the best I could do in a rush," she explained. Her hair hung loosely on her shoulders.

Dely fretted, "We didn't have time to prepare her properly." But to James she had never looked lovelier. Her heart seemed a gleam in her eyes in the reflection of the lamplight, to James perceiving her more desirable than ever.

"Never mind. We are going straight from the wedding into the boondocks. Even so, I am as happy as I have ever been," James said, basking in a brief reprieve from the fear that now stalked the wakeful moments of everyone present.

The padre spoke frankly in fluent English. "Ordinarily I would not perform a secret marriage. However, church canon law provides exceptions for secrecy of matrimony if the circumstances would place the couple in grave danger if known. It is all too obvious that these are such times, with our country under the tyranny and prying eyes of cruel invaders. So, I consent. The celebration of this marriage must be in secret."

He surreptitiously looked around before continuing. "This is not the ideal time and place for a wedding. I am sorry we must dispense with the traditions of a full wedding, the symbols that remind you of your love—the cord, veil, and coins." At the mention of these objects, Maria briefly closed her eyes as if invoking memories of these items: the cord draped over the couple symbolizing the shared bond of matrimony; the veil that they belonged to each other and no one else; the coins for the reciprocity of give and take in a relationship. "But it is the love of James and Maria we are formalizing in Holy Matrimony tonight, which is stronger than mere symbols of ceremony. With that said, tonight we are gathered here to witness the union of mind, heart, and body, man and woman becoming one, together and forever."

The padre recited Corinthians 13:1-8, The Way of Love, finishing with "Love never ends." Transitioning the ceremony to the exchange of vows, he asked James and Maria, "Do you promise to love, cherish, and protect each other, whether in good fortune or in adversity? Both responded emphatically, "I do." Jocelyn produced two heirloom gold rings from her personal jewelry, which they slipped on to their fingers. After pronouncing James and Maria husband and wife, the padre culminated the ceremony with the pronouncement, "Bless their marriage, O God, as they begin their journey down the road of life together and guide their path through the trials to come in these turbulent times."

James and Maria clasped hands as the padre sprinkled holy water from a flask onto them. "You may kiss the bride," he said.

After sealing their nuptials with a formal kiss, Maria released a muffled squeal. James swept her into his arms, asking, "Well, Mrs. Novak, how do you like your new name?"

"I love it as I love you," she sighed. They exchanged a long kiss, each reciprocating ardently on full display in that all too brief interval, amidst whispered sighs in place of joyful cheers and applause, warily repressed by all, sensing the necessity.

"The Japs! Do the townspeople talk to them?" James asked.

161

"Most not willingly. While you and Walter were gone, about the same time as your ambush of the Jap convoy, enemy troops came here. They arrested a dozen people and drove them away in a truck heading west toward the coast to their home base. None have been seen since." All feared to their core that any taken by the Japanese would be transferred into the custody of the Kempeitai, the dreaded military secret police, akin to the German Gestapo.

"Now people make themselves scarce at the approach of Hapon," Cesar said.

"I am so sorry," James said. "Keep your eye out for ones who don't make themselves scarce. We will want to know about those in good time."

Cesar fixed James with a resolute gaze. "The Hapon sons of bitches would tear this town apart if we killed so much as one soldier, but they don't much care what happens to their Filipino kampons [slaves]. They are expendable. The Jap devils can always recruit more tangas, by torture, bribery, or both. They will probably kill them anyway when they are useful no more."

The two young women transferred the contents of their suitcases to canvas knapsacks and musette bags. "I know your lives in the bundocs of Abra will be hard," Jocelyn said, tears on her cheeks. "We will pray for your safety every day."

Shedding uncontrolled tears, Maria hugged Jocelyn. "You are more than a friend; you are as much a mother to me now as my real mother was, may she rest in peace." Jocelyn embraced Maria who pressed her face onto her shoulder.

Dely hugged Jocelyn and kissed her cheek. "I will miss you so much and always cherish your kindness." Then she said gravely, "Walter told me if the Japs tried to stop us to run and hide in the bush. I swore I would."

Jocelyn squeezed Dely's hand and kissed her cheek. "Now is not the time for such talk, silly girl," she said, dabbing at her eyes with a handkerchief and wishing all a last farewell.

"Felix, you'll have to ride in the truck bed to make room for the women."

"Of course. The night air is fresh." he said and clambered into the back. Driving the truck in the dark, steering gingerly, James drove with the headlights off on the straight stretch of road until he was well east of Bangued, relieved not to encounter other vehicles of the only type traveling at night—Japanese patrols.

On his return to the mine, James followed the glowing kerosene lamps signaling him to the gulch. As soon as he parked the pickup truck against the steep cliff side, dark figures began covering it with branches. "Take the battery out first, you tangas and siphon the gas. Add it to the troop truck," Lt. Ruiz barked, kerosene lamp in hand. Within minutes, the guerrillas had the truck hidden behind a camouflage of vines and limbs.

Ruiz came stalking through the headlights. "Congratulations on your marriage," he said stiffly. "We're heading out. Everything is ready to go—the truck will carry a dozen men, the two women and our equipment. I will drive. The route is confusing. I know the land."

"I hope the Japs find it confusing as well," James said.

Maria changed into her khakis and carefully folded the dress, hugging it for an instant to her breast. "It was over so quickly," she said, pouting, with a forlorn look on her face.

"I cannot sit in the back with those lice-ridden, lasings [drunks]," Dely hooted in protest. "They pretend to help you, but it is really just an excuse to grope. I feel their eyes all over me." James could not help but notice the men's looks directed at her, a mix of approval and wanton leers, but considered the sultry way in which she stuck out her hip when annoyed hardly helped her cause.

"I would rather sit on the groom's lap than back there."

"You are bad, Dely! That space is reserved for me," Maria joked in mock affront.

"Come on, I think we can all squeeze in," James said.

Ruiz locked his jaw as if gritting his teeth. He drove the truck off the main road onto a wagon track, the truck bouncing and trundling along to the northwest, reaching San Juan as dawn broke. Not even the rose-gold light of sunrise, breaking through the river mist, could enhance the sight of the dilapidated settlement before a rickety-looking bridge crossing the Abra River tributary. Late morning, they reached the final barrier at the end of the road, weary from lack of sleep, the beautiful but vexing Tineg River materializing out of a background of heavy, dense forests. The river's frothing turquoise waters cascaded over low falls, filling terraced rock pools, vexing because no immediate crossing or drivable track to the other side presented itself.

"We'd run out of gas before we'd find a crossing," James concluded glumly.

"It looks so inviting," Maria chirped. "I am hot and sticky. I would love to wash here."

"Yeah," James conceded, "We might as well freshen up before we start hiking." All the men shared this sentiment except for Lieutenant Ruiz who stood by in characteristic disapproval, unable to restrain his men as they stripped unabashed, flinging themselves naked, hooting and hollering into the clear, bubbling waters. James led Maria and Dely downstream around a bend from the men. "Enjoy yourselves, ladies."

"Aren't you going to join us," Dely cooed. "Don't feel embarrassed. You two are married, and I am a fallen woman with no shame." With mock reproach, Maria pointed at Dely with her lips, a Filipino trait. Dely slipped out of her plain white dress and dived into the clear water naked, like a shimmering water nymph. "Aye it's wonderful, come in."

Maria quickly removed her clothes, "Oh, what the heck. The war has changed even my sense of modesty." For a couple of seconds, she revealed herself to James's delight, nude in all her feminine grace, before leaping into the water, squealing with pleasure.

James hesitated for an instant until Dely called, her impish eyes teasing. "Don't be silly. What's a little nakedness among friends?"

"Dely, I don't know if I want you leering at my husband's naked body." Maria laughed, her eyes sparkling under wet lashes. With that, James quickly stripped to his birthday suit and splashed into the water faster than a peep show. Dely giggled with mirth, and Maria's initial pout gave way to a muffled snigger.

Before exiting, they all scrubbed away the grime of the trip as best they could.

James rubbed his legs with a handful of limestone sand he had scooped off the bottom.

"My goodness, I forgot the soap." Maria sighed.

"Ladies, the limestone sand right under your feet, should be a good skin cleanser, the finer the better. It breaks down dried sweat. If you want to know, I can explain the chemistry."

"No thank you," Dely said, bobbing her pretty head above the water. "I am not scientific."

When fully refreshed, they dressed and returned to the truck. Dely and Maria, who had just been gaily frolicking naked as jaybirds, resumed a poised manner, avoiding eye contact with the men, before reentering the cab. For an instant, Ruiz arched his eyebrows critically as they appeared from around the bend. Judging by Ruiz's wet hair, James concluded even he had found the cool waters too tempting to abstain.

Scouting the country south of the river, James noted the paths becoming increasingly narrow, ending further travel by truck. There was no chance of fording the river, which dropped precipitously in a rushing surge from the hills. "Ruiz, I thought you said you knew the country."

Ruiz's face flushed dark with anger. "Most of Abra. Some tracks have washed out since I was last here."

Having driven the truck as far as he could, to the end of the road, Ruis reversed course to the last village they had passed. He purchased three carabao, and hired a guide named Sulyan from their reserve of silver pesos, the only currency the natives considered worth a damn. He claimed to know the countryside, the 'bundocs.' "Yis! Bery good," Sulyan nodded vigorously.

The guerrillas hid the truck behind jungle brush and branches on a hard rock glade off the trail. From the moment they left the last road, the isolation of the Abra highlands closed in around them. In this tangled world of limited visibility and blurred sense of direction, James realized how easily one could become lost in its maze.

CHAPTER 15

The Tangadan Tunnel

A S JAMES AND RUIZ'S PARTY TRAVELED into the remote countryside of northeast Abra searching for a suitable site for the evacuation camp on Mt. Bawao, Cushing began his plan to block the 62-meter Tangadan Tunnel. Blocking it, he reasoned, would thwart marauding Japanese troops from the coast access into the fertile rice valley of Abra. In advancing the plan, Cesar Villa introduced him to an excavation contractor Roberto Cruise from the town of San Quintin. Being the only heavy equipment operator in Abra, before the war he had contracted with the Philippine government for provincial road maintenance, the contract now ended because of war. Having the only caterpillar tractor in Abra, with a mounted bulldozer blade, Cruise's support was essential for the plan to blockade the Tangadan Tunnel.

Cushing had just learned that Dely and Maria had gone with the party of Lieutenants Ruiz and Novak into the wilds of northeast Abra, after the Japanese raid of the Rainbow mine. A wise decision, he conceded, relieving his anxiety about their safety. With a Japanese manhunt for him underway, their lodging at the Villas placed them and their hosts in perilous danger.

Having clearly fingered Cushing for the Candon raid, the Japanese had extended their manhunt for him into eastern and central Abra, in increasingly brutal search and destroy missions and merciless interrogations of residents. As if the abuses and abductions perpetrated by the small-scale patrols to date were not bad enough, the very thought of a large, permanent Japanese garrison horrified the populace. The only thing restraining the Japanese army from an all-out dragnet and carnage in Abra, he realized with mounting dread, were their transient, low numbers inland, thanks to troop shortages due to their stymied campaign in Bataan.

Although on board with the plan, Cruise's fear had become palpable. "The work of a D6 caterpillar tractor is obvious; there is no mistaking its tracks. It won't take much for the Japs to guess my role in the plot."

Cushing paused, giving this careful thought. "What if the guerrillas steal the dozer against your will, take it at night, make a commotion? Then you rant and rave bloody outrage to your neighbors at the top of your lungs. Scream that the bandit guerrillas have robbed you. If the Japs question your neighbors, they can vouch for your story. We can't pay you much for the D6 at this time; how about a thousand pesos in silver now and a promissory note for the rest after the war?"

"That would not even cover the down payment, not to mention large payments on credit. And who guarantees the loan? The U.S. government?" Cruise lamented. "Doubtful! So, I give you the D6 for free. The Japs would steal it anyway, and if they catch me with silver, they will ask questions harshly, then I'm done fore." He swallowed hard, "Keep your silver; you will need it soon enough. When you are finished, destroy the tractor, please. Otherwise, the Japs will know for sure I am complicit."

"Sure thing, I hope the bank doesn't try to collect missed payments after the war," Cushing snickered.

"I wouldn't put it past them. Damn Pensionados [monied elites]! I'm not aware of them defending our country," he said with sarcastic sneer. "Can't wait till they try to repossess it," he said, snickering. "What's left of it. Also, I must ask you, when you stage the robbery, can you hit me a half-dozen times in the face, hard enough to bruise? That will make my story more believable."

Cushing frowned, "I don't like striking allies, but I can see your point."

"Believe me, it may spare me far worse treatment from the Japs."

The next day at dusk, Cushing and his guerrillas moved up the winding road to the tunnel entrance. A scout reported that a Japanese motor patrol had entered the province earlier in the day and had not returned through the tunnel. Cushing sent a group of his men up to the ridge top with instructions to take positions hidden among the scrub brush and rocks and to wave a black signal flag when the daily Jap patrol cleared the tunnel, heading west back to the coast.

When the daily truck entered the tunnel on its way back to the coast, he bawled out the stand down order, "Let the truck go. Huwag magpaputok [Do not fire]." He hoped the truck was not transporting captives, as had been the case on other Japanese forays into the province. Shooting up the truck would have likely killed anyone inside; a rescue of possible captives was out of the question. When the truck exited from the west end, an observer on the ridge waved the flag, giving the all-clear signal. With conflicted ambivalence, the guerrillas allowed the truck to put away in an unhurried departure back to the coast.

With Abra free of the enemy, Cushing directed the emplacement of the dynamite, calling together a crew of twelve of his men. Scrambling up the rise, Cushing led the men carrying the case of dynamite, the reel of ignition wire, picks, and shovels, to four locations above the tunnel entrance on the eastern San Quintin side of the ridge. Dividing the dynamite into four lots, he directed the men to dig four sink holes into the stony dirt beneath the crusty topsoil—a laborious task with the men probing the tough soil with their tools, jabbing into fissures to free rocks. They were all former miners, robust men used to hard, demanding work. After examining the holes, Cushing grunted with satisfaction. In each of the strategically positioned holes, he directed the placement of twenty sticks of dynamite, then inspected the continuity of circuit from the leg wires to the detonator.

After dark, Cushing with a squad of guerrilla riflemen, returned to Cruise's shop to conduct the elaborate charade. His men beat on tin, shouted in loud, strident voices until making themselves hoarse, obliterating the tranquility of the neighborhood. One fired several rounds from his .45 into the ground and yelled, "sayaw ka asong babae [dance you bitch]."

Cushing said to Cruise, "I'll strike you with an open hand. I do not want to knock out teeth or break your nose. Yell and beg at the top of your lungs." As if striving for realism, Cushing slapped Cruise across the face hard with an open hand—"for the cause" he muttered as if an atonement. Cruise shouted in pain, as if his life depended on it. "Please, no more, take what you want," he yelled after the sixth slap.

From houses nearby, lamps flickered through the open shutters, his neighbors undoubtedly peering through windows. A few of Cushing's men shouted menacingly, "Mind your own business! Stay inside if you know what's good for you."

"That should raise a few welts. You put on a good show," Cushing said.

"I wasn't faking. It hurt!"

Cushing clapped him on the shoulder. "I am sorry my friend," and asked, "How much diesel do you have?"

"A hundred gallons. You might as well take it all. If you don't, the Japs will. I am now out of business for the rest of the war." His men loaded two diesel drums onto the truck. As they shook hands, Cushing advised in dark jest, "You can tell the Japs you have been robbed by the bandit guerrillas. Implore them to find and punish us. After we leave, go talk with your neighbors; make sure they see your face, your alibi." He feared that no alibi, no matter how plausible, would diminish the enemy's appetite for retribution.

As Cushing drove the caterpillar tractor down the road to the tunnel, Cruise ran out into the neighborhood yelling outrage. His neighbors emerged astonished, peppering him with questions and expressions of concern. He waved his fist in the direction of the departing bulldozer, cursing the thieving bandits stealing. With a look over his shoulder, Cushing could see Cruise's animated silhouette in the glow of the kerosene lamps, bobbing his head like an agitated turkey, gesturing stridently before his gathering neighbors. *Good show ol' boy.* He hoped it was convincing enough, unable to hear him above the roar of the diesel engine.

Cushing parked the D6 a safe distance back from the Tangadan Tunnel entrance, then climbed up the slope to a sheltered spot above the dynamite bore holes. He hoped that the dynamite, placed next to a great rock slab, would undermine the substratum layer beneath and trigger a collapse of the hillside. With his men positioned well back, he shouted out the warning "Take cover," waiting a minute before pushing down the detonator plunger. The hillside exploded in a rolling cloud of dark billowing earth, with dust and debris thrown upward. For an instant, the fireballs illuminated the dirty plumes. The avalanche released tons of earth, gravel, and boulders, which cascaded down the hill above the tunnel, piling onto the road before the tunnel entrance.

Cushing descended the steep grade through the precarious rubble, zigzagging cautiously. After starting the bulldozer, he lunged the heavy earthmoving machine repeatedly into the debris mass, pushing the tumbled piles of rock and earth deeper and deeper into the tunnel. As seen in the light of kerosene lamps and the D6's headlights, men with picks and shovels moved earth and rock into the path of the dozer blade.

Other men climbed up the grade of loosened earth, digging with tenacious resolve and shouting warnings, pushing more loosened dirt and rocks down the hill to the waiting road crew.

Inside the tunnel, sweating, bare-chested men shoved wheelbarrow loads up the growing earth mound in the tunnel center on ramps of wooden planks, raising the pile toward the ceiling. Cushing reveled in imagining the bewildered chagrin awaiting the next Japanese patrol on encountering the impassable barrier in the middle of the tunnel. He marveled with pride at the men's dogged determination; they showed no letup in their all-out effort to push more rock and earth onto the road, lessening his concern about whether enough blasted rubble would be available to complete the task. As the piles of earth kept coming, he concluded the explosions must have blasted through ancient fractures to account for the large quantity of freed earth. He still had two sticks of dynamite left to destroy the bulldozer.

Once dawn broke, the efficiency of the work crew improved in the light of day, the rubble pile growing far longer than it was high. Filling the last gap beneath the tunnel ceiling did not matter. Nothing, not even another earth mover, was going to push through the blockage. Any Japanese engineer crew approaching the tunnel would be easy targets from the ridge above. In setting booby traps for the enemy, he placed three hand grenades in the pile, pulling the pin on each and securing the safety handles in the depressed position under the weight of rocks. It would not take much disturbance to release the handle and detonate the grenades, giving a Japanese work crew an unwelcome surprise and a reason to slow their pace, not knowing how many more bloody booby traps lay hidden in the rubble.

At midmorning, the sentries on the hill signaled two Japanese troop trucks heading east toward the tunnel. Ecstatic, Cushing whooped, "Come on, boys, put down your tools and grab your rifles. This you got to see." In battle fervor, the men charged up to the ridge top, rifles in hand, intent on delivering a righteous blow, settling scores. Clearing the steep crest, his fighters spread out into firing positions among the ample boulders and brush overlooking the western approach to the tunnel. He passed the message, "Nobody fire until I do. Let them enter the tunnel," he yelled with an aid bawling out the translation.

Of the two trucks, the first drove into the tunnel at a leisurely pace. Its horn blared from inside as the second truck entered. At the sight of the trucks caught in the trap, the guerrillas waited on the verge of manic glee. A couple minutes went by before the two trucks backed out of the tunnel, bumper to bumper, with the last truck controlling the pace out.

On exiting, the Japanese trucks maneuvered in frantic skid turns, with wheels spinning in the roadside gravel, the panicked drivers grasping the impending threat. Cushing started the attack on the trucks, firing the signal with his .45 pistol immediately followed by a fusillade of rifle fire from his men. The sluggish diesel acceleration of the trucks slowed their escape, as rifle fire from above shredded the bed covering enveloping the hapless troops inside. With the following truck screening out the cab of the first truck, it escaped down the road, no doubt Cushing presumed, with a lethal cargo of casualties. The second truck careened off the road into a ditch as the guerrillas continued to pour rifle fire into it from the ridge.

No one emerged from the partially tipped over truck, but agonized screaming emanated from inside. "Sair, at least one of dem bastards still alive," Juan said. "Maybe more."

"If so, they can bleed to death. We're not going down there," Cushing answered, as the screams became fainter and intermittent.

Juan nodded in agreement, "What if more Japs come back here when the truck don't return and charge up the ridge?"

Cushing looked down on the steep slope. "Would you want to storm this hill against concealed gunfire from above?" Juan shook his head no. "We'll probably be gone by then but it would be a turkey shoot," Cushing declared. "Okay boys, show's over. Now let's pack up and leave." First, his men stacked a pile of wood on the crest of the ridge. A delegation of curious men from the town arrived at the base. He instructed them, "If the Japanese return in force, light a signal fire. If it is just a small scavenger squad collecting their dead and equipment, do not light the fire and stay out of sight. A few Jap buzzards are no threat to anyone."

A signal fire visible from a long distance would give his forces more than enough time to arrive and repel enemy engineers sent to clear the tunnel. Before leaving, he destroyed the D6 crawler in a whomp of a dynamite blast, leaving behind a mass of mangled metal. He still believed in the imminent return of American forces, though further out in time than he had hoped.

Still possible by the end of the rainy season in October? He hoped, like a prayer that depended on the tunnel blockage prevailing until then, an impassable obstacle to Japanese incursion into Abra.

CHAPTER 16

Raids and Consolation Prize

E lsewhere in Ilocos Sur, Cushing aggressively hatched daring plans for new offensive actions against the Japanese. In the pall of darkness of an overcast night, a party of Cushing's guerrilla fighters silently climbed in single file up a slope in a drainage gulley to level ground after following the course of a creek below to reach a Japanese base on the bluff above. Occasional muffled Japanese voices broke the otherwise still of the night, either from sentries or drift from the barracks.

Just below the lip of the gully, gravel loosened by one man's foot cascaded down the slope; at the sound, all froze. They waited breathlessly until Cushing signaled forward by inserting a cigarette lighter into a small wooden box with embedded red stained glass, a gift from a sympathetic padre. As Bob Arnold had explained, red light cuts down on the visibility from a distance, reducing the chance of the enemy detection, which made sense to him. For an instant he regretted their irreconcilable differences. He had no quarrel with Arnold's competency.

Armed with Springfield rifles, three BARs, and Cushing with a Thompson submachine gun, to his knowledge the only one in northern Luzon, the guerrillas halted at the perimeter wire fence. They waited until a guard inside walked by, marked in the dark by the glowing end of a cigarette dangling from his lips, on which he puffed, unaware of the raiders crouching in the foliage. One man, after sliding through a cut made in the wire fence, rose behind him with a straight razor in hand. He simultaneously jerked his head back with his hand over his mouth and, with a powerful swipe of the sharp blade, sliced through his throat and carotid arteries. He covered the soldier's mouth with his hand until his stifled moans ceased, releasing the body when the soldier stopped thrashing.

More men slithered over the edge of the gradient into positions on the level ground before the wire fence. Two more of Cushing's men quickly slid through the cut in the wire. Behind the fence, long, dark silhouettes of the barracks materialized from the opaque darkness. With his men now committed, Cushing trusted that none would break communication silence.

A second guard, retracing his steps, unaware came within an arm's reach of the men inside the fence before spotting the crumpled body of the dead soldier and dark shapes of the guerrillas rising out of the grass. He uttered a startled shriek before a guerrilla cut him down with a strike to the neck with a razor-sharp bolo. From the heavy slapping sound of the bolo on flesh, Cushing knew that the strike was fatal, but his crying alarm had been enough to rouse a squad of enemy soldiers who rushed toward the fence.

Yelling "Fire," Cushing began the skirmish with a burst from his Thompson. The thumping BARs joined him in mowing down the advancing enemy, roused from the camp, in their tracks like blades of grass. Having lost the element of surprise, Cushing realized what happened next had to happen fast. Responding to his exhortations, a half-dozen more men squirmed through the breach in the fence in quick order with canvas musette bags filled with dynamite, lighting the fuses on the run with cigarillos. They hurled the bombs through the doors and windows of the long, low steel-roofed barracks in swift, simultaneous attacks before the Japanese troops could rally. The same sets of startled screams issued from within each of the barracks before the dynamite bombs exploded in flashes of bright fireballs that for an instant lit up the sight of buildings shredding apart in the blasts.

In a mad dash back to the fence, his men dived one after the other into the cut in the fence, dragged through with frantic tugs in the hands of their comrades on the other side, as stunned, howling Japanese staggered out of the barracks. The Japanese that escaped from the nearest burning structure quickly succumbed to the withering salvo of guerrilla rifle fire.

Elated, Cushing called out. "Well done, boys, move out. Sige na!" His men retreated as fast as their surefooted agility allowed in the dark down the gully. No longer concerned about the cascading sound of debris and sliding feet, only in making haste, they put the destructive aftermath and the enemy's ineffective rifle fire further behind them. Stray shots continued to emanate from the camp, but the enemy refrained from pursuing the guerrilla raiders escaping into the ink-black jungle. The guerrillas followed the creek, where the thick, foreboding jungle foliage favored evasion and ambush.

The enemy came to know Cushing's guerrillas by their sudden, nighttime attacks, their deadly calling card, dynamite hurled without warning through windows and doors, infuriating the enemy by their uncanny ability to evade pursuit. Anecdotal stories reached Cushing that Japanese soldiers had taken to sleeping in trenches rather than in the barracks, believing they were safer in the event of nighttime bombing raids. Well into May, the Japanese could only guess the guerrilla's movements by the colored pins on their situation maps, identifying the dynamited bridges and garrisons along the eastern coast, and attacks that their officers insisted on calling bandit activity. The guerrillas dynamited facilities while the soldiers were away in futile pursuit of the same guerrillas, returning afterwards to take in the destructive aftermath. Attacks on Japanese engineering crews and equipment frustrated Japanese efforts to repair the damaged bridges, to Cushing's satisfaction, along with the mounting enemy casualties.

In late March, with 7,000 Japanese troops combing the coast of northern Luzon for the phantom Cushing, he led a contingent of guerrillas, brazenly traveling at night in trucks on the same roads of the Luzon west coast used by the enemy, to the northernmost province Ilocos Norte. A credible report from a guerrilla scout said the Japanese had stored captured American ammunition in a warehouse. With low clouds fortuitously darkening the land, the men of the Abra Battalion moved stealthily through the brush up to the chain link fence and barbwire enclosed perimeter surrounding the warehouse. The overgrown grass in which they crouched grew beyond the fence into the compound, providing favorable concealment. Treading along at regular intervals, shadowy guards revealed themselves in puffs of glowing cigarettes. *Puff away, assholes* Cushing thought, figuring the flickering end in front of their faces impaired their direct vision. Still green, the Japanese had yet to fully grasp the intensity of hatred and the malevolent storm of resistance gathering about them.

Now, a stockpile of .30 caliber rifle ammunition lay forty yards away in the darkened warehouse, a bounty too hot to pass up. At Cushing's direction, one of his men, a skilled woodsman, uttered convincing calls of nocturnal animals, signaling instructions to the men of the squad in the darkness. In response to his piercing call of a grass owl, his men dropped prone on the ground. When he emitted chirps like a gecko, a couple of men with wire cutters crept over to the fence. Cushing directed them to cut access through a section of the fence obscured by the foliage.

Living up to their cunning reputation, several Ifugao tribesmen crawled through the cut in the fence and across the ground through the tall, uncut brush. The heedless guards staggered along a well-trampled path in predictable cycles, as if following the cigarettes in their mouths, never veering from the path in the dark into growth possibly concealing snakes. The mountaineers synchronized their forward creep to the lapses in the guards' patrol.

After slithering under the raised floor of the warehouse, Cushing's Ifugaos cut through the bamboo flooring with their razor-sharp bolos. Over the course of the next six hours, they lowered 124 cases of .30 caliber ammunition, 150,000 rounds, through the floor. Forming a relay, crawling on their backs with the cases of ammunition on their chests, they passed the loot from one man to the next back to the hole in the fence in the intervals between the rounds of the guards. Squatting on his heels, Filipino fashion by the fence, Cushing watched amazed, giddy, as the cases kept coming. Outside the fence, silent cargadores waited and snatched up the cases, carrying them like a line of ants back to the collection point at the base of a mountain to the waiting trucks. He relaxed, releasing a sigh of relief. He had left orders with the drivers to flee with the trucks without a fight if the Japanese discovered the operation in progress.

Once fully loaded, the trucks packed with ammunition and men, some clinging to the outside of the now filled trucks, delivered the stash to a hidden depot in the mountain forest of Abra. Relieved, Cushing thanked his lucky stars that the retreat order had not been necessary. His chest swelled with pride. Cushing looked on in awe at the men unloading the truck in quick order. *A crack team*! They had pulled off a heist flawlessly in coordinated secrecy. The men slapped and clapped each other about the shoulders and back. With the silence order lifted, Cushing crowed with delight, "Boys, fill your bandoliers and ammo pouches with as much ammo as you can carry. No more going into fights unprepared."

At that moment, he did not want to think about the inevitable Japanese rage the mission would trigger. Distressing beyond measure to the Filipinos, Japanese loss of face usually resulted in violent reprisals; Colonel Watanabe was no ordinary homicidal maniac. Humiliation by a conquered people whom the Japanese believed did not know their place drove them to wanton brutality. With Watanabe, that probability magnified in the recesses of Cushing's psyche, a nagging remorse, festering. The Japanese wanted the people to believe that the guerrillas were responsible for reprisals against them. Though he

178

desired absolution from the people, he saw no alternative to the cycle of violence until the Japanese were driven from the islands and received justice for their war crimes. But that hope seemed to stretch ever further into the future, like a moving goalpost on a long, deep play!

Major Candonia Gaerlan received a tip that Colonel Masanobu Tsuji, a special envoy of Imperial Japanese Headquarters and architect of the Japanese army tactics in Southeast Asia, would travel in a staff convoy, from the Japanese sea base at Tagudin, Ilocos Sur to Manila. On April 19, Gaerlan, Cushing, and Barnett met at a safe house in La Union province to plan the ambush. Major Gaerlan wore his trademark sombrero and bandoleers over his shoulders, looking more like a Mexican revolutionary than the managing engineer for an electric utility. Though his outfit may have appeared flamboyant, his reputation as a serious man preceded him. He had a firm mouth and the calculating eyes of an intelligent man. Though a head taller, Barnett seemed his natural complement, wearing a leather cartridge belt around his waist, the pockets stuffed with .30-caliber clips, a Colt .45 model M1911 pistol on his hip, and a long fighting bolo in a scabbard. The three men now huddled together in conference, finalizing mission details for the ambush of the Japanese motorcade.

The reports from a resistance spy stated that imperial high command had appointed Col. Tsuji as an adviser to General Homma and a troubleshooter on a fact-finding mission. "He wields considerable power for a colonel. He is a ruthless bastard, a confirmed sadist and butcher. Even generals are afraid to cross him," Gaerlan explained. "Tsuji wants to execute all detained Filipino-American military prisoners, even the civilians of enemy nations. For now, General Homma will not allow him to implement the 'Kill All' order, but Tsuji encourages brutal mistreatment and casual murder of POWs. He is an advocate of what Japanese call the Three Alls policy: kill All, burn All, loot All—the scorched earth tactics they adopted in China."

Cushing shook his head, "Fucking ghoul! How did you get this information?"

"Every bar girl between here and Manila is a spy," Gaerlan said. "However, in this case it is intelligence from a well-placed spy, Homma's mistress. He hates Tsuji's guts with good reason, for questioning and subverting his authority. He can't stand being saddled with him. Apparently, General Tojo is upset about how long it took General Homma to defeat the Allied forces at Bataan and that Corregidor and the southern islands have yet to fall. Tsuji complains to Imperial command that General Homma is mismanaging the occupation, that he is too lenient with the Filipinos, encouraging impudence."

Cushing smirked. "I almost feel sorry for Homma. I'd be happy to rid him of the pest." Barnett and Gaerlan chuckled softly. "As for the fate of the POWs, I'm still in the dark about the details." The sketchy reports that had reached him were grim, but damn hard to confirm from his remote locale in northern Luzon.

"We all have pieces of the puzzle. Together, a fuller picture will emerge," Gaerlan said.

Cushing grimaced, "I would love to question Tsuji alive."

Gaerlan shook his head, dismissing the thought. "If he is truly a Bushido warrior as he claims, I doubt he'll give you the chance. But then again, maybe he is not what he pretends to be. Sometimes sadists like him have inflexible codes intended for everyone but themselves."

Gaerlan said he knew of a promising spot for the ambush on Tagudin-Cervantes Road. Cushing stared at the map Major Gaerlan had spread out. Gaerlan pointed to a section of the road that oscillated north and south." There's an S-curve in the road west of town with a high bank on one side with shoulder high cogon grass, good concealment for the ambush. Any vehicle between the two curves of the 'S' has to slow down. That's when we hit them. They will have no chance to speed up fast enough to escape our trap.

"Excellent!" Cushing said. "Now that we know the quarry, let the hunt begin."

Cushing took George Barnett aside and asked him how things were going with Major Gaerlan. "Very good! To be honest, I would be at a total loss here in La Union without him. He has the organization and knows how to use it." Cushing regarded Barnett's assessment with unequivocal confidence.

On the expected day before sunrise, sixty men from the La Union Regiment and 121st assumed hidden positions in the tall grass on the hill overlooking the double curve in the road with rice paddies on the other side. The men had barely settled in when the lookout signaled three cars approaching. As the cars slowed into the center lap, Gaerlan fired the opening shot. The guerrillas poured lethal rifle fire on the little motorcade, halting the lead car that careened onto the grade in a jolting crash with its hood pointed uphill and its rear end sticking out into the road.

The cars behind the lead one braked to avoid colliding with it. In the salvo of bullets, the drivers slumped dead at the wheel with more bodies visible through the shot-out windows.

A stocky Japanese officer in a green tunic spilled out the door of the last car, slipped, and then picked himself up as he ran in a crouch into a rice field. Ducking and trying clumsily to dodge as the bullets splattered the paddy mud, he slowed to a panting slog. A quick-thinking farmer in the field with a bolo in hand ran along the dike to intercept him. He swung the blade in a clothesline strike to the officer's throat, bringing him down on his back in the mud. Running down the hill to the field, Cushing, Barnett, and Gaerlan arrived on the scene where the farmer stood victorious, the bloody machete in hand, over the felled officer. Blood pumping from a deep gash in his neck mixed in a maroon tint with the mud.

"Holly shit," Cushing said, looking down at the officer dying in spasms. "We bagged a general."

"But not Colonel Tsuji," Gaerlan said, "This one is Major General Hara! We believe the harsh treatment of Filipinos in Northern Luzon is on his orders."

"I guess Hara's the consolation prize," Cushing said.

"Probably. Tsuji is clearly the architect of the harsh policies and Hara only too willing to carry them out. But Tsuji can always find another high-ranking patsy to do his bidding."

"Right you are. There's no shortage of psychopaths in the Jap army," Cushing muttered. He bent down and removed the yellow patches, each with a silver star designation of a major general, from Hara's uniform. He pinned the silver stars onto his lapels. "Hey, look boys," Cushing shouted. "I've been promoted a Jap general," he announced. The fighters cheered, hooted, and laughed in a mixture of derision and exhilaration. At that instant, with a high value target, a dead general, to their credit, all believed with pride their successful ambush could not fail to rattle the enemy's confidence to their core. They had just sent a clear message: no more safe passage on Philippine highways. But as the elation wore off, all realized that Japanese reprisals against civilians entrapped in their dragnet by proximity to the attack were now imminent. The death of a Japanese general would demand it.

Cushing waved the farmer over, who held out his bloody bolo for inspection, beaming with pride. "Well done, my friend!" Cushing said, placing his hand on his shoulder. "But trouble is just beginning. Now go to your barrio. Tell the people to prepare to evacuate if the Japs come. I wish it were different." *Where to and for how long?* He had no satisfactory answer to give the stalwart tao. Gaerlan stepped in, "I want the same message sent to all the barrios in the area. You must all cooperate to get through this."

"I understand trouble come. But I would kill him again," the man said. Cushing saluted him with a full, precise salute, for the first time revering the military ritual that had previously felt so awkward.

CHAPTER 17

Evacuation Camp

A S CUSHING'S COMPANY CONDUCTED ATTACKS throughout northern Luzon, the party of Lts. Novak and Ruiz set out on foot leading hired caribous laden with provisions, foodstuffs that included sacks of rice, camote, and dried mung beans, critical for staving off the ravages of beriberi, the curse of a mostly white rice diet. The party moved up the circuitous mountain paths into the Abra highlands. James regarded the men in his squad with a growing confidence in their survival skills for living in the far reaches of highlands, especially those of Sergeant Conrado Potencion.

He had first met the resourceful sergeant during the Candon raid, and now, walking together along the path, listened to him describe in-depth the availability of food foraged from the forest. Potencion described a cornucopia of wild foods, including edible leaves and flowers, tubers, starch from fruit palms, seeds and plants. He said these could be dried and ground to create a flour substitute for baking. How you could get potable water that seeped from the stems of certain plants when cut, and tangy red fruits that, from his description, sounded to James like raspberries. For protein, he named a mixed bag of edible wild fauna, including large reptiles. "At night, you can hear a python from a long way." Their burps as they digest sound like a mix of grunts and growls.

"And how long do pythons grow?" James asked.

I have heard over thirty feet. The largest one I've seen, maybe twenty-five feet." *Digesting what?* James thought. The big ones, he had heard, could swallow a man whole. For other palatable meals found in the forests, Potencion included brown deer, monkeys, bats and, the most sought after, the wild warty pig, distinguished by stiff, spiky hair on its head and back. But then Potencion admitted, "Finding enough food can take all your time, and some days you may come back with little. At least you do not starve, but you do not grow fat."

As they advanced into the countryside, the grassland transitioned to the tall trees of the virgin forested hills. "You know where we go?" James had asked the hired guide Sulyan.

"Go! Oh my, yis," Sulyan said, smiling though betelnut-stained teeth, with assurance that James found less than convincing.

"Does he understand what we are looking for, a suitable place for an encampment?"

Ruiz frowned, "Unfortunately, his pidgin Ilocano is even worse than my Tinguian. He knows the words for trail and camp. Even with hand signs, it is hard to tell if this tanga fully understands me."

"Well, I guess we'll just keep following him and hope he knows where he's going," James said, with a resigned shrug.

"We should know soon enough. If he is just selling us rumors, I will take back the money we paid and keep his Carabaos," Ruiz grumbled. *Hardly any appeal to the man's better nature,* James thought. He concluded Ruiz increasingly distrusted Sulyan, deriding him as some 'low-bred dolt' of the bundocs.

Upon emerging onto a slope with an unobstructed north view, James began to envision the topography of the land through which the party moved. From the north-facing slope, an immense, sprawling mountain appeared in the near distance that made the highland foothill from which they gazed seem like a mere hummock.

"Bundoc Bawao! See bery near!" The guide Sulyan chimed happily. Clouds hid the mountaintop from view. The sides supported a rising mass of jungle forest over a vast landscape. Sulyan looked at the view, awed like an explorer on a journey of discovery. Ruiz scowled at him, as if wondering whether he'd ever been to Mt. Bawao before.

"I bet you could play hide-and-seek with Japs there forever," James said, thinking how the Japanese search and destroy missions against guerrillas kept moving deeper into the Luzon interior.

As all were aware, in the back and beyond, security came at the expense of food and supplies, a nagging conundrum and bane of guerrilla existence. "Food is going to be a problem despite of Sergeant Potencion's bushcraft," Lt. Ruiz concluded.

"Well, maybe the locals will have a good harvest and be generous," James said.

Ruiz gave him a disdainful look. He was already advocating for a patriotic food levy for the armed men in the forests and insisted that it would not unfairly burden the local population. James had his doubts. Ruiz's talk about a patriotic levy sounded more like a shakedown of people with little concept of nation. *Maybe they'll sacrifice for their village, but a nation?* He wondered. For the time being, he pushed these impending dilemmas into the recesses of his mind. Their mission was to prepare a camp for the time when the 121st would need it, an absolute certainty he believed, considering enemy advances inland.

Speaking a mix of Ilocano and limited Tinguian, Ruiz questioned Sulyan. "I think he says there is one path from the south up Bawao to a high table land."

"What about escape routes if we have to abandon the mountain?"

"There are game trails all over the mountain. We can clear them, giving us a way east to the Cordilleras. Then we can link up with Colonel Horan."

"Maybe Horan will have to come to us," James said, thinking of Colonel Horan's tenuous HQ now at the Batong Buhay copper mine in Kalinga province. He wondered if Cushing's decision to commit the Abra battalion to Horan's command as the 121st Infantry would yield any strategic advantage or just create a caretaker burden for the 121st. Since no reports of Colonel Horan taking the fight to the Japs were forthcoming, James concluded Horan needed Cushing's battle-tested

185

organization more than Cushing needed him. But he thoroughly believed the old advice about making the boss look good.

The party trudged up the mountain grassy slopes and over forested ridges in single file behind the pack-laden carabaos, surprisingly docile for 1,000-pound beasts, James observed. Under the shroud of tall trees, they found passing relief from the sunbaked grasslands. All moved at an even pace up the rising gradient. The two women, Maria and Dely, shuffled stoically along with resigned determination, wearing kerchiefs wrapped around their hair like turbans. Their banter became terser, as they walked with their heads bowed, watching the ground for snakes, occasionally emitting squeals, "Ngek!" More likely their imaginations, James concluded. The oppressive, encroaching wall of green forests threatened to take back the trail, leaving all traveling within it lost with no bearings.

Maria and Dely would tease each other calling one another, he guessed, the Filipino equivalent of 'scaredy-cats,' before resuming their monotonous plod forward. He reckoned loose stones and exposed, twisted tree roots that could turn an ankle were a greater danger on the trail than snakes. Though he assumed the hidden rustlings, emanating from the brush along the side of the trail, indicated some kind of agitated reptile presence.

James looked at the mountain spurs radiating symmetrically from the heights of Mt. Bawao. "If we hold the ridges, the Japs will have to attack up through the canyons."

Ruiz turned his head. "The only path they would find would be one we recently used. Unless you have lived here, you don't realize how fast the jungle takes back what people touch. But I know eventually the enemy will come. They only have to torture enough people to learn about Mount Bawao."

Clouds obscured the summit. When the whisps of clouds receded, steep ridges appeared, stretching outwards for miles in all directions revealing valleys. "Kampo, see, see!" Sulyan pointed excitedly to a level clearing on a mountain shoulder.

Looking through binoculars, James whistled. "Looks very encouraging," he said, perceiving the ridge shoulder a natural citadel. He could imagine an ancient encampment of nomadic people favoring its heights for defense.

"Up there, a few men with plenty of ammunition could easily hold off a larger force, and, with pickets, have plenty of warning," Ruiz said. With his doubts about the old guide dispelled, James sighted his binoculars in the direction he was pointing. Two hogback ridges extended from the table bluff, forming a deep box canyon between them.

The shoulder is high enough to move men quickly between the mountain ridges," Ruiz said. No matter what path the Japs attack, we can flank them from above. Catch them in a crossfire."

One of the Filipino soldiers said, "The Japs will never take that mountain."

Another muttered, "If a Jap general in Vigan tell Jap soldiers you take Bawao or die, you think they no fight? Japs fight to the death." He plodded along the trail, cackling.

As the shadows of the Luzon Cordillera mountains settled over the land near dusk, the guerrilla band stopped to make camp. Tomorrow, they hoped to reach the box canyon on the sprawling west side of Mount Bawao, and the next day ascend to the mountain shoulder, and investigate the site, hopefully for a secret base.

The men launched into the brush, gathering from the forest materials with which to make improvised shelters for the night. When completed, the lean-tos consisted of two forked branches pounded into the soil, supporting a horizontal, long, reasonably straight sapling trunk between them. They laid angled sticks upon the trellis and then covered the structures with large, palm-like leaves, from the small samak trees, creating water-resistant enclosures.

"Look Maria, our honeymoon suite—rainproof provided it doesn't rain too hard" James Novak said, with wry appraisal, now a fugitive and out of work gold mining engineer in Japanese occupied Philippines with a new wife, married in a secret nighttime ceremony behind a closed village marketplace. He reflected back to when he had first met Maria, an office clerk working for the Itogon Goldmine, now decommissioned due to war. "Sorry, it ain't the Baguio Pines Hotel."

As the Novaks wearily stared at their slapped-together shelter, his thoughts revisited that safer, pleasanter time before the outbreak of war to the most enchanting romantic night of his life. He had booked a room for a night at the Baguio Pines Hotel, a celebration with Maria of nothing more complicated than a growing awareness that their relationship had entered a deeper stage of commitment, in which both felt comfortable enough to see where it led.

The Pines Hotel ranked as one of the finest examples of boomtown gold wealth in the growing city. Then, he had considered himself carefree, a young man with money to spend in a land where the American dollar went far. He liked to have a good time, enjoyed the company of women, but was not recklessly extravagant. Now, instead of pine scent in the air from the pine forests that thrived in the temperate Baguio Mountain climate, the fetid smell of rotting vegetation permeated their jungle bivouac.

On weekend nights, the Pines Hotel had been the place where the who's Who of Baguio gathered, the nightlife flourished ostentatiously in full swing. Maria's eyes had radiated in awe as red-suited, black-striped uniformed doormen ushered them inside. The usual crowd included the upper echelons of the mining industry, vacationing bureaucrats of the Philippine protectorate, and businesspeople, the ambitious sorts found throughout the Orient, *where opportunity knocked*, James surmised.

Also, ever-present, were the American officer corp. They lodged free at Camp John Hay, the exclusive military retreat for General MacArthur's USAFFE command, and had money and time to burn. He recalled the guests, sanguine, drifting between the crowded bar, the dance floor, the restaurant, and the large crackling fireplace in the main lobby, inviting after entering from the cool mountain air. Narra wood panels, a reddish-brown rosewood prized for its ribbon striped grain, finished the walls and ceilings. The restaurant boasted an extensive menu and wine list, steak from Australia, and seafood from the coast, with an overflow crowd waiting for tables in the bar. The music of tango and jitterbug floated in from the dance hall, the Crystal Room.

With an inward smile, he remembered how mortified Maria had been thinking that the desk clerk might realize they were not married. "I do not wear a wedding ring. He will know," she whispered.

"Nothing I can do about that now," he told had her with a wink. The desk clerk having seen it all—adulterous couples, high-end escorts, and obvious charlatans—pass through the doors, a registration by a romantically infatuated young couple, one named Novak and the other Lopez, would fail to tweak his jaded indifference. With the Pines Hotel always doing a brisk business, an advanced reservation was the important criterion. Maria smiled, relief came to her face, watching James sign the register, 'Mr. and Mrs. James Novak.

Stepping through the door of their room, Maria had been awestruck by the elegant décor, French oil paintings above the enticing bed, cream-colored drapes, fresh flower arrangements of roses, gerberas, orchids, and hanging ferns, at once forgetting her qualms.

On the dance floor that night, James and Maria danced among men in white dinner jackets and women in evening dresses under dimmed chandeliers. While some dances were new to Maria, she learned quickly, proving nimble on her feet with a good sense of rhythm. The orchestra struck up Glen Miller's 'In the Mood.' "My favorite!" she squealed, swinging her curved hips gracefully in fluid sway to the pulsating music.

The tune made popular around the world, James concluded. Maria wore a pink v-neck party dress, accentuating her graceful neck, with a flared skirt allowing for the flurry of jitterbug and the long dance strides of the tango. "You look beautiful," James said, and she laughed. On the dance floor, he directed her through the five-step tango: Quick right foot back, quick step left, slow forward, slow forward, pivot right and around we go for another five steps. Very Good! You'll be ready to learn the Argentine eight-step next, if I can remember how it's done."

Maria chortled happily as James leaned her back, supporting her with his arm as her right leg spontaneously lifted off the floor, her dress hemline cinching up her leg, delighting James with a flaunting glimpse of her shapely thigh.

For their last dance, they swayed in a self-absorbed slow rhythm and embraced fully to another Glenn Miller hit, the enchanting ballad 'Moonlight Serenade.' The spell had been cast—her head on his shoulder, soft breath against his cheek, the aromatic scent of perfume in his nostrils, the invitation in her almond eyes, and the perfect closing song on which to retire to their room.

Maria met his eyes and demurely turned her gaze toward the exit into the hallway. With her hand in his, James led the way down the hallway to their bedroom. Once alone together, they embraced in the bedroom foyer exchanging kisses. "Your eyes are like stars, brightly beaming," James crooned, staring deeply into her dark eyes.

"Bravo, my darling, we Filipinas love a good moonlight serenade." Her eyes probed his and lips pursed invitingly.

"What a shameless mimic I am," James said before kissing her deeply. Maria squealed happily. Uninhibited from all constraints, she responded eagerly to his lead, clothes discarded at her feet. Though her dress she carefully folded and placed on a chair before presenting herself in all her naked allure for his approval. James freed himself of clothes as though they were encumbrances he couldn't rid himself of fast enough, as Maria giggled. Wrapping their arms around each other, they fell together onto the bed, both laughing. They returned passion in ardent embraces, deep kisses and probing caresses consummating in joyous lovemaking, and cuddled in contented sleep.

The next morning before checkout, James and Maria enjoyed breakfast in bathrobes with room service provided—eggs, ham, coffee, and tropical fruit cocktail with chunks of pineapple, banana, mango, lime juice, and fresh mint—on a private balcony, complete with a view of the morning sun in all its warm hues rising over the east-facing mountains, sensing checkout time approaching too soon. The lush potted plants offered a secluded haven from prying eyes.

"I love you," Maria murmured. "Nothing can ever change that." Falling in love in Baguio, he remembered nostalgically, had been easy, the perfect escape from the disturbing thoughts of war sweeping the world—Nazi aggression across Europe and Japan's imperialist conquests in Asia. In the mountains of Luzon, all that amounted to mostly were news bulletins on a shortwave radio, newspaper headlines, or cinema newsreels.

Now lying on his back, Maria sleeping by his side, in one of the most remote areas of Luzon, James looked up at the fan leaf cover of the lean-to and took stock of their ominous reality, war all too close for comfort. Water droplets from the night drizzle seeped between the fan leaves. In the morning, they would eat cold rice for breakfast, not tropical fruit cocktail. The Japanese aerial bombings had changed everything in an instant, upending their complacent lives like a nightmare from which there was no awakening. Their new reality would amount to survival, hiding in the forests of northeast Abra on the slopes of Mount Bawao.

The day after the scouting party finally reached the foot of the mountain, they began the ascent to the level clearing they had spotted high up the slopes. To reach the camp site, the guerrillas had to traverse a main trail along switchbacks that reached up the box canyon between the extending ridges. Up close, they noted the natural defensive features of the mountain. Observing the mountain sprawl, Lt. Ruiz pointed out, "We can spy any approaching enemy well in advance."

Scanning the ridges, James envisioned the defensive advantages of terrain provided by the steep slopes of the canyon. "A properly armed machine gun nest guarding the last stretch of the trail will make a bloody mess of any enemy choosing that route," Ruiz observed with foreboding certainty. "But since we don't have the damn guns, we have to make sure our camp is well hidden."

They all felt dread of a world suddenly turned dangerous. General MacArthur's promise, "I shall return" was the flame of hope intended to keep them going, but all wanted his return before they had to put the defenses of their mountain citadel to the test. No one doubted the Japanese would eventually find them. "All it will take is the capture of one supply cargodore or guerrilla for the enemy to learn of our secret camp on Mount Bawao," Maria said.

James watched Maria staring at the Bawao mountain scape, seeing her apprehension. "Today we are safe," she said. "Tomorrow? I don't want to think that far ahead."

He embraced her, "Tomorrow I will be right here with you," James said, with his arm around her shoulder. "Nothing can ever change that."

CHAPTER 18

Reprisals

FOLLOWING THE FALL OF BATAAN, Cushing continued his operations along the west coast, confounding Japanese pursuit, and in the process blowing up ninety percent of the bridges in the northern provinces of Luzon. In April 1942, having stirred up the hornet's nest and with the Japanese troops scouring the coast for him, Cushing retreated to Abra, the birthplace of his movement. For two months, the blockade of the Tangadan Tunnel had provided Abra with a much-needed respite and security from enemy presence east of the tunnel. Reportedly, the unsuspecting Japanese laborers had sprung the grenade booby traps, he hoped with deadly, intimidating effect.

Finally, the Japanese resorted to the one access the guerrillas could not block, the expansive Abra River. A Japanese division of 7,000 soldiers simply floated up the wide river in a flotilla of troop rafts, past the blocked coastal road, into the province interior intent on retribution. Cushing now realized that the Japanese final victory on the Bataan peninsula had freed up their troops for search and destroy missions against the guerrillas. With angry vengeance, the disembarked troops fanned out into the defenseless countryside.

Wherever the Japanese troops went, they conducted themselves abominably, coercing the terrorized population into submission, seizing food, burning homes, torturing, their firing squads and sword wielding soldiers staging public executions. At the approach of patrols, the alarmed villagers did not wait to take stock of their disposition. They grabbed what they could carry and fled to the hills and forests to survive somehow, sleeping under crude, quick-to-erect lean-tos and slowly wasting from malnutrition on a scavenger diet.

What seemed like madness to the people, the horrors of Japanese custody, had a diabolical purpose to the Japanese. If the guerrillas were the fish and the people the sea, as Mao Zedong had written in his 1937 pamphlet, the Japanese reasoned simply poison the waters. Each scrap of information they got through torture and fear added to their growing jigsaw puzzle of the resistance. Everyone knew someone who was a guerrilla or a sympathizer. None could sustain prolonged torture—days of beatings with whips and bludgeons; being hung from a crossbeam, arms spread behind them in a torture euphemistically referred to as the butterfly swing; or suspended upside down, their head over hot coals. And there was the fearsome water cure, in which interrogators would pump the victim's stomach full of water and stomp on it rupturing organs—all too familiar to Cushing from the execution of his caretaker Felix Albio.

The Japanese had arrested his caretaker Albio and hauled him to the garrison in Lagangilang. Albio had allowed his maintenance visits to the mine to take on a too predictable routine, attracting unwanted attention. No one ever knew for certain who informed; all knew that someone had breathed a word to the Japanese.

In the village plaza, on Colonel Watanabe's order, the Japanese subjected the elderly Albio to interrogation by water cure. His pitiful bleats of ignorance only enraged his inquisitors. When they stomped on his bloated stomach, water flushed from his body cavities When his resistance to interrogation crumbled, the Japanese extracted from him the names of Cesar and Jocelyn Villa of Bangued and their role in the sheltering of two women, Cushing's mistress Dely Valanciato and the Filipina wife of an American guerrilla Maria Novak.

Once Colonel Watanabe decided that there was no further useful information to gain from the old man, he could still use him as a ghoulish object lesson to compel the villagers into horror-stricken submission. He ordered the citizens to watch Albio's execution, cordoned as a group at gun point on the plaza by soldiers, under penalty of punishment by death to any attempting to leave. A soldier with a fixed bayonet on his rifle poised above the maimed Albio, readying to deliver the fatal thrust. "Cut open his stomach," Colonel Watanabe ordered, "This man has no honor, do the honors for him." He gave an order to the soldier, "Junonjigiri [cross-shaped cut]!"

For an instant, the soldier looked stunned by the order, then in response to Watanabe's glare, plunged the bayonet into his abdomen below the waist on the left side and drew it slowly across to the right side; then turning the bayonet in the wound, gave an upward cut. Throughout the village, Albio's shriek pierced the souls of the people, with Watanabe noting those who dared to lament. "Let him die here," Watanabe sneered. "Tomorrow, I expect to see the body where it lies." The soldiers ordered the residents to disperse. The moans of the mortally wounded man subsided in muted rasps and finally silence.

As dawn broke in Bangued, a Japanese truck pulled up outside the Villas' residence in the Casmata Hill neighborhood. Japanese soldiers removed the gate from its hinges in seconds and banged loudly on the door. "Stand back," Cesar ordered Jocelyn. As soon as he twisted the handle, the door burst open and a squad of short, muscular men rushed through, surrounding the Villas. A lieutenant strode up to Cesar. Performing the dictated bow from the waist failed to spare him a hard knuckle blow to the face. He announced, "You unde' arrest fo' shelte' fugitives of impe'ial Japanese justice." A squat sergeant grabbed Cesar, roughly binding his arms behind his back. He barked an order, and another soldier grabbed the cringing Jocelyn with force intended to hurt. Quickly, the soldiers thrust the Villas with prodding bayonet pricks into the back of a truck. Their neighbors watched sorrowfully from windows. Outside, a few bolder residents made out as if they were doing chores. The lieutenant yelled to one slow to avert his eyes, "Not'ing fo' you see hea'. Mind yo' business o' we take you." Grief-stricken and fearful, they retreated into their houses, knowing they would never see the Villas again, their neighbors for many years.

The truck with the Villas in custody drove through the streets to Japanese headquarters. Cesar and Jocelyn, shoved into the truck bed, sat on to a wooden bench with their hands tied behind their backs. When pushed onto the bench seat, Cesar felt a metal support bar for the truck bed panel against his back. On the drive, he assumed an expressionless face, while monitoring the soldiers' reactions out of the corners of his eyes. They barely acknowledged him with their focus on Jocelyn, staring at her with evil intent. She flinched as one reached over, gripping her hair. They reacted in harsh cackles and smirks as she failed to pull away.

Cesar began rubbing the bindings tying his wrist against the bar. He curled back the fingers of one hand until he could feel with his fingertips the bindings beginning to fray. By the time they reached the Japanese garrison, Cesar was certain he had almost worked through the bindings. He hoped that with a hard tug he could pull his arms free or break the worn cord, but for the moment he just prayed silently that the guards did not examine the bindings.

With no explanation, the soldiers jostled the Villas into a room with all the trappings of an archetypal torture chamber, a table with sharp implements that looked like surgical scalpels and shears, bamboo canes and a couple of straight-back chairs, and manacles attached by chains to the wall. The guards pushed Cesar onto a chair. One guard placed a razor-sharp bayonet against his throat beneath his chin, forcing him to lift up his head and watch as the other two guards wrestled a crying Jocelyn against the wall, forcing her wrist into the shackles. "Why you c'y now? Fo' you Ame'ican friends? We not hu't you—Yet," the interrogating lieutenant said, sneering, then spat in her stricken face.

When the lieutenant gave an order, the guards stripped off her clothes, ripping them roughly from her trembling body, the shreds discarded at her feet. His eyes crawled up and down her, as if appraising her vulnerability. "You look at table, wha' you see." He tapped his fingers on an electric hand generator of the type used to power field radios. "You tell me where Majo' Cushing."

"I don't know!" Jocelyn wept.

"Maybe you remembe'," the lieutenant said, picking up the leads of the electric hand generator on the table, with one lead attached to a metal dowel and the other ending in a copper clip. He held the dowel and clip in front of Cesar, leering before he stepped toward Jocelyn trailing the wires with the contacts. "You know where this go," he said, holding the dowel in front of her face. His eyes studying her were cold, deliberate. She writhed in her restraints as he attached the clip to her nipple.

"Please, no, no!" Jocelyn cried shrilly and sobbing, her eyes flicking up and down in terror and tears. The guard next to Cesar cackled evilly, distracted watching Jocelyn's shackle-bound body struggling in futile contortions, screaming in fear and desperation, and relaxed the bayonet at Cesar's throat.

Hunching his strong shoulders, Cesar pulled with all his might and resolve at the bonds. As if God had answered his prayers; his hands came loose. At that instant, perceiving time in slow motion, he grabbed the guard's wrist, pulling him off balance with more strength than he knew he possessed. Freeing the bayonet from the guard's grip, he shoved him away, gaining the split-second he needed. He lunged across the room at Jocelyn, driving the blade into the throat of his wife of thirty years, twisting it before the Japanese soldiers could disarm and restrain him. With blood flowing from her neck and down her body, she jerked in a series of waning spasms, then slumped like a dead weight in the shackles.

With the two guards holding Cesar by the arms, the lieutenant beat him repeatedly in the face with the but a pistol, bloodying his mouth. "You reg'et that." He gave a terse order, and one soldier rushed out of the room, returning with a Japanese colonel with a face etched with malice. "I am Colonel Watanabe," he announced. "Perhaps you have heard of me?" He frowned in response to Cesar's dazed wooden stare with a shrug. "No matter. Before long, the people of Abra will all know my name through the fate of those who defy Japanese rule. Your bamboo telegraph will confirm that." He spoke clear English, barely missing an 'r.' "Like in your Christian prayer, thy will be done." With no need to interpret, the pidgin-speaking lieutenant stood aside. "I have only one question for you. Where is Major Walter Cushing?"

"I don't know," Cesar mumbled.

"Yes, I believe you," Watanabe said, staring at him with narrowed eyes, like a snake coiled to strike. "But if you truly know nothing, your example is still useful." Watanabe leaned close to him with a look of grim finality, with eyes devoid of mercy. "As a lesson to other misguided ones who dare to provide aid and comfort to the bandit guerrillas. Because you killed your wife to steal her from justice, you will receive punishment twofold. We will see how desperate you are to die, but not until you have received righteous justice."

"Japanese injustice," Cesar croaked hoarsely.

Watanabe smiled with evil portent and said in English, "Lieutenant Nagumo, erect the butterfly swing in front of the market, with the cross beams wide enough to give this pig room to swing."

The news of Albio and the Villas deaths reached Cushing from a messenger who spoke with a downcast gaze at the ground while relating their horrific fate. He believed the Japanese had executed Jocelyn in isolation. As with Albio, Watanabe had Cesar executed in another of his gruesome public spectacles. Cesar's executioners stripped him naked and pulled his arms behind his back, tying the ropes to his wrists, and hoisted him, arms spread, to swing from the crossbeam, screaming as his arms dislocated from his shoulder sockets. The punishment alternated between the slashes of whips and blows of clubs as they flogged his back raw, rendering his face unrecognizable. Sadistically, his tormentors tied a cord around his genitals, swinging him with vicious jerks back a fourth, laughing maniacally.

Helpless, the villagers suffered pangs of pity, revulsion, and terror, realizing all their lives were in the grip of a sadist's whims. As night fell, the sound of the whip carried in the dark, his screams ceasing as his vocal cords gave out. By the next morning, he hung dead in the sling with flies swarming over his wounds. Whether he had died from a heart attack, shock, or internal bleeding, a combination of these things, no one knew for sure. The bamboo telegraph would conclude, "The Hapon must be mad. Who else but a madman would think of doing these things?" Bangued had lost a valued citizen and pillar of the community, hideously.

Colonel Watanabe walked up to the hanging body, wrinkled his nose in petulant disgust. "After only one day? Despicable weakling! He shouted." In one last act of barbarity, Colonel Watanabe ordered his head decapitated and stuck on a pole in front of the market. He threatened that anyone tampering with the grizzly display would receive punishment in kind, and none did.

On hearing the names of Watanabe's victims, anguish gripped Cushing's heart like a cold vice. With the deaths of Albio and the Villas, a terrible loss all too personal had come home to roost. He hung his head and murmured, "An abomination!" His face twisted grotesquely, "This motherfucker prides himself on gore." Feeling helpless and overwhelmed, he concluded if he could not defend the people; the only succor that he could give them would be to remove himself as far away as possible, to the remote region of Northeast Abra.

With his plans for a Japanese-free Abra thwarted, friends murdered horrifically, Cushing packed up, feeling lower than a dog with its tail between its legs, and retreated with his company of men on a course toward the Abra—Kalinga border country. There he would regroup, assess his resources and options, and plan his revenge, with Colonel Watanabe in the crosshairs of his wrath. With the name Watanabe now imprinted in all minds as the personification of Japanese evil, his only certainty was that his punitive campaign had not run its course. For now, Cushing kept this thought to himself, not wishing to further provoke his men to unfocused rage.

Despondent, Cushing and his men moved along a path following the Langas River east to avoid contact with Japanese troops on the main road. His path would pass through the small village of Bonglo, a short distance northeast of his Rainbow Mine. He had dealings with the community, hiring men as labor and buying basic food supplies, rice and vegetables from the village, *injecting a little prosperity into the community*, he liked to think. Because the terrain and brush made Bonglo too difficult to bypass, he would pass through it, an agreeable prospect, out of concern for the wellbeing of the familiar community in troubled times.

As the guerrilla company approached the village near the riverbank, the acrid smell of lingering smoke drifted alarmingly in the air, triggering their collective gut instinct. On heightened alert, his men moved forward, covering their noses, and flicking their heads from side to side like horses sensing danger. The pungent charcoal smell of burnt structures blended with a musky scent like pork grease and putrid, rotten egg in their nostrils. A faint, metallic taste like copper, the odor of boiled blood, settled in their mouths. Wide-eyed looks of dread from his guerrillas reinforced Cushing's apprehension.

Careful not to bunch up, the column approached the outskirts of the village, rifles at the ready. Around the bend, the sight of the torched village remains confirmed their grim foreboding; thatched huts on either side of the path burnt to the ground. Here and there, skeletal beams of blackened wood still stood.

Suddenly, the lead soldier shrieked, alerting Cushing and his men to his grisly discovery. Under the remains of collapsed huts, charred faces defied recognition. Amidst the fiery destruction, the dead revealed burnt evidence of rope binding. None were intended to escape the fiery fate. The evidence applied to victims of all ages, who perished under the raised homes that had burned like pyres above them. The immolated body of a mother protectively covering the remains of her dead baby revealed her last futile efforts before both succumbed to the fire. None witnessing the aftermath could have prepared themselves for the ghastly sight. The guerrillas gazed in horror, gasped, retched, others made the sign of the cross, "Susmariosep [Jesus, Mary, and Joseph]!"

"Those motherfuckers!" Cushing bellowed, looking upon the corpses of people so recently roasted alive before their burning homes collapsed in flames on top of them. He stomped the ground with futile rage, receiving helpless looks from his men. Recovering from their initial shock, the men likewise gave rising vent with threats, oaths and curses howled heavenward, "Murdering Savages! Eye for an Eye! Devils! Send them all, every last Hapon, to Hell!" Men shook with fury, faces contorted, unable to let their anger run its course.

Then out of a smoking rubble pile, a body rose like an apparition on hands and knees and crawled toward the sound of the voices. The fire had burnt his clothes away, leaving his face and large patches of his body charred black and skin sloughed off from pink flesh, hanging loose from his body. When the man directed his clouded white eyes toward him by the sound of his voice; Cushing realized he was blind. Spent from the effort, he dropped prone on the ground, body jerking. "Goddamn, get me the morphine and first-aid kit," Cushing yelled, kneeling over the man. "Watanabe," the man gasped in a hoarse whisper, the name, now tantamount to savagery and sadism, of the monster leaving a trail of atrocities behind him as he moved east through Abra.

"Please! Don't talk! I know why this happened," Cushing implored him. Because of the proximity of the barrio to his mine and its association with him, the bloody colonel must have concluded the residents had colluded with him.

An orderly scampered over with the first aid kit. Cushing drew a full syringe of morphine from the unit's precious few vials. "Sair, is that not too much?" the orderly enquired.

"No! This is the best we can do for him." He inserted the needle into his neck, injecting the morphine through his carotid artery straight to his brain. After he had administered the injection, the man's breathing slowed, his last gasps, then ceased altogether. Cushing closed the man's eyes with his fingers and rose unsteadily to his feet. Tilting his head back, he howled heavenward, "Why? They were just trying to make a living. I promise, as God is my witness, I will send that son of a bitch Watanabe to eternal Hell." For the first time since the start of the war, Cushing wanted to believe in something greater than man; but revenge was a realm of man. He gazed at his men through raw eyes. He wanted to cry but did not dare coax the tears. "We can't bury them. We have to keep moving." His voice sounded to himself like an echo from a nightmare. One of his men began rasped out a prayer, "Our Father, who art in heaven, hallowed be Thy name. Thy kingdom come…"

"Amen," the men answered in hushed tones at the end of the prayer, with heads bowed and hands to their breasts. *No one who survives this war will come out of it with their soul unscathed and sanity intact*, Cushing concluded prophetically. Poor decisions had contributed to too many deaths. At that moment, he feared a descent into madness even more than death. The company proceeded east through the Abra back trails like a solemn, funeral cortege, with rage and horror roiling in all minds. Killing Watanabe began to take on a fixation in his mind with the moral atonement of penance. His one comfort amidst the horror was that Dely and Maria had escaped to northeast Abra. But the thought of telling the two young women the fate of the Villas mortified him, fearing the knowledge of their cruel deaths would crush them.

CHAPTER 19

Chief Puyao's Stand

BEFORE THE DESPONDENT CUSHING had reached Mount Bawao, news of his arrival in northeast Abra preceded him. A runner reached him with news that eight hundred Japanese troops were deployed to the east of the Abra-Kalinga border. In the aftermath of the Bonglo massacre, his report stated that Colonel Watanabe was on the move. Cushing had sworn an oath, which now felt sacred, to eliminate Watanabe to end his wanton scourge of violence, a justification that superseded his personal desire for vengeance. However, he knew killing Watanabe would not put an end to the Japanese scorched earth campaigns, with *no shortage of sadists in the Jap army to replace him.* But he believed that if he could stop one maniac from doing any more harm in this world, it was his destiny. With the rogue colonel on the loose in eastern Abra, Mt. Bawao would have to wait.

As Cushing and his guerrillas moved east through Abra, they skirted the main body of Watanabe's regiment bivouacked at the foot of the Abra highlands. Cushing deployed Tinguian scouts east to the Abra–Kalinga border country. The scouts had orders to monitor and report on enemy movements but not to engage, barring unavoidable skirmishes.

On studying the marked map recovered from a dead Japanese officer, he grasped *Hell just broke loose*—the enemy's final destination Lubuagan, Kalinga, and their objective, the capture and elimination of Colonel Horan's headquarters at the Batong Buhay copper mine.

Despite their orders, his scouts had spotted an exception to the no-engagement order. "He too busy taking shit, forget his men move on. How we not take advantage?" the scout explained apologetically.

Cushing just waved his hands with a resigned shrug. "Thank God for dysentery." He realized Watanabe's troops would pass through the Kalinga border town Balbalasang, the most eastern enclave of the proud, independent, pro-American Tinguian people.

With Horan's command the apparent Japanese target, Cushing deduced the obvious. Watanabe's overextended regiment, beyond quick resupply by the enemy main body in central Abra, would resort to banditry, plundering for food and supplies.

"Watanabe is going out on a limb," he told his officers and non-comms. "Too far from the main Jap forces to reinforce in a pinch. For us, it's an opportunity too hot to pass up."

Quivering in excitement, the scout concluded, "Hapon no see it coming."

"We can pick them off in small groups, bombings, the usual guerrilla stuff at the time of our choosing, whittle 'em down, the sooner the better." He considered Bob Arnold's tactical viewpoint that guerrillas can't win standing battles. He pondered a counterargument: "But if we can hit, run, and regroup for another strike, they cannot defeat us." Cushing roared, "I want Watanabe, the sooner the better." Cushing glared at his men, seeing no waver in their eyes. Then in a more subdued voice, "My pressing reason for wanting to stop Watanabe from reaching Lubuagan, Colonel Horan has the only radio transmitter operational in this sector. We goddamn can't afford to lose it."

"The radio might be the only thing of value in Horan's whole damn command," Sergeant Goldblum sneered. Confidence among USAFFE guerrillas in the leadership of the former career bureaucrat in a peacetime army had declined to the point of merciless grumbling with his perceived inaction. Increasingly clear, he appeared out of his depth as a guerrilla leader. By his tepid actions, partially decommissioning roads and copper mines, Cushing doubted Horan even wanted the mantle of guerrilla leadership, although Cushing disliked open denigration of superior officers among the men.

Avoiding encounters with Japanese traffic on the Abra-Kalinga Road, Cushing and his company moved from Abra province on a three-day march into Kalinga province. A guide, the PA soldier Corporal Odah Mawangga, a native of the northeast Tinguian hill tribes and formerly with Captain Arnold, led the company through the mountains. The company followed his lead up from the trailhead at 2,800 feet, through grass-covered hills of Abra with patchworks of bamboo groves, into pine forested mountains cresting at 5,500 feet before dropping from the heights into the hot plateaus and isolated jungle valleys of the Saltan River.

As the guerrilla company moved into the opening of a glade, the tracker Louis Heuser whispered to the nodding Corporal Mawangga, "Odah! Hobnailed boots!" Noting the trampled boot prints and broken twigs in the soil, he eyed the boot outlines in the condensation of trampled grass, "They're fresh as dew." Characteristic of the self-reliant people of the rustic North Virginia back country, the sharp-eyed Heuser had from the beginning shown superior woodsman skills, steeped in Appalachian tradition. "Patrol size at best sir. I'd estimate eighteen Japs. I reckon we can take them."

Cushing regarded Heuser as an exceptional tracker and daring warrior, but now responded curtly, with his nickname, "Probably damn it, Apple, but for now I would prefer they don't know we're on their tail."

Heuser gave him a crooked grin. "As you wish, sir. Whenever you give the word. The bastards are way out in front of Watanabe's troops on the other side of the Saltan River, all by their lonesome. Lots of damn nasty rapids between here and Balbalasang. Nowhere to cross till you get there."

"Couldn't be happier," Cushing hissed with a thumbs up. Heuser continued his reconnaissance of the trail ahead, which led to a small clearing with a few rustic houses. Blue tinted smoke from cooking fires curled lazily up from vents in the roofs of the rough-hewn pine huts. Dogs barked excitedly at the approach of the guerrillas across the open ground. An old man with a thin face and deep eyes stepped up, as if he was the leader, while the other adults and timid children stayed behind.

A tough place to eke out a living, Cushing concluded. He directed Odah, "Ask him if he knows Chief Payao of Balbalasang." Mawangga translated Cushing's question into the local dialect. "Sair, he say everyone know Puyao."

Cushing explained to his squad leaders, "Chief Puyao is the local strongman among the eastern Tinguians before Kalinga territory. I met him before the war while gold prospecting in the area. Pro-American and forward-thinking for these parts. He had an elementary school built and invited the Episcopal Church to establish a mission."

Cushing instructed Corporal Mawangga, "Odah, ask him about the Hapon. How many? When?"

At the mention of Hapon, the old man began to gibber, pointing east. Mawangga questioned him, turning his palms outward and slowly downward to induce him to calm down. "He say eighteen Hapon went through here just before you arrive." Cushing looked awestruck at Heuser, his count of troop strength by footprints confirmed.

Mawangga continued the questioning. "He say men gathering wood saw them come. In time! The people ran into forest with animals and hide." Mawangga cupped his ear, listening as the man spoke excitedly, pausing before translating. "They hear the Hapon steal and sometimes use women, even if old or child, but praise God the devils no stop."

Heuser scurried back in a crouch along the trail that ran east of the village. "We're gaining on them," he announced, gauging the pace of the patrol by length of the stride clear in their tracks. "Stompin' their hobnails all over the place."

"Cushing produced two silver pesos and a can of sardines for the old man. "Thank you, good fellow."

Unprompted, the old man spoke excitedly. "Sir, Puyao post guards in valley outside village. All with rifles."

Cushing directed his two stalkers to the head of the patrol, with Heuser in the lead setting the pace and Mawangga behind him. The company set off on a stealthy pursuit. Cushing now knew where he would stage the ambush, on the outskirts of the Balbalasang valley, in a pincer attack between his squad and Puyao's guards. Sure enough, when the Japanese stumbled onto the guards, a fight would ensue, but success rested entirely on stalking the enemy undetected until they could spring the trap. Both Heuser and Mawangga grasped the point— no accidental encounter.

Cushing calmed down, watching the men follow the example of the two stalkers as they moved with stealth along the trail. The attack would have to be quick and decisive. Japanese squads carried hand generator powered radios. They could not allow the enemy squad to raise the alarm to Watanabe's forward troops across the river. Cushing caught up with Heuser, whispering, "Louis, looks like you're going to get your wish. Will catch the sons of bitches in a crossfire between us and Puyao's guards." The men relayed the whispered message down the column line: "Do not fire until Cushing fires, not when Puyao's guards fire."

Cushing recognized the excitement in Heuser's eyes, by the quiver in his limbs, his eagerness for the fight, the same zeal for killing the enemy, he had to admit, as himself. Though he considered it had no bearing on his sanity, killing had become the new normal. He took pride in his successes. Heuser whispered back the Biblical Proverb, "When justice is done, it is a joy to the righteous but terror to evildoers." When he quoted proverbs, Cushing struggled to cancel the smirk he could feel forming on his face. And if Heuser took notice, he never let on. For now, he just said, "I swear, sir, they won't see shinola."

Cushing clapped Louis on the shoulder and motioned with his thumb, "Continue on lead."

Heuser snapped a quick salute. Scooping up damp dirt, which he rubbed on his face as camouflage—a white man's compensation for the lack of natural pigment. In a hunched, silent slither, a posture that seemed natural to him, he moved ahead through the forest as if part of it, down the jumbled trail intersected by a confusing maze of dead-end game trails. He tracked the enemy quarry like any other animal, estimating their pace by the depth of footprint and stride. By their deep footprints, Heuser could see their pace was slow, men heavily weighted with gear. Sporadically, with increasing regularity, faint Japanese voices reached them. With a forward chopping motion with his free hand, Heuser signaled the men in the single-file column to spread out.

Coming to a bend in the trail, Heuser raised his palm, signaling 'stop' to the squad behind him. He lowered himself on all fours and crawled around low brush at a twist in the trail, moving out of sight. Returning in a duck walk squat, he motioned Cushing and Mawangga forward to a clearing with a sweeping view of the trail below. As they crouched low, Heuser pointed out the now visible Japanese squad, still beyond accurate rifle range. The enemy worked their way down the hillside, plodding along indifferent to the heavy crunch of decaying and down vegetation underfoot and the rustle of plant leaves. Unlike ambush-wary guerrillas, who moved at least ten paces apart, the enemy soldiers bunched up, oblivious to their tailing pursuers. "Practically treading on each other's heels," Heuser whispered to Cushing.

Cushing nodded, "Damn sloppy," realizing his men could mow down the lot of them in seconds. He guessed the enemy were too arrogant even to imagine a serious challenge, considering the local natives just primitives, unworthy of such caution.

The Japanese patrol briefly disappeared from sight into the wooded lowland leading into the valley of Balbalasang. When the first villagers sighted the approaching enemy squad, a gong from the village, a stick striking the hollow bamboo, resonated out a warning. Realizing they'd lost the element of surprise, the Japanese soldiers now advanced in a sprint toward the village along the dikes of the adjacent rice fields with rifles and fixed bayonets at the ready. Focused on cutting off any villager's escape, they disregarded their rear where the men of the 121st stealthily closed the gap.

When the village guards opened fire with their captured Arisaka rifles on the approaching Japanese column from the concealment of high cogon grass beyond the tree line, Cushing saw one Japanese soldier fall. The Japanese soldiers fanned out before the trees to avoid becoming caught in a clump.

Listening to the sharp zing reports of dueling Japanese Arisaka rifles firing from opposing directions, Cushing perceived a tactical advantage, based on his men's known aversions. They all knew the pings of lighter caliber Japanese rifles from the deeper booms of American .30-caliber rifles. In nighttime engagements, his men disliked using Japanese rifles, fearing the return of friendly fire in the dark. Like a revelation, he realized the obvious, how confusion of night might work to their favor.

A burst from a Type 6 Japanese light machine gun strafed the grass before   where the guards had fired. Cushing signaled hurry, pumping his fist. His fighters picked up their pace, advancing behind the unsuspecting patrol, closing range. Cushing fired his .45-pistol signaling the attack, shooting the Japanese squad's unsuspecting, sword-waving lieutenant commander in the back.

The startled soldiers turned to meet the unexpected threat from behind, firing wildly. The light machine gun swung around too slowly to meet the new threat; its muzzle fire extinguished by concentrated return fire from the Abra guerrillas. Caught between the Balbalasang guards and Cushing's guerrillas, the enemy squad quickly succumbed to the inescapable crossfire. Before that happened, one Japanese soldier fired a self-propelled grenade from a light .50 caliber mortar, the shell exploding harmlessly behind the advancing 121st before return fire united him with his bushido ancestors. Then the shooting from the Japanese ceased altogether.

Cushing's fighters and Puyao's guards appeared out of the cover of the brush into the open, greeting each other with jubilant cheers. "We're not through, damn it," Cushing roared. "Check the bodies. Make sure they're all dead." The guerrillas moved among the bodies on heightened alert, knowing full well the possum ruse of a wounded Japanese soldier with a hidden grenade, intent on making a final honorable sacrifice. "Careful! Don't be fooled! They're down but still dangerous," Cushing called. Razor sharp bolos flashed in every hand. The fighters tread cautiously among the dead and dying Japanese, dispatching with heavy butcher chops to the throat any showing signs of life–quivering, twitching, or labored breathing. *A bloody job well done*, Cushing thought grimly. With the fighting over, they scavenged through the firearms, ammunition, and belongings of the fallen foe, a necessity for guerrillas chronically short of armaments and equipment.

"Does anyone want shoes?" a guerrilla fighter called out.

"No! Not with goddamn hobnails. Too easy to track" another fighter called back. The village guards came out from the carnage with their own prized victory trophies, severed ears. Cushing could hardly blame them. With more Japanese soldiers expected, all recognized the intimidation value such war trophies had on enemy morale. "Let them come in fear," a village guard sneered with grim resolve.

A ruddy-faced man, reddish-brown, of late middle age in work khakis separated from the guards, burly chested and with a prominent aquiline nose like an American Indian. By the deference the guards showed him and recollection, Cushing recognized the approaching Tinguian leader Chief Puyao. His contagious wide grin spread across his chiseled, weathered face like a boy getting his first bike. "Greetings, my friend!" he said, shaking Cushing's hand vigorously. "You arrive in good time."

"I try to be prompt, don't like to keep my host waiting," Cushing said with an impish grin.

"Aha, Walter!" Puyao gave a hearty laugh, hugging his shoulders and slapping him on the back. "Now you return to us a leader of fighting men. All of you, rest and refresh yourselves." His eyes narrowed, appraising the butchered Japanese patrol, in the skirmish's aftermath of the skirmish. "With the Hapon, one cannot be too careful. We know how to make bodies disappear."

Heuser approached, "Sir, we found their radio. They never had a chance to use it."

"The Japs will soon know they have a missing patrol," Cushing said, summing up the dilemma. "Maybe no radio, no bodies, but no evidence is the most suspicious of all. Damn it either way."

Chief Puyao shrugged resigned. "Nothing else we can do now but defend ourselves." He led the Abra guerrillas into the village, where they continued down a main street bordered by thatched roofs and rough-hewn pine houses, strutting like gamecocks, to the Chief's home on the outskirts of town. It was a larger version of the homes lining the main street, supported solidly off the ground by sturdy, thick timbers. The house had a deck porch along one side, which faced an open, well-tended yard, where there were long serving tables set. Women in wrap skirts and sleeveless blouses were already at work preparing a feast of food for the triumphant men, with cups and pitchers of strong basi set out. The women beamed at their men with smiles and crinkle-eyed pride.

A woman spoke, bringing a wide smile to Chief Puyao's broad face. "She know we have a victory party when she hear the first shot. Her faith is strong." With drinks in hand, cups of basi, the smell of chicken stew and roast pig in the air, the guerrillas hungrily consumed the feast, and the food kept coming. "Flenty, flenty, fo' all," the serving women said. The basi worked its effect, inciting spontaneous merriment. As they ate and imbibed, the soldiers boisterously relived the fight, teased the bunglers for slip ups, dropped ammo, one who didn't realize the safety was on frantically squeezing the trigger, and in solidarity toasted each other to victories ahead.

Upon joining chief Puyao for cheroots on the porch of his home, Cushing received a welcome surprise. The Anglican priest Father Alfred Griffiths, or "our Padji [priest]" as the Tinguians referred to him, waited with Puyao. "Al! Well, bless my eyes!" Cushing exclaimed, enthusiastically shaking hands with the American with wavy brown hair, angular face, and expressive green eyes. "Dang good to see you again." Cushing bore fond memories of the Anglican priest's hospitality from his prospecting trip through the area before the war, at the same time he had met Puyao. Reverend Griffiths now held a brevet rank of lieutenant in the 121st, serving as its military chaplain. When inducted into the 121st, he had said with a wry smile, "Not sure my Bishop will approve my involvement in guerrilla activities." He said, "Now we have a problem." He explained the imminent threat to Colonel Horan's command by the Japanese force, believed to be on course to Lubuagan.

"There are already 800 Nip troops on the western edge of the Kalinga-Abra border, under the command of a murdering son of a bitch, Colonel Watanabe," Cushing explained. "Based on a captured map, the evidence indicates they hope to catch Colonel Horan at the copper mine and eliminate his HQ. Unfortunately, that will take them through Balbalasang." The haunting memories of Bonglo stirred in his mind.

Father Griffiths took in the news with resigned acceptance. He said with determination, "We need to warn Colonel Horan about what's coming his way. I know the trails. I believe I can speak frankly to him." He shook his head and rose on the balls of his feet. "Time's a-wasting. I better get going."

The two men shook hands emotionally in parting. "Look forward to a good chat when you get back. Be careful and stay alert," Cushing cautioned the resourceful Padji.

"I'll be fine," Griffiths said, taking his leave with a salute.

"There is no choice. We must fight," Chief Puyao said. "But also, our women and children must evacuate with our livestock to Maatop, a safe camp in the mountains. I knew the Hapon would come after us. It is only a matter of time before the devils finger us for the rifles and burn the village, slaughter our animals and surely kill us, leaving any who escape without food. So, we prepared Maatop. We make sure the trailhead is well hidden. The people will be as safe there as anywhere, as long as the food lasts."

"What are your arms?"

"As you see, captured Japanese rifles from a Japanese arms depot near Tubuk. It was easy. The Hapon never thought we would do it. And now thanks to the generosity of the recently departed Jap patrol, we have a light machine gun, a mortar and a few shells."

"An idea came to me like a vision," Cushing said, "about the Jap rifles you stole." Feeling as if putting his foot in it, he corrected himself with a snicker. "I mean liberated. American rifles have a deeper report. In the darkness of a night skirmish, with both sides firing the same rifles, it is hard to tell friend from foe. The Japs might not know who they're shooting at."

Chief Puyao laughed, eyes widened. "Ah I see, the confusion of battle. It could work for us. Maybe Japs shoot each other. Hot damn! As you Americans say." He clapped Cushing enthusiastically on the shoulder.

Before the banquet ended, a runner arrived with alarming news. The Japanese column had reached the Kalinga border, doubtless on a rendezvous course with Balbalasang. "I didn't expect them so soon. What men can you spare?" Cushing asked.

"Other than the guards, most of our men are gone, foraging for supplies.

In this part of Luzon, foraging could mean anything from harvesting the bounty of the forest to banditry of other communities. *The right skills for stealing a cache of rifles from the Japs*, Cushing thought. He frowned now noting other than the guards the stark absence of grown men, though Chief Puyao's eyes radiated hopeful confidence.

"But we make do!" the chief exclaimed.

With the brief celebration abruptly over, the women and children shifted to preparations for evacuation to Maatop, gathering necessities and rounding up livestock for the trudge up the mountain to the evacuation camp.

Though relieved by their preparedness, after the Bonglo massacre, Cushing nonetheless looked taken aback when Puyao's guards rounded up a couple dozen early adolescent boys of ages twelve to fifteen, besides the guards. He presented them as a group for Cushing's inspection. They stood straight, holding their heads erect, trying to look like men. "They are just boys," Cushing objected.

"By the traditions of our people, they are fighting men," Chief Puyao insisted. "I assure you they will fight well." Each boy had been issued a captured Japanese rifle, on average, nearly as long as they were tall, ten rounds of ammunition and minimal firing instructions. Chief Puyao directed the boys' attention to the sights on the rifle and, on a chalkboard retrieved from the school, drew a picture showing the alignment of the rear aperture site and front site on a target. Puyao called one boy forward and asked if he understood. "Yes," said the boy.

"Then show me." He pointed to a thick tree stump fifty feet away. "Shoot it." The boy shouldered the rifle, squinted, and fired. The bullet struck the ground in a puff two feet to the right beyond the stump. Grabbing the startled boy by the earlobe, Puyao led him back to the chalkboard. Admonishing him, he directed his attention to the chalk picture showing the alignment of the sights on a target, while the other boys looked on. Holding the rifle, he asked, "Show me which is which." The boy pointed out the pictured sights on the rifle. He gave the rifle back to the boy. "Pull the rifle tight against your shoulder, let your breath out slowly, now shoot the target." The boy drew his breath, took a bead on the fence post, and squeezed the trigger. This time the bullet struck true with a loud smack into the stump. The boy whooped in delight. With one boy after another he repeated the drill, giving each boy two shots. "That is all we can spare," Chief Puyao said.

"My guess is the Japs plan to bivouac here for the night," Cushing said. "Unless we stop them, there won't be anything left of Balbalasang but ashes."

"Then we must go now. We can catch them at the pass we call Lamonan," Puyao said. All business, Chief Puyao led the boys, his guards, and men of the Abra battalion on a fast march on a well-traveled trail to a hilly location. Derelict abandoned shacks, now nothing but shells, were all the evidence of a failed effort to create a barangay at the remote, barren place. The guerrillas took positions overlooking a narrow mountain pass. Flattening themselves on the ground, they waited in the tall grass back from the road.

Cushing placed dynamite along the road, wired to his detonator. Chief Puyao and the newly promoted Sergeant Heuser scurried about, shooing the pubescent soldiers off the road to hiding places a safe distance from the dynamite but close enough to the path to take advantage of point-blank range. Cushing would wait until the oncoming enemy column had come fully abreast of the guerrillas' position before detonating the charge, beginning the attack.

Waiting in the dark around midnight, the guerrillas discerned by the crunch of brush and the silence of crickets, the approach of the Japanese. Then, revealing silhouettes materialized through the vapor of fog. "They're coming four abreast," Goldblum hissed, gripping his BAR. On they came in a tightly bunched column of marching men, bareheaded, most having placed their helmets over their rifle barrels to protect their weapons from rain. Complacent in their strength in numbers and perceived superiority, the Japanese had made all the fatal mistakes, the most egregious in Cushing's judgment, not sending scouts ahead. *Overconfident bastards! Haven't learned a damn thing since Candon and Lagben.*

When the lead soldiers closed to within ten yards of him, Cushing detonated the charges, producing a sudden fireball and an earsplitting explosion, with a shock wave that rolled over the forward files of the Japanese column, flattening soldiers to the ground.

Sergeant Goldblum sighted his BAR and swept the dispersing Japanese column with thumping automatic fire, joined by a mixed salvo of rifle reports—the zinging of the captured Arisaka rifles with the heavy bangs of the 121st guerrillas' .30-06 ammunition. The guerrillas fired from the vantage of pointblank range, overcoming limited marksman proficiency. As rifle fire shredded the forward formation of the Japanese column, soldiers broke rank, racing for the cover of brush. In the murky dark, the guerrillas could see by the orange muzzle flashes of their rifles, enemy silhouettes falling, felled on the road, fleeing in confusion before collapsing short of the shelter of the tree line.

With the distinct reports of .25-caliber ammunition crackling from multiple directions, an elated Cushing realized his hoped-for advantage, utter Japanese confusion. The enemy soldiers were firing wantonly at muzzle flashes, as the toll of friendly fire casualties of their own comrades mounted. His ruse working, Cushing marveled with vindictive satisfaction at the unfolding mayhem. The baffled Japanese at the rear of the column were firing on their forward guard. He passed the word to withdraw. One boy refused to budge. "Move out, damn it," Heuser ordered.

"But I have two bullets left," the boy protested. Heuser ruffled his hair and then shoved him along after the other retreating youthful fighters. In the darkness, the receding din of rifle reports, whines of bullets, and screams of the Japanese confirmed that their internecine battle continued well after the guerrillas had left the area. Days later from scuttlebutt, an anecdotal casualty count would state about 160 enemy killed and many uncounted wounded. The Japanese withdrew to Abra to tend to their wounded and dispose of their dead. Cushing conceded the time-honored military wisdom— more often than not, mere blundering separates victory from defeat. *Balbalasang would not be another Bonglo,* he concluded, He intended that it stay that way. With a vague plan forming in his mind, he hoped to assassinate Watanabe before he wised up.

When Cushing and his men arrived back in Balbalasang, all but a few of the inhabitants had deserted the village, fleeing to their mountain evacuation camp Maatop. "We hope the rains come soon so the waters rise," Chief Puyao said. "Maybe Japs don't swim any better than they shoot."

The rivers will become like moats around castles, Cushing thought. "The flooding will hopefully buy you another four months," seemed the best consolation he could give resolute Chief Puyao and his people, along with a wish for General MacArthur's punctual return.

Concerned about the burden of his guerrilla force on the local food and resources, Cushing sent his men back to Abra with directions and contacts at the secret basecamp at Mount Bawao, except for Sergeant Heuser and Corporal Mawangga.

Two days later, Reverend Griffiths returned from Labuagan. Cushing explained to him the outcome of the battle, that for now, had halted the Japanese incursion into Kalinga. "How did things go in Lubuagan?" he asked.

"I am sorry to say, Colonel Horan has holed up in the mine and will not budge. It's like he's paralyzed by indecision, unresponsive to any entreaties."

Cushing asked, "What about his radio? Did you see it?"

"No!" he grimaced. "Horan said he gave the radio to a Lieutenant Colonel Everett Warner for safe keeping."

Cushing shook with uncontained fury. "He gave a shortwave transceiver to that drunken rummy! Wouldn't surprise me if he trades it for a case of whiskey."

Lieutenant Griffiths slowly shook his head, somberly, "And Horan has now lost contact with him."

The news left Cushing dismayed, feeling nauseous.

With Griffiths in the lead, they hiked in silence up the remote mountain, into the pine forested secret refuge of Maatop, with a collection of hastily erected wood cabins and bamboo thatch shelters. The Tinguians milled around, sorting out their animals and shelter needs for their families. Griffiths' family were waiting, his wife Nessie, a tall, lean woman of curly dark hair and pale white skin as though resistant to the tanning effect of the tropical sun, with their two-year-old towhead daughter, Katherine. Awed by the little girl's blond hair and unable to resist, the Tinguians would touch her tresses in passing as if reaching for golden rays of sunlight. Though charmed and despite best wishes of all, Cushing suffered the loss of the radio too deeply to stay longer. He told Reverend Griffiths that he would leave at dusk, wishing goodbye and for the prospects of a longer, more pleasant visit next time.

CHAPTER 20

Hunting Colonel Watanabe

FTER SHELTERING OVERNIGHT AT MAATOP, Cushing summoned Cpl. Heuser and Cpl. Mawangga. "Louis, Odah, I held you two back for a special mission for which you two are well suited. I'm going hunting and want the two of you with me."

Mawangga nodded and replied with a terse, "Yes sair."

"Sir, I'll do whatever you want," Heuser said. "What game we huntin'?"

"Colonel Hidemi Watanabe."

Heuser's face twisted; Mawangga's eyes widened, and brow narrowed. "Son of a bitch! It might as well be Lucifer himself," Louis erupted. The fiery massacre at Bonglo haunted their memories.

Mawangga's face darkened like a thundercloud. He issued an invective in his native dialect and spat, "A bullet is too good for him."

"I agree, but a bullet's distance may be the closest we get to him. I'm asking both of you to do something dangerous, above the call of duty."

Mawangga acknowledged with a composed nod of his head. Heuser muttered, "The Lord is my shield. The righteous will rejoice when he sees his vengeance."

Cushing nodded thoughtfully; *each finds solace in his own way.* He retrieved a slender canvas pouch from his musette bag and removed a cylindrical metallic tube.

A riflescope!" Heuser exclaimed.

"That's right, a Weaver Model 330, 3x magnification. "You can adjust windage and elevation with these two screws. With this, you have a range of fire accurate up to 600 yards, hopefully far enough away to have a good chance to escape."

"How about 900 yards!" Heuser said with a wry smile. Cushing knew it was one thing to line up the cross hairs on the target. There was no substitute for experience in knowing the drop of the bullet and lead on a moving target varying with distance, and that judgement only came with experience, which Heuser had plenty of. "Louis, you are the best shot of the three of us."

"Well, growin' up, we couldn't live year-round harvesting apples. Somebody had to keep food on the table. I remember a time…"

Cushing cut him off, sensing the start of a garrulous soliloquy. "I want you to make the fatal shot. You're our sniper."

"Yes, sir!" Heuser bobbed his head in agreement. "Colonel Watanabe, I'll serve em up with an apple in his mouth," making a pun of his nickname! "My pleasure."

Cushing looked at Mawangga with gravity. "Ang Kasama ko [my companion], you know the paths and trails. Our mission depends upon it."

"I am at your service," Mawangga said. "But these Japs are not that hard to track. You can smell where they go."

The enemy marked their course with discarded refuse. There was no mistaking a column of men on the move. Wherever the Japanese stopped or encamped, a fecal odor permeated the spot. The stench lingered as if they slept amid their own garbage and excrement. Cushing wrinkled his nose in disgust. "Damn, before the war I thought Japs were known for cleanliness…sticklers for bathing and hygiene."

"At least you know where they've been," Heuser said, fanning his hand. "My ol' hunting dog Lily May coulda sniffed 'em out anywhere, no trouble, in the whole damn Luzon boondocks."

The three men moved west of Lamonan, following the trail the Japanese had taken in retreat to the Abra foothills. Coming over a rise, a smell of carbon resin like burnt pork and the copper smell of burning blood greeted their nostrils, in the air like a bad memory from Bonglo. "They're burning their dead," Cushing said. Coming around the bend, they saw the remains of funeral pyres punctuating the highland meadow ahead. "They must have layered the wood and bodies."

Scores of black wing vultures alighted on the vestiges of the pyres, jabbing their heads into the ashes and incomplete burned wood, gorging on the partially burned bodies. "By the smoke, looks like they used too much green wood for complete cremation," Heuser said. "Left a hell of a meal for the buzzards."

With the cremation site behind them, Cushing's party hiked up to the crest of a hill where they could see wisps of smoke rising above the nearby foothills. After cautiously picking their way in that direction, they climbed to a hilltop overlooking the Japanese encampment on the plain below. Through binoculars, Cushing noted the camp features. "He's surrounded by damn near a full battalion."

A ramshackle abundance of tents and hastily erected structures occupied the grounds. A couple of large rectangular tents appeared on the opposite side of the encampment. He focused his binoculars on the soldiers rushing in and out, emptying basins of liquid into a slit trench, others fetching supplies. He surmised they were medical personnel and the long tents, a makeshift field hospital for the wounded from the Lamonan ambush. *One bit of good news* Cushing noted. *Watanabe's force ain't as mobile now, burdened with wounded men.*

"Most of the land around the camp is hilly with thick brush, super cover for sniping, if I could only catch him near the perimeter," Heuser said.

"We'll watch Watanabe's comings and goings, see if there is any consistency that can help us pull off this bushwhack. My guess, he's too cocky to be evasive."

Peering through the binoculars, Cushing surveyed a log-fortified dugout. A steady traffic of officers and non-coms entered and exited from the structure. "That's got to be Watanabe's command post. It would be hard to get close enough to it to get a proper shot." He observed a Nipa hut inside a barbwire enclosure. "Now that looks rather well constructed for this camp."

Soon, their watch produced clues. An officer exited the log bunker. Cushing noted the bow and scraping deference the soldiers showed him as he strutted toward the hut, a riding crop in his hand. A guard saluted and opened the gate. "That must be Watanabe," Cushing said. With the windows shuttered, Cushing could not spy into the house. About half an hour later Watanabe exited, buttoning his tunic. After he had gone, a Japanese soldier carried a basin and a water jug to the house, entering through the door without knocking.

"He must have a woman in there," Mawangga said. "Though not willingly! Why barbed wire? The guard just enters as he pleases. Hardly the respect one shows an esteemed lady, even a mistress."

"A comfort girl?" Cushing asked.

"A hostage. With a comfort girl, the men would be lining up outside."

"There's thick brush along the road leading into the perimeter right up to that drainage ditch. Gives us cover to move to the ditch. That's close enough to make the shot into the compound," Heuser said.

A Filipino with a loaded stake bed truck arrived at the camp before dusk. From their hideout they watched the Japanese unload the truck of live chickens in crates, and sacks, Cushing assumed rice and corn, and baskets of vegetables and fruit. "I knew it. They are living off the land, my guess exacting tribute from the locals."

They moved along a trail parallel to the road and set up a bivouac on a glade with a view of the road leading into the camp. The next morning as the cool of the early morning subsided, the sunrise turned molten yellow in the sky. The men drank sparingly from their canteens, aware of the fickle availability of water. But the dilemma, as they knew, heavy rain would enliven the land with parasites in less than a day, making for a miserable bivouac.

"That truck could be the way in, if the delivery is regular," Cushing said. "If so, I want to stop the driver and request the use his truck."

Mawangga and Heuser snickered. "The Japs probably got pickets along the road in," Heuser said. "They radio in when the truck is approaching the camp."

"We can't just seize it on its way out. We don't know if and when the Japs expect it back. On its next run in, we got to stop it."

"There is a curve in the road," Mawangga said, pointing. "We can drop a tree in front of the truck when it drives into the curve."

Cushing nodded. "That should work. Doubt the delivery driver will do anything too bold."

Using his bolo, Mawangga cut most of the way through the trunk of a medium size tree beside the road. In the breeze, the tree creaked against the narrow section of solid wood holding it up. "Only a few more chops, it fall," Mawangga said. Cushing smiled and clapped him on the shoulder.

With rations and water good for at most five days, they hoped for a break—that the truck would return soon with another delivery. "We're not prepared for a longer wait," Cushing grumbled. However, mid-afternoon on the second day they spotted the stake bed truck trundling down the road from the west. Cushing took a position across the road from the tree placing him on the driver's side of the truck. Mawangga remained on the other side of the road with his bolo ready to fell the tree. Heuser moved up the road and hid in the rushes with his rifle ready to prevent the driver from trying to reverse out of the trap. As the truck entered the curve, Mawangga delivered the final chops to the trunk, dropping the tree in front of the truck. As expected, the driver slammed on the brakes, bringing the truck to an abrupt halt.

Cushing jumped on the running board and leveled a cocked pistol through the window at the startled driver. "Get out," he ordered, opening the door.

The driver stumbled out from the truck with his hands raised, making no sign of resistance. "Please, no shoot," he whimpered in English.

Give us a hand," Cushing ordered. The four men dragged the tree to the side of the road. "Louis, get this truck off the road." He hoped the tall grass and jungle growth would obscure the sight of the truck from the road. Heuser hopped aggressively into the cab on the passenger seat, covering the driver with his .45 pistol, ordering him to back up onto a path off the road near the glade. Soon after a Japanese scout car drove by as the men hunkered down silently with the truck backed into the foliage, the driver with Heuser's .45 to his head. Cushing exhaled hard, wondering if the scout car had received a radio call from a lookout that the truck had arrived. *Too close for comfort.*

"Sair, I must tell you, I am not with the Hapon," the driver protested. "I hate the bloody Jap devils. I deliver supplies because I have no choice. The Japs tell us to give them our food or they punish us. And now they have something as good as a gun to our head."

"What's that?" Cushing asked.

"They hold the daughter of our Alkalde [municipal mayor] hostage. Colonel Watanabe say they make her comfort girl for his troops unless we do as he say. Her safety depends on how well we follow instructions."

Cushing's face contorted, tormented by the implication of the Japanese euphemism 'comfort girl,' for military sanctioned gang rape and sex slavery. From stories he had learnt about the practice in China, their lives were short and brutal, death preceded by beatings, sexual trauma, and physical neglect. That Watanabe had already raped her seemed a foregone conclusion, explaining his visit to the hut yesterday. Cushing believed a comfort girl's fate was inevitable once Watanabe tired of her but refrained from saying so.

"What's your name?" Cushing asked.

"Arturo," the driver answered.

"Arturo, I want you and your truck to get us inside the Japanese perimeter."

His eyes widened. "May I ask what you do when you get there?"

"Kill the commander Colonel Watanabe like a mad dog. He has done much harm and if not stopped will do a lot more. With a little luck, we can rescue the Alkalde's daughter. But I believe Watanabe has already violated her."

223

"I know her father will want her back, no matter what done to her. She is a victim."

"She is how we get to Watanabe. He'll use her again. Why else go to the trouble of building a trysting hut."

"She's now bait, like a tethered goat staked out by a hunter to bait a cougar," Heuser said. Arturo looked stricken.

Cushing blanched at Heuser's coarse depiction. "Louis, show Arturo your rifle!" Heuser produced the Springfield rifle with the attached scope. "Let Arturo look through it." Heuser handed him the rifle. "Now Arturo, hold it to your shoulder and look through the scope." As instructed, he pulled the rifle into his shoulder though hesitantly, as if unsure how tight to hold it. With the cross hairs in front of his eye, he gasped in amazement at the enlarged image through the scope. "This is how we intend to kill Watanabe," Cushing paused, resting his hand on Heuser's shoulder. Heuser glanced back at him with a grin and a nod. "We now know his habits, where he goes, so obvious. All we have to do is hide nearby and wait."

Arturo handed the rifle back to Heuser. "I believe he will continue to use the Alkalde's daughter. She is beautiful."

"The drainage ditch is plenty close to the hut," Heuser said.

Arturo nodded sagely, now privy to the plot. "Yes, I see why you need my truck, to get near. They are expecting me. Soon they will wonder why I late. We must make haste."

"Drop us off in the scrub brush after the checkpoint, and we'll do the rest," Cushing told Arturo. "I have to trust you. We will need your truck to escape, with or without you."

Mawangga's hard, expressionless eyes did not waver from Arturo's face, deliberately letting him feel his stern gaze.

"I am with you," Arturo said. "After I drop off my load, I will park in the track off the road before the sentry. I can cover the front of the truck with brush, so it not seen. I wait there and come for you when I hear the shot, yes? If the sentry try to stop me, I run him over."

"It could be a long wait, Arturo."

"I have a large can of water if you need to refill your canteens. And I can steal some fruit and vegetables, enough for us all."

"How we going to get her out of that compound alive, as well as you?" Heuser asked.

Mawangga answered with his brand of harsh reality. "If we cannot rescue her, she better off dead. I would advise shoot her."

With Arturo looking visibly distraught, his eyes frantic, Cushing shrugged his shoulders, with 'ah hell' resignation, acknowledging their unexpected dilemma. "We didn't plan on a rescue mission but now we got one. But since we can't pop Watanabe without her, I think we owe her." Pondering the realities, he said, "In my experience, the Japs don't react well when they're leaderless. After Lewis shoots Watanabe, I need a diversion at the same time, that will have the Nips runnin' in circles like headless chickens." Mawangga gave a solemn nod, acknowledging the onus was on him. "If I fail, you two bail out of here," Cushing said.

Both Heuser and Mawangga stared back in disdain, rejecting the very notion. "What kind of diversion?" Mawangga asked.

"I've got six sticks of dynamite. Odah, tonight you move to the other side of the camp behind the hospital tents and place the dynamite as near to it as you can without the Japs seeing you. This is about diversion, not about blowing up Japs. When you hear Heuser's shot, light the fuse. It is a short one, so run fast. After the explosion, take cover and fire a burst with the BAR. Then beat it back here and wait for Arturo to come with the truck. My hope is the Japs will think an attack is coming from the direction of the explosion and BAR fire and rush over there in a confused mass, giving me a chance."

Mawangga saluted. "Yes sair, by God's grace, I believe it will work."

Arturo said, stuttering, "I-I will do my best."

Cushing clapped his shoulder encouragingly. "When is your next delivery?"

"This is supposed to be the last load until they tell us they want more. I just hope the Japs do not ask for another delivery while I wait here. Then they know something wrong."

225

Cushing wiped sweat from his brow with an agitated swipe of his hand, fretting about coincidences and unpredictable threats thwarting the assassination plot. "The longer we bivouac on Watanabe's doorstep, the greater the odds of detection." Cushing, Heuser, and Mawangga stretched out in the truck bed, hiding amongst the load of sacks and baskets as best they could. Cushing feared that the cargo cover gave them more protection from the beating sun than from the prying eyes of the enemy.

Anxious about Arturo's reliability, Cushing thought about removing the coil wire to the truck distributor in case he lost his nerve; too much time waiting could weigh on his mind. Without the coil wire, he could not hotwire the vehicle, if he knew how. He dismissed the idea, considering the difficulty of reconnecting it amidst the confusion of a skirmish. They had no choice but to trust him. But Arturo seemed genuinely concerned about the safety of the girl, enough to risk his life in a rescue operation.

The truck came to a stop. From close by, they heard a Japanese voice, "You late," and then Arturo's muffled remonstration. "So sorry san. radiator water low." He pointed to the grill of the truck. "Must fill." He patted the grill of the truck, pantomiming opening the hood.

With relief they heard the sentry grunt impatiently, "Move. Speedo! No mo' excuse." Pleased, Cushing allowed himself a smile. Arturo had just passed his first test.

As the truck rounded a bend, Cushing peered through the gaps in the cargo and the stake frame at the thick, disorienting growth of green jungle marking the edge of the road into which they would stealthily exit from the truck. Arturo slowed to a creep. "Go now," he hissed from the cab. The three men spilled over the railing with their equipment, landing in the thick foliage, a dark green tangled mass too dense to see more than three feet in any direction.

They crawled on their hands and knees finding a natural tunnel in the tangle of plants, trying to keep their bearings and find a path that led to a secluded bivouac. They settled down on a sheltered, rocky rise above the low ground. *Thank God it's still dry season*, Cushing thought realizing the rainy season was fast approaching, repelled by the idea of holing up in a wet fetid morass besieged by leeches and mosquitoes.

That night Cushing and Heuser moved toward the drainage ditch. Mawangga split off toward the opposite side of the camp, carefully hugging the jungle growth. All tried mightily to avoid any disturbance that might reveal their presence. Cushing and Heuser stopped short of the drainage ditch. For camouflage, Heuser had smeared charcoal residue on his face and covered his head in a burlap hood. "Shooting Watanabe is going to sure stir up the hornet's nest," he said.

Cushing said, "I just hope Arturo hasn't flown the coop."

"I think he's still around. I heard him drive a short way down the road, the engine coughed, and the truck went silent."

Cushing nodded, reassured. "Alcohol in the gas. Damn Japs! Glad your hearing is as sharp as your vision. The bait is set. Just hope Watanabe's feeling randy tomorrow."

Yeah, but it feels damn crummy using the girl this way." Heuser quoted from Deuteronomy, "If in the open country a man meets a young woman, and the man seizes her and lies with her, then only the man who lay with her shall die."

"Then Watanabe is a dead man walking. Let's do God's work," Cushing said, stifling a grin, patting Heuser on the back before they moved out in a stealthy creep to the drainage ditch in search of an optimum sniper position. The ditch was deep enough to covertly hunch down in without being spotted.

The next morning came with thick grey mist rising out of the jungle. As the sun rose, Heuser and Cushing lay sweating lightly with their weapons beside them amongst feathery grass that grew in the shade of the trees. Just before noon, an officer emerged from the log bunker, receiving deference from the soldiers along his path. Cushing watched with rising anticipation through his binoculars, sensing the hunt moving toward a climax.

Watanabe headed in the direction of the Nipa hut. He had made it about halfway to the compound when a subordinate officer raced from the command post and intercepted him. The officer bowed and scraped, looking most uncomfortable, blurting something out. Watanabe appeared to glare at him, kicked at the ground in frustration. *Grin and bear it asshole, I'm as frustrated as you are*, Cushing thought, watching him return in a huff back to the HQ. The excitement of the moment seeped out of him, leaving him feeling maddened and drained.

Cushing didn't have to ask Heuser, the eternal optimist, how he felt. "I think we're going to get another chance tomorrow," he whispered. "I was watching Watanabe through the scope. He looked pissed that his nooner got interrupted. I'm betting he'll be back again tomorrow to pick up where he left off. Strange he's so fixated on noon."

Cushing hissed, "Maybe at night he gets drunk with his officers."

"At least we know one habit we can exploit. In nature, that's what you look for in prey, predictability."

"I don't want him to even imagine he's prey." Cushing replied in a quiet voice. He sensed Heuser preparing himself for a long wait.

As a hazy dawn on the next day broke, bugle notes of reveille drifted over the Japanese encampment. The soldiers assembled for calisthenics to the shrill exhortations, slaps, and bullying from non-coms. "There's fewer of them now than before the Lamonan ambush," Heuser said.

"And three of us. With those odds, the Japs will just have to take their chances," Cushing said with a dry chuckle. "Louis, when I move to the compound, take out the two guards at the gate, but no further support fire until I get her out of the hut and on my way back. Timings got to be near perfect for this to work."

The morning sun rose, and in the heat of day, the air turned hot and sticky. As expected, Watanabe emerged about noon from the command bunker, walking with a fierce swagger and step that defied unwelcome approach. "Look at that arrogant son of a bitch. He's coming this way."

"The camp smoke is rising almost straight up," Cushing whispered.

"No need to compensate the scope for windage," Heuser said, making a fine adjustment to the elevation turret. He stretched out motionless in the prone position with one arm through the rifle sling at ready and the rifle stock resting on his closed hand. "You are my hammer and weapon of war, a destroyer of kingdoms," he murmured.

"Wait until he enters the compound," Cushing hissed. As the guard opened the gate, Watanabe strutted through. Heuser steadied his breath, zeroed the scope crosshairs on the back of his head, then squeezed the trigger. As the shot rang out, the bullet drilled through the hapless colonel's skull with blood spraying from his face, dropping the embodiment of evil like a lifeless stone.

From across the camp, an explosion erupted in a burst of heaving earth near simultaneously with Heuser's shot. In quick succession, Heuser dropped the two stunned guards at the enclosure gate, with the blast dampening the sound of his shots. Then, the burst of Mawangga's BAR thumped from across the encampment. From his vantage point, Cushing could see the enemy soldiers doing exactly as expected as the undirected herd instinct took hold, moving in mass and returning fire towards the location of Mawangga's automatic rifle fire. For a minute, the enemy appeared unaware of their commanding officer and two guards lying dead on the ground in the opposite direction.

Seizing the moment, Cushing leaped from the trench with his Thompson submachine gun at the ready. The compound lay before him unguarded and open. Sensing his luck burning like a short fuse, he sprinted with unwavering resolve toward the compound, charging through the open gate. Close enough to hear Heuser's shot, a squad of Japanese soldiers ceased their forward rush to the far side of the camp and pivoted as their screaming officer spotted the body of Watanabe face down on the ground.

Cushing kicked the locked door of the hut off its hinges. A frightened, wide-eyed young woman in her teens with a delicate, fine-featured face stared back at him in terror, her mouth agape, beginning to shriek. She wore a simple, white linen dress like a smock. Cushing noted satisfactorily the sandals on her feet, thinking better than nothing for running over the thorny, rough ground. "Shush," he said putting his finger to his lips. "I am here to rescue you." He clasped her hand firmly.

"Come, dear. Now!" Either trusting or seeing no other alternative, she allowed him to lead her. "Can you run?"

"Yes," she squeaked, her flight reaction coming alive.

"Stay with me. I'll get you out of here. I promise." Her feet gained traction, keeping pace with him as they rushed through the door. Two soldiers charged through the gate. Cushing dropped both of them with a sweeping burst of metal from his Thompson. With deadly accuracy, Heuser squeezed off shots from the drainage ditch, picking off the officer and two more soldiers. "Don't look back. Just run," Cushing roared. She proved fleet-footed, running at his pace.

Hope set in as bullets fired at them kicked up dirt behind them, with every step the drainage ditch beckoning. Fifteen yards more he reckoned in midstep. His poor opinion of Japanese infantry marksmanship did not extend to their fearsome .50-caliber light mortars. The two running full out, only seconds left to the oncoming trench, Heuser chambered and fired in quick succession rounds, scoring precision shots against the pursuing Japanese. Others hesitated in their forward rush as if sensing suicidal folly without an officer directing it.

Bullets struck the ground short and wide. When no mortars joined the fray, Cushing realized they had made it, *by the skin of their teeth*. He grabbed the girl around the waist, hurling them both into the ditch, pulling her on top of him to cushion her fall. He directed her attention to Heuser, who winked and gave her a reassuring smile. "Crouch! Move like he does, sweetie." They followed the trench out of the open field and into the cover of jungle growth. Back strapping his submachine gun, he pushed his way through the thick foliage with one hand, and with the other coaxing the girl along by the hand, retracing his route along the narrow game trail. With his arm around her waist, he swung her bodily over encroaching obstacles, while vaulting roots and thrashing his free hand through the entangling brush.

Thankfully, she remained silent throughout the ordeal. Thudding explosions of small mortar shells detonated around the drainage ditch well back of them, proving they had eluded enemy sight. When he came into view of the road, a confused guard appeared in the middle turning and swinging his rifle in frantic arcs from side to side, trying to anticipate the direction of an unseen attack. Mawangga waited silently, crouching low in the brush. Cushing raised his finger to his lips indicating silence to the girl and motioned to the lethal jungle fighter, tracing his finger across his throat.

Mawangga handed Cushing the BAR. His eyes narrowing like slits, he nodded. Cushing lost sight of him as he slithered away serpent-like into the dense undergrowth toward the road. From farther down the road, an engine revved. The guard turned toward the vehicle. In the same instant, Mawangga rose from the brush with the bolo in hand clearing the distance to the cringing guard, giving him no chance to turn. With a powerful strike of the long knife, the lithe fighter chopped through the guard's neck, leaving him splayed on the ground with a partially severed head, and blood surging from dead soldier's open neck.

Though time seemed to move in slow motion, it had taken Arturo only a minute to arrive with the truck. Cushing jerked open the passenger door and shoved the young woman onto the bench seat. He and his men scrambled over the tailgate into the truck bed. "Go!" he yelled to Arturo, who stepped on the gas, throttling the truck in a lurching getaway.

From behind, a new squad of enemy soldiers appeared onto the road. Cushing and Mawangga fired their automatic weapons at them over the tailgate until the truck accelerated over a rise in the road, shielding them from return fire. Simultaneously, a vehicle appeared behind them. "It's that damn scout car," Cushing bawled. Racing up the road in pursuit, the car quickly gained on them. Arturo weaved the truck as a machine rifle opened up from the pursuing vehicle. Several rounds penetrated the tailgate panel passing too close for comfort before .30 and .45 caliber return fire from Cushing's team sent the car careening off the road, riddled with bullets. Cushing slumped back against the stake bed, the emotional toll of the recent days descending on him like a cloud of lead.

In the cab, Arturo glanced at the slender, glassy-eyed girl trembling on the seat next to him. "You are safe now, Loling. I will take you back to your family."

She raised her head looking back at him, anguish in her dark eyes. "Will my family want me? I am soiled, with the stain of sin."

As soothingly as he could manage, Arturo said, "If it was against your will, it is not a sin."

"Of course it was," she whined, her tears flowing down her face. She pulled up her dress, revealing slash welts on her legs like the type left by a switch.

"Shush now! What happened to you cannot be helped. Your father and mother love you and want you back very much. Those men in the back risked their lives to save you. They are heroes. You must honor their deeds by going on with your life. Believe me, time heals." She leaned against Arturo, sobbing as he drove in the direction of the municipality of her family. He felt sure the Japanese would hunt for the men in the back. The less he knew about their whereabouts, the less he could say if interrogated.

As for Loling, he hoped the Japanese would just forget about her, with their attention focused on more pressing quarry. If not, there were always the evacuation camps, now becoming ubiquitous as Japanese abuses mounted. He hoped that Lola had not been impregnated, considering her options. He knew of an old woman, a healer it was said, who could make potions that could solve that problem. Sin or not, the very thought of the spawn of Watanabe seemed an abomination.

As Cushing watched Arturo's truck pull away, he hoped that the assassination of Colonel Watanabe would strike a psychological blow to the enemy's self-confidence, just when the resistance seemed increasingly vulnerable.

The Miner Warrior of Luzon, Walter McKay Cushing

On his return back to the eastern high country of the Abra-Kalinga border, Cushing received a report carried by a runner who intercepted him in route from Colonel Horan. The handwritten letter informed him the fortified bastion of Corregidor Island, the last Fil-American defense on Luzon, had fallen. General Jonathan Wainwright had ordered the surrender of all Filipino-American forces in the Philippines.

Horan wrote, "General Homma gave General Wainwright an ultimatum. He would not accept surrender or guarantee the safety of the POWs until all forces in the Philippines obeyed the order to surrender." Cushing considered Homma's warning more likely a bluff, though at this time reluctant to call it. He had no intention of surrendering, not while a single Japanese soldier occupied the island archipelago.

He considered himself at a crossroads that required a new strategy of how best to proceed. His options were to continue armed resistance, Homma's ultimatum be damned, or pursue more clandestine forms of resistance, reconnaissance and intelligence. As Colonel Horan had told him, a cavalry officer, Captain Praeger, was operating a radio transceiver in Apayao province in the far north of Luzon, a hopeful possibility of communicating gathered intelligence. The sooner the strategy emerged from the disorder of general surrender, the sooner he could sort out his tactical options.

Hard facts dictated his choices; there was no imminent American military rescue of the Philippines. That dilemma would weigh heavily in his consideration of the struggles ahead. He would fall back to Mount Bawao to clear his head and consider his options dispassionately. Colonel Watanabe was no more, and at the moment that strengthened his resolve.

About The Author

Before writing my debut novel *The Miner Warrior of Luzon*, my career experience included technical writing, in chemical production and telecommunications equipment and wine grape farming in northern California. My inspiration for *The Miner Warrior of Luzon* derives from my experience of living in the Philippines at the impressionable age of 11 to 13 from 1963 to 1965. At that time, memories of the World War II and the Japanese occupation were still fresh in the minds of the Filipinos. I heard numerous stories, most harrowing and disturbing, which have been rattling around in my head since, requiring an outlet through publication. I became familiar with the heroic exploits of Walter M. Cushing from reading *The Intrepid Guerrillas of North Luzon* by Bernard Norling. My goal in writing this book is to preserve the memories and contributions of Walter M. Cushing, posthumously awarded the USA second highest decoration The Distinguished Service Cross, and others like him in the Philippines guerrilla resistance from becoming forgotten heroes.

www.ingramcontent.com/pod-product-compliance
Lightning Source LLC
Chambersburg PA
CBHW060318260626
47160CB00007B/2654